# THE WATER
# GARDEN

# THE WATER GARDEN

Louise Soraya Black

MUSWELL
PRESS

*For Gus, Alex and Beau*

First published by Muswell Press in 2021
This edition published 2022
Typeset in Bembo by M Rules
Copyright © Louise Soraya Black 2021

Louise Soraya Black has asserted her right to be identified
as the author of this work in accordance with
the Copyright, Designs and Patents Act, 1988

Printed and bound by
CPI Group (UK) Ltd, Croydon CR0 4YY

A CIP catalogue record for this book
is available from the British Library

ISBN: 9781739966041
eISBN: 9781916360280

Muswell Press
London N6 5HQ
www.muswell-press.co.uk

# Sarah

*Surrey, Spring 2010*

Light-dappled woods shade her from the sun. Tiny birds call to each other and dart from branch to branch. The path is a carpet of dry leaves, turning slowly to dust.

Sarah is free to walk at her own pace. Jack, who would be stopping to study beetles or collect sticks, is at school. Charlie, tugging at her hand or sitting on her hip, is at nursery. Her body feels weightless, as if she might float away without the anchor of her children.

For a moment, she imagines that Paul is beside her, his arm brushing hers, their shadows blending together, but he's hardly ever here any more. His absence compresses her, wearies her heart and empties her, and she can't remember a time when it was different.

The path begins to climb and her legs work harder. A breeze lifts the hair from her face. She loosens her scarf. A twig snaps and something rustles in the undergrowth. Perhaps it was some shy creature, a squirrel or a rabbit.

She is alone. There is no sign of the man who walks his

muzzled Alsatian, pulling the lead tight when they pass, or the two Lycra-clad women who jog and converse in low, breathless voices.

The ascent takes longer than she remembers, but at last she reaches the top and is rewarded with the view: sloping green fields, divided by hedgerows and wooden fences, enclosed by leafy trees. A train sounds its horn, winding through pastures and villages whose names she has forgotten but will remember as the months pass. In the distance, there is the muted roar of the motorway.

The sky is blue, there is no cloud, and she stretches her arms over her head. The sun warms her face. Her body feels loose, limber, and the ache in her shoulder melts away.

There are horses in the next field and she thinks of Charlie, who waves to them as if they are friends. They look cosy in their blankets. Although the afternoons are warm, it is still cool in the mornings.

The path becomes narrower and uneven, with cropped grass. Yellow flowers have sprung up in the foliage and she studies them carefully, noting the size and shape of their petals; later, she will look them up. Catkins decorate some of the trees, which she thinks are silver birch. After so many years in the city, she has forgotten these things. She wants the boys to grow up outdoors, not in front of the television; this is why they have come here.

It is a homecoming of sorts, but her grandparents are long gone, buried in the cemetery at St Michael's, and her mother has moved overseas. She doesn't often think of her father; they haven't spoken for years. People she doesn't know live in her grandparents' old house and she avoids driving past. A glimpse of the white farmhouse and the honeysuckle by the front door makes her throat tighten. There is only Aunt Edith now, living in a smart gated estate, and she's nearly ninety.

2

An ancient tree stands in her way like a guard; its thick, ridged trunk and crooked branches look fossilised. She circles past, brushing her fingers over the knotted bark.

The ground begins to drop down into the woods again. The trees tower above her, fragmenting the sky. It is suddenly cold and she pushes her hands into her pockets. She has never walked this far from home. She wonders if she should turn back. It will soon be time to collect Charlie.

Something glitters, gliding through the bracken and the brambles. A stream is flowing beside the path. She didn't notice it before; perhaps it's been there all along. She follows the stream, wondering where it will lead her, and comes to a wooden plank bridge. Through the silhouettes of trees, the pale mist, the horizon shimmers. She crosses the bridge.

The trees thin, the light grows stronger, and birds are flying above. A lake, as smooth as a plate of glass, appears before her like a mirage. Reeds line the rocky edges and a willow tree drips into the greenish water. A white swan floats past and its reflection is a painting. Red-brick houses with striped lawns slope down to swept wooden jetties and rowing boats. A few deckchairs are positioned to catch the sun. It is quiet.

She's never heard of a lake in Littlefold. She searches her childhood memories, but there is nothing. Perhaps this was once the water garden of an old country house, knocked down and developed into new properties.

She follows the path circling around it. Here and there, trails lead down to the water. Up close the lake is murky, with wreaths of tangled weed. A black-and-white duck paddles in the shadows; a bigger, brown one dives and resurfaces, its wet head glistening like an emerald. There is a sign for the Littlefold Anglers, but she can't see any fish. Perhaps it is quite deep.

She comes to a bench and sits down. The trees are wrapped in ivy and tiny buds of new leaves sparkle like fairy lights. The lush vegetation hums with invisible insects and bees.

Across the lake there is another, larger seat. Carved from polished dark wood, it looks more like a beautiful piece of artisan furniture than an outdoor bench. The sun pulses, the woodland seat glows, and she suddenly longs to touch it. She follows the path around to it and there is a name, Samuel Thomas, and two dates. The boy, Samuel Thomas, was thirteen when he died. The wood is as smooth as walnut, the grain flecked with amber and gold. She runs her fingers over the blackened inscription. *A flower in His garden. In the stars and in our hearts.*

She doesn't know how his parents have managed to go on living. She can't imagine a life without one of her sons.

'Sarah, darling. And little Charlie,' Aunt Edith says, looking pleased. She is in the sitting room, folded into a high-back blue velvet armchair drawn up to the fire, a copy of *Pride and Prejudice* and her spectacles on a table beside her. The damask curtains are tied back, but it is overcast and Anna has switched on the lamps. Beneath the heavy gilt mirror, on the marble mantelpiece, are silver-framed portraits of family weddings: Aunt Edith, tall and elegant in a veil and long flowing gown, standing beside Uncle George on the steps of St Michael's; Grandpa Jim and Grandma Maggie in their uniforms in wartime Rome; Catherine, her blonde hair falling around her shoulders, in an ivory dress with puffed sleeves; Harry in a grey coat and tails, stepping out of a Rolls. And there are Sarah and Paul, on their honeymoon in Barcelona; it wasn't that long ago, but they both look so young, their faces glowing, their eyes bright with the promise of a life together. She remembers strolling hand in hand with Paul along the tree-lined avenues, admiring the flamboyant Gaudí architecture, sitting close together for candle-lit suppers by the marina. It seems like a dream now.

Sarah leans down to kiss her great-aunt and is nearly tipped over by the weight of Charlie, who has refused to be put down. A blanket is tucked around Aunt Edith, but her cheek against Sarah's is cold. There is a trace of perfume that is almost medicinal; it is probably Chanel, and fifty years old.

Sarah sits on the Parker Knoll sofa opposite Aunt Edith, a glass-topped coffee table between them. Charlie sees the wooden toy chest in the corner, wriggles out of her arms, and she flinches as he narrowly misses the sharp corner of the table. Aunt Edith watches Charlie rummaging through toys that once belonged to Harry. Her white hair hangs in limp waves around her angular, still handsome face. Her grey eyes are inquisitive, but softer than they used to be when Sarah was a child. There is a loud, crashing noise as Charlie empties a box of cars over the parquet. Sarah begins to get up, but Aunt Edith says kindly, 'Let him play.'

Charlie is at that unpredictable toddler stage, equally prone to giggles or tears, and sometimes Sarah feels as if she's guarding a ticking bomb. At the moment he's on good form, smiling winningly at Aunt Edith and making *vroom-vroom* noises as he pushes a car along the floor, then up the leg of her armchair. The car journeys across Aunt Edith's lap, bumping over the blanket, but she doesn't seem to mind. 'They grow up quickly,' she says.

Charlie looks every bit the cherub, with his blond curls and blue eyes. When he wraps his arms around Sarah, she feels a pang, knowing he's her last, and drinks in his infant smell. Even so, there are times when she wishes Charlie would grow up: these early years are trying, and there are times when she wishes she could leave him in the garden. It is difficult to express these mixed feelings, and she is accustomed to the nostalgia of mothers with grown-up children, so she says, 'Yes, indeed.' One day she too will feel the emptiness that comes when children leave.

Anna carries in a tray with a teapot, two china cups and saucers, and a plate of digestive biscuits. Charlie sees the biscuits and drops the car, but Sarah scoops him onto her lap before he can lunge at the tray. 'Hello, little man,' Anna says, smiling at Charlie. She puts the tray on the coffee table, gives Charlie a biscuit and pours the tea. 'How's he enjoying nursery?' she asks Sarah.

'He cries when I leave, but settles quickly.'

'Bless him,' Anna says. 'He's a good boy.'

Anna has sons of her own who have long grown-up. She doesn't ask, unlike others, if Sarah and Paul will try for a girl.

Aunt Edith lifts her teacup and saucer to her lips, but her hand shakes and tea spills into the saucer. She puts the cup down. Anna wipes the saucer with a cloth, then leaves, closing the door quietly behind her.

'How are Harry and Catherine?' Sarah asks.

'Harry is as busy as usual, working all hours in town. Catherine might bring the girls this summer.'

'That would be lovely,' Sarah says, cautiously. Aunt Edith's daughter lives in Australia and has been promising to visit for years. Sarah feels sorry for her aunt, growing old without her children near. At least she has security and neighbours, living on a private estate.

Sarah's mother says that Edith used to live in one of the grandest old houses in the village, with acres of grounds, tucked away at the end of a winding lane. After George died and there wasn't as much money, Edith said it was too remote and moved here. She has one of the last red-brick thirties houses on the estate; most of the original homes have been demolished to make way for neo-Georgian

6

mansions – sweeping paved driveways, double garages with staff annexes, cavernous marble halls, two, if not three staircases. At night the mansions are lit up like landmarks. 'These new builds are ridiculous, with their pocket-handkerchief lawns. They've been squeezed into plots meant for smaller houses,' Aunt Edith often remarks. 'Gardens have gone out of fashion.' Her own garden is large and secluded, with ancient conifers and oak trees, fragrant lavender and roses, an overgrown lawn, and a wild, wooded area where the boys like to hunt for beetles and peer into foxholes.

'Anna pops in all the time,' Aunt Edith goes on, as if she must reassure Sarah. 'She looks after me.'

'Yes, Anna is wonderful,' Sarah says. Anna has been with Aunt Edith for years. It's difficult to believe that she is now in her seventies – she's fit and energetic, never ill. She's more like a family friend than a housekeeper; loyal and kind, with brown eyes full of the wisdom and patience that comes from caring for people and their homes.

'How is Jack? Does he like school?'

'Yes, but he misses his friends. He's the new boy and it can be difficult at playtime.'

'You'll have to do your bit. Have a few children round.'

Sarah knows she should, but it's not easy with Charlie, who always wants to join in, and she finds the other mothers intimidating. When she collects Jack, they huddle in small groups, speaking in low voices, and she can feel their eyes flick over her as she walks past. The morning drop-off sets the tone: women arrive in four-wheel drives and then teeter in on high heels, one hand steering their children, the other displaying a designer handbag. Their sunglasses are oversized, their hair glossy and highlighted. Sarah doesn't have the time for, or interest in, all this preening. She rarely wears make-up; she prefers to look natural and she's lucky to have inherited her mother's porcelain complexion. Her brown, shoulder-length hair is straight, if a little fine, and doesn't need to be blow-dried. She wears jeans, trainers and a parka: clothing suitable for the school run, grocery shopping and the often-inclement weather. It's practical and comfortable, and she doesn't miss the tailored suits and court shoes that she used to wear to the office. She is smarter today for Aunt Edith, in chinos, a navy blouse that deepens the soft blue of her eyes, and a cardigan. The chinos are smudged from Charlie's shoes when she carried him in.

Starting school was a milestone for Jack, but Sarah hadn't realised it would be a challenge for her too. There was a lot to remember: the uniform, with its permutations, to launder and name; sports kits for football and swimming to deliver on the correct days; homework to supervise and log books to complete; parent-teacher conferences and open mornings; packed lunches for school trips; birthday parties to organise and attend; coffee mornings and school fairs. The run-up to Christmas was a gathering storm of nativity plays, teachers' gifts and class parties. By the new year she was worn out. Her academic achievements and City career were no use. She was not qualified.

She reminds herself from time to time that life could be much worse. She is lucky in so many ways. She has a loving husband, happy children, her health, a comfortable home. There are many women in the world who aren't as fortunate, who struggle with illness or relationships or money. Some women face unimaginable hardship – poverty, disease, war. It's easy, living in Littlefold, to lose perspective.

Aunt Edith leans forward and pats Sarah's hand. 'Don't fret. Children are adaptable. If it's the mothers you need to win over, put on a nice frock and go to a charity lunch.'

'Yes,' Sarah says, but it's up to Jack to make friends. Friendships orchestrated by mothers are artificial.

Charlie has been quiet, eating biscuit after biscuit, but the plate is now empty. 'More?' he says, his mouth full, showering crumbs. Sarah hunts in her bag for baby wipes. 'No,' he says, trying to twist away while she cleans his mouth and fingers. He breaks free and points to the plate. 'More,' he says firmly.

As if Anna has heard, the door opens and she comes in. Charlie runs to her and holds up his arms. She swings him up, kissing his face. 'You smell of biscuits,' she says. 'Have you had the lot already?'

'I'm afraid so,' Sarah says.

'More,' Charlie repeats absently, studying Anna's dark hair, which glints with silver. He touches it carefully, as if it's treasure.

Anna takes a bottle of pills from her apron pocket and puts them on the side table beside Aunt Edith.

'Thank you, Anna,' Aunt Edith says. She puts on her spectacles and looks at the label, then shakes out a tablet and drinks it down with cold tea.

'And you, young man, can come with me,' Anna says. 'I'm sure I can find something for you to play with.'

Charlie is happy to be carried away by Anna, and Sarah feels the relief of not having to supervise him. Aunt Edith's ornaments – little china figurines and lacquered boxes, displayed on low console tables, are irresistible to the fingers of an inquisitive little boy.

Without Charlie to mind, Sarah remembers her question. 'I've been walking in the fields near our house. There's a lake in the middle of the woods. Do you know it?'

Aunt Edith's eyes flicker. 'Yes, the old brickworks pit. When the clay ran out the council filled it with water.' She's silent for a moment, then says, 'You shouldn't be walking in the woods on your own. If you want to keep your figure there's no shortage of gyms. I hear Zumba is all the rage with the mothers around here.'

'Yes,' Sarah says, but she has no intention of joining a gym. It's peace and quiet she's after, not small talk with the women she sees at the school gates. She says nothing more. She can't help feeling disappointed. She'd imagined that the beautiful lake was once a water garden in the grounds of a Victorian house, perhaps commissioned by a lord with a passion for horticulture or landscape painting, not a dusty quarry pit with machinery and miners extracting clay.

Aunt Edith has sunk into her armchair. She looks pale and exhausted, and Sarah knows it's time to go.

'I should take Charlie home for his nap. Thank you for having us.' She kisses her aunt's powdery cheek.

Aunt Edith's fingers brush Sarah's face like feathers. 'Little ones can be tiring,' she says, and Sarah wonders if her aunt misunderstood. 'Come again soon, darling. It's lovely having you near.'

Anna is playing with Charlie in the kitchen. They have made a train track with two loops and an eclectic mix of toy spectators – a cow, a dinosaur and Postman Pat. Charlie sees Sarah and reaches for her. She picks him up and he rubs his face against her neck.

Anna walks Sarah to the door. 'Your visits do her good,' she says, kneeling to help with Charlie's shoes.

'I'm glad,' Sarah says, although her feelings about these visits are tangled. She feels beholden to Aunt Edith, who has always taken an interest in her – even though there were times when Sarah did not wish it, but she used to come to the Laurels with Grandpa Jim and it's strange to be here without him. It's as if she and Aunt Edith are waiting together for an important guest, passing the time with polite conversation, but the guest never comes. Still, she tries to visit every few weeks. 'I saw her hand shaking,' she says to Anna.

'That's the Parkinson's, but the pills help. And her mind's as sharp as ever,' Anna says. She stands and her knees click. She sighs. 'Neither of us is getting any younger.'

Outside the cloud has cleared and a cat is lying on the sunlit roof of Aunt Edith's Peugeot.

'Looks like the afternoon will be nice. I expect you and the boys will be in the garden,' Anna says.

Sarah wants to ask Anna about the old quarry lake, but instead she says, 'Yes, I expect so. See you soon.'

# Maggie

*Italy, 1944*

Maggie is hiding in the broom cupboard from Matron. She doesn't want to go to the party. She's come to Italy to tend to the wounded, not entertain officers. But the cupboard is dusty, she sneezes, her hiding place is discovered, and she is dispatched along with the other nurses to brush her hair and put on lipstick.

The journey to the Foggia airfields was tiring and she longs for bed. Instead she's in the officers' mess, a crowded and stuffy marquee, sipping red wine and making small talk. This is not what she'd expected when she joined the RAF.

A young man is walking towards them. He is tall and fair, and has the lean build of a sportsman. She thinks he's heading for Nancy, a thin blonde who looks his type, but instead he touches her arm and says, 'Would you care to dance?'

'Me?' she says, before she can stop herself.

The other girls titter. Nancy pats her hair.

The young officer's grey eyes make her think of a misty morning and she feels a sudden pang for England. He smiles warmly at her, as if they already know each other.

He holds her close, his hand resting lightly on her waist, and leads her in a waltz. He smells clean, of soap and water, and beneath it a green musky scent like the woods in the spring. She feels stiff and awkward, aware of the eyes of the other nurses, but he's a considerate dancer and she soon loses her self-consciousness.

'I'm Jim Howard,' he says.

'I'm Maggie Jones,' she says.

'I'm going to marry you, Maggie Jones. You're my kind of girl.'

He is smiling again and she thinks it's a joke. A laugh bursts from her. 'Don't be silly,' she says.

The music is fading, the song coming to an end, but he keeps his arms around her. 'A few of us are going to the coast tomorrow. A day in the sun before we leave. Please say you'll come,' he says.

She hesitates. She doesn't know this man.

'Bring your friends. We've got the transport,' he says, as if he's guessed what she is thinking.

She wants to see him again. And it would be lovely to bathe in the sea. She decides not to listen to the voice in her head, whispering of impropriety. The risk is nothing compared to the war.

The three girls sit on their towels, the white cliffs behind them, the turquoise bay beyond. Sorrento is an oasis, undisturbed by the war; the empty hotels and the quiet cobbled streets are the only sign. Alice and Nancy are gossiping about Matron.

'I've never seen her smile,' Alice says, leaning back on her elbows. She is wearing a two-piece, and her bare midriff is smooth and creamy.

'I can't imagine it,' Nancy says, brushing sand from her

long, coltish legs. 'She wouldn't look herself at all.' She's in a glamorous floral one-piece, with a halterneck and a short skirt. It looks new and must have been expensive. Maggie's own costume is second-hand; she chose it for the colour, a brilliant cobalt blue that suits her complexion, but it clings to her hips and she has to keep tugging at it.

The girls laugh, poking more fun at Matron, and Maggie hears them as if from a distance. She's watching Jim swimming in the sea, the sunlight flashing off his shoulders, his hair wet and slick. He is strong and fast in the water. She has a sudden, childish urge to race him.

'You'd better snap that one up,' Nancy says archly.

Maggie feels her face go pink. Before she can speak, Robert and Tom arrive, carrying two large umbrellas. They seem keen to live up to Jim's introduction; 'good sorts' from his regiment, the North Irish Horse.

'Thank you, darlings. It was getting rather hot,' Nancy says.

The boys look pleased, as if they'd do just about anything for her.

Jim is swimming back to shore. He emerges, the water streaming down his face, his arms, his chest. 'Come in,' he calls. 'It's glorious.'

'I've just done my hair,' Nancy says, smoothing her blonde waves. 'I don't want to get wet.'

'The water looks cold,' Alice says, wrinkling her nose.

The boys have finished setting up the umbrellas. 'We'll keep you company,' Tom says, rolling out his towel.

'Don't tell the CO, but I'm not much of a swimmer,' Robert confides, joining them.

'I'll go,' Maggie says. Her childhood holidays were spent at her grandparents' home on the Welsh coast. She is accustomed to bracing swims.

14

She stands on the beach. The waves cascade over her feet then pull away, leaving effervescent foam on the flaxen sand. The sun warms her hair. In the distance, a shadowy Mount Vesuvius rises up out of the sea like a sleeping mythical creature. The air is scented with lemons and oranges, and carries the salt tang of the sea. The war seems far away here, as if they are in another country. Jim is further out, floating, drifting on his back. The tides tug at her, tease her, seem to be calling her. She takes a deep breath and runs headlong into the sparkling water. She swims, the shock of the cold eases, and hidden currents that are more powerful that she'd expected carry her towards him.

It's late by the time they get back to Foggia. Jim parks his truck and walks her to her apartment. Her face feels warm, but she doesn't know if it's from too much sun, the wine at dinner, or the thought of being alone with him. At the door, they stand together quietly. He strokes the hair back from her face. He kisses her and she tastes the salt sea on his lips. 'Will you write to me?' he says.

Her throat tightens, painfully. 'Yes,' she says, but her voice is a whisper. 'I will.'

He gently wipes the tears from her face. 'Everything will be all right. It has to be.'

She's afraid to say goodbye; she has already lost her brother to this war that claims life after life and is never satisfied, but she must be strong and brave for him. 'It will be all right,' she says, as if repeating this will make it real.

'Tell me when you get your next forty-eight hours. If it's quiet, we could meet,' he says.

'Yes,' she says, feeling her heart lift. She will find a way to see him.

Maggie rolls over, sighs, gives up on sleep. The nights on the ward are exhausting, but it's difficult to rest during the day;

sunlight seeps through the curtains, it's hot, and there is the constant drone from the airfields.

She reaches for the letter she received from Jim the day before. He can't divulge the regiment's location because of the censors, but she's guessed from the news and his other letters that he is travelling north. Wherever he is, it sounds enchanting. Even though it would be dangerous, she wishes that she were there with him, instead of here in hot, dusty Foggia.

> Ltnt Howard
> The North Irish Horse
> 24th June 1944

My dearest Maggie,

I received your letters of the 15th, 16th and 17th all at once today. I can't think why there was a delay, but I suppose we shouldn't complain. I must admit that I was getting a little concerned, so it was wonderful to hear from you, darling. I do hope that you're managing to get some rest. Night duty must be tiring. How very resourceful of you and Nancy to organise deliveries with the local farmers – they sound most obliging.

I've been monitoring the wireless as usual, but it's fairly quiet here at the moment. We are staying in an abandoned castle, with a rose garden and views over the green valleys. When it's misty, it feels as though we're at the edge of the world. I've been feasting on cherries and peaches in the orchard, so you mustn't worry. I'm not going hungry.

The vino is rather scarce, unfortunately. The Germans and French Moroccans have taken it all. Last night, I played piquet with the CO. We made some dubious cocktails and I felt quite ill this morning. I think it's a good idea to keep in with the CO, so that he's helpful when I ask him for leave. I may be able to get away for a night in a couple of weeks. Do you think you could take your 48 hours? If you can hitch a flight to Rome, I could meet you there.

There isn't any more news. It's late, and I'm writing this by candlelight, so I'm sorry if the writing isn't as neat as it should be. Just know that I'm thinking of you all the time, missing you, and longing to be with you again.

You mustn't doubt my love for you, my darling. You're so different to the other girls I've known: honest and brave, and strong. Sometimes, I think I see you in the castle rose garden. You turn, I stroke your cheek, and you smile at me, the way you do with your eyes. You're my angel, guiding me.

Love,
Jim


At last she has the answer to the question that she'd finally dared ask; from time to time she's wondered why he chose her instead of Nancy or one of the other girls. When she's tired or unhappy, she returns to this letter, reading again the last few lines, and it comforts her.

The days pass; the long nights on the ward pass; she writes to him every day and waits impatiently for his letters. Jim manages to get leave from the CO, no doubt persuaded after several rounds of cocktails over piquet, she is allowed her forty-eight hours, and they have one night together in Rome. Jim is thinner, with stubble on his face, but his smile is the same. He holds her close and she breathes in his smell, the green scent of the woods. They kiss and she can almost taste the cherries from the orchards in the north. In the morning, neither of them want to part.

'We are one now,' he says softly, tracing her cheekbone with his finger. 'Will you marry me?'

There is a rushing sound in her head and she feels suddenly faint, as if looking down from a great height. They've only known each other for a few months. Even so, she can't imagine a life without him. 'Yes,' she says. 'Of course I will.'

He pulls her to him. 'My angel. We're going to be so happy.'

Autumn arrives, bringing cold winds and rain. Jim is a captain now, still journeying up through Italy in his wireless truck with the Eighth Army. 'If this carries on, it won't be long before we're clear out of the country,' he writes. Maggie has been made a sister, with responsibility for the burns ward. Both of them are busy, but they write to each other as often as they can. She is anxious about Jim. He tries to be cheerful in his letters, but it's clear that conditions are deteriorating.

Capt. Howard
The North Irish Horse
15th November 1944

My dearest Maggie,

I'm sorry that I haven't been able to write. We had to move again, and the muddy fields and boggy tracks made progress slow and difficult. Still, we've reached our new place now, and I think we'll be here for a few days. I've been busy with the wireless at night, keeping communications open, and haven't been getting much sleep – now I know how you feel on night duty. It's hard to get much rest, in any event, with the shells whizzing past my tent. I've dug a trench and when it gets too noisy, I take cover in there. If it rains, the bedding gets soaked, and it's hard to get it dry again. I've started to fantasise about having a bath. You can't imagine how dirty I am. You'd be appalled.

The food isn't as good now – bully and biscuits, sardines, dehydrated potatoes. How I miss the summer, when we could pick cherries and peaches! There isn't much vino, either. The CO and I have a brandy or whisky when we play piquet. When things are quieter, I'll speak to him about our wedding. I'm hoping that he'll give me leave in December.

I had letters from Mother and Edith today. Mother was pleased to receive your letter – thank you, my darling, for writing to her. The family seem a little shocked by our engagement, but I suppose that's to be expected. I'm sure they will love you, just as I do, when you meet. Edith has suggested that we marry once we're back in England, after the war, but I don't think we can wait, do you?

There isn't any more news. If you don't hear from me for a few days, it will be because we're on the move again.

> All my love,
> Jim

She doesn't want to wait until the war is over either; now that they are engaged, she is as impatient as he is to be married. His family's reaction to their happy news unsettles her – she'd expected surprise, not shock – but she's too worried about Jim to dwell on it. It isn't easy in Foggia, but at least she has decent food and a roof over her head. She can't bear the thought of him cold and wet, sleeping in a ditch, living on bully and dehydrated potatoes. If this carries on, he'll fall ill. One of the soldiers on the ward is going back to the Front in a few days. Lieutenant Peterson is a kind young man. He might take a parcel for Jim.

Capt. Howard
The North Irish Horse
23rd November 1944

My dearest Maggie,

Thank you for such a wonderful parcel! The almonds and chocolate are delicious, a most welcome change from bully and biscuits, and the woolly socks are just the ticket. You're so thoughtful and clever, arranging it all. Peterson seems a good sort. He spoke very highly of you.

It's quieter here now and everyone is in better spirits. We're staying in a farmhouse and it's wonderful to have a roof over our heads again. The mobile shower unit came today. It really is the most amazing contraption; pipes bring water from a stream and a burner heats it. Being clean again feels like the epitome of luxury!

Yesterday, the CO confirmed that I am to be given a tank, so it's farewell to the wireless truck. I asked if I could get married first. He wasn't keen, but eventually he agreed. I don't think this war can go on much longer, but I can't go into a tank without knowing that you would be looked after if anything were to happen. I've spoken to the Padre, and he's trying to organise a church in Rome. I'm hoping that you can get leave within the next couple of weeks – do you think Matron will agree?

All my love,
Jim

She loves him even more after this letter. He will be the one in greater danger, yet his first thought is about her.

Arranging a wedding during wartime isn't easy. It proves difficult to find a church, neither of them being Catholic, and the CO becomes evasive about leave. There is nothing to do but wait and make the necessary preparations, so that when the time comes, they are ready. She wonders about a wedding dress, fashioned from silk parachutes, but it doesn't seem right to go to such lengths during a war. It would be better to wed in their uniforms. Gold is scarce, so Jim has their wedding rings made from the gold used by dentists for fillings.

At Jim's request, Maggie has her portrait taken by a photographer and sends it to his family. She tries to look her best; she hopes they will approve. Jim tells her that his father has given them his blessing, and his mother and sister thought her photograph very nice, and this reassures her. She knows how important family is; her mother died of polio when Maggie was ten, and her father drank himself to death. She aches for them, and her dear brother. They would have adored Jim.

One weekend in mid-December, she travels to Sorrento to gather a few items for her trousseau – a lace nightie and a dressing gown, and returns to find a telegram from Jim.

*Leave granted. Service arranged in Rome, 24th December.*

On Christmas Eve, at the Anglican All Saints' in Rome, she and Jim are married. The red-brick church is elegant and stately, with marble columns and pillars, stained-glass windows and wooden floors. After the service they emerge, arms entwined, and snow falls on their hair like confetti. It's all happened so quickly, it feels like a dream, but here are Tom and Robert congratulating them, clapping Jim on the back, and she receives kisses from Alice and Nancy.

The Army surprises them by putting them up in the Grand Palace, a luxurious hotel usually reserved for senior personnel. Two nights; this is their honeymoon, and they are separated again. Jim goes back to the Front and Maggie returns to Foggia.

It feels unnatural to be apart now that they are married. Everyone is saying that the war will be over soon, the Germans can't carry on for much longer, but somehow it drags on. Maggie worries even more, now that Jim is in a tank. If his letters are delayed, her heart slows and her blood stills, and she can think of little else until an envelope addressed to Mrs M. Howard in his slanting writing arrives.

She is holding the hand of a dying soldier when she hears that the war is over. The soldier is young, just a boy; another life lost, laid waste. Others around her are celebrating, but she feels numb at the pointlessness of it all. Still, she knows that she is lucky. She has survived, and so has Jim. They can make a new life: pick up the pieces, rebuild, begin again.

She and Jim return together to England, to the village of Littlefold, where Jim's sister lives. They buy an old farmhouse, painted white, with low ceilings and beams, and honeysuckle by the front door. It has a comfortable, rambling feel to it. Maggie knows that the farmhouse will be more work than a modern property, but she prefers character to convenience; this is a family home, somewhere she and Jim can settle down. The large garden, with its expanse of lawn and neat borders, looks out onto fields and a copse where the ponies from a neighbouring farm rest on hot days. She can imagine children playing happily here.

Now that she is expecting, nursing will have to wait; instead of caring for the injured, she tends to bantams and nurtures tomatoes. She kept house for her father after her mother died, so she knows how to run a home. She is thrifty and organised, and enjoys cooking. She tries her best to be the good wife that Jim had judged her to be that evening they first met in Foggia.

When Vivien comes, a tiny child with green eyes and auburn hair, she looks so like Maggie's own mother it makes her wonder if she's been reborn. She loves her baby, but it's some time before she can look at Vivien without feeling her chest tighten with longing for her mother, who is gone. Two years later, Michael arrives, dark like Maggie, but with the Howard grey eyes. With a baby and a toddler, her hands are full.

Jim is working as an accountant in London. He leaves on the seven o'clock train, coming home in time to kiss the children before they go to bed. Maggie prepares a three-course meal every evening. Jim is fond of roast dinners and steamed puddings, although you'd never know it: he burns it all off playing squash and tennis.

Housework and children are as tiring as nursing. Washing and ironing clothes, shopping, cooking, tidying, dusting ... it is never-ending. There are times when she misses nursing, the bustle of the ward, the camaraderie of the other nurses, her own money; but a woman's place is at home now, and there is no one else to look after Michael and Vivien. Still, running up and down the stairs all day long keeps her fit. And a family and home are precious; she knows not to take it for granted.

23

It's a different life from when they were in Italy. Their wartime love affair has been replaced by stability, family, routine. And although this is what they both dreamed of there are times, fleeting moments, when Jim kisses her cheek almost chastely or half listens to her recounting an anecdote, when she wonders if he found her more interesting during the war. She is content with this quieter life. She tells herself it's only natural, in a marriage, for the romance to fade.

Jim's sister, Edith, often calls in for a cup of tea at the weekends. She's a handsome woman, tall and fair like Jim, but aloof, not as warm – or at least, she's like that with Maggie. Edith and her husband, George, have more money than they know what to do with. They live in an elegant six-bedroomed house at the end of a beech-lined drive. Edith doesn't have to lift a finger; they have a nanny for their two children, a housekeeper and a gardener. She is always beautifully dressed, a chiffon scarf tied loosely around her neck, her blonde hair set in waves.

Edith is never unpleasant to Maggie, but she doesn't seem to want to be friends either. 'You must come round for tea, Maggie darling,' she says in front of Jim; but later, when he's speaking to George, 'Unfortunately, next week is terribly busy,' and she talks about her children's piano lessons, coffee mornings and appointments. If she and Edith meet at all, it's by chance while shopping in the village. Maggie revises her expectations. Perhaps a polite, arms-length relationship with her sister-in-law is for the best. She is grateful that Jim's parents have retired to France; at least she only has to contend with Edith.

One Sunday lunch, several years later, Maggie finally understands. It's a bright summer's day and, at Jim's suggestion, they meet at the Anchor. The pub's low ceilings and beams seem to trap the heat, and there is a stale smell of chips and beer, but their table is by a window and looks out on to a pretty walled garden and golden fields.

Edith brushes the wooden chair before sitting down, smooths her floral-print swing dress and removes her white gloves. Maggie hopes that Vivien and Michael are behaving themselves with Edith's nanny; they are younger than Harry and Catherine, and can be impulsive.

Jim and George go up to the bar to order. The pub is busy and the two men wait their turn. The barmaid seems to know Jim. She speaks to him and smiles while pulling pints. She is a striking young woman. Dark eyes, smooth olive skin; her shining black hair falls in waves to her waist.

Edith sighs, fanning herself with her hand. 'I'm parched, but at least Jim's got the barmaid's attention.' She gives Maggie one of her tight smiles. 'My brother's always had girls after him. There was an heiress who was terribly keen, before the war. What's your secret, darling? How did you persuade him to settle down?'

Maggie is aware of the way women look at her husband, but it has never troubled her. 'I don't have secrets,' she says lightly. 'Just lucky, I suppose.'

They both watch Jim, leaning against the bar, speaking to the dark-haired girl. She reminds Maggie of the girls she saw in Italy during the war.

'Yes,' Edith says softly, almost kindly.

There is no need to say any more. Jim could have married an heiress. Maggie is a disappointment.

# Sarah

## *Spring 2010*

On the weekend, Paul takes the boys swimming. Sarah clears away the breakfast things, rinsing cornflakes from milky bowls and loading the dishwasher. She makes beds, puts on laundry and redirects the drift of trucks and tractors from the playroom. It's easier to do the chores without the interruptions of Jack and Charlie. She mulls the contents of the fridge – the boys will be hungry when they return – wondering how there is never enough food, even though she is always at the shops.

No matter how she prepares, packing swim bags the night before and setting the table, Saturday morning is always chaos: Jack hopping about in his pants, his hair unbrushed, demanding to know where his Spiderman t-shirt is, Charlie taking off his coat and shoes as quickly as Sarah puts them on, and finally Paul, bellowing at everyone to hurry or there will be no point going at all.

She makes a cup of tea and sits in the glasshouse. There is more evidence of spring in the garden: white blossoms on the apple and plum trees, crocuses and daffodils, buds of leaves. The overgrown lawn glistens with dew. In the field that borders their garden, the willow tree sways, the mole has been burrowing and two rabbits potter near the brambles.

Beyond, the woods are deep, tangled and dark. The inscription for Samuel Thomas has been in her thoughts for days, circling like a song. A bird takes flight, its white breast a lantern over the black woods.

The field is as waterlogged as a rice paddy and she wades across, the mud sucking at her boots and splattering her jeans. The sun is climbing into the sky and she tips her face to the warmth. She looks back and sees their house as a passer-by might: sandy brick walls, wisteria, a grey tile-hung roof, a pitched glasshouse. The palm tree fans its long delicate leaves and the bamboo is a jungle beside the stone patio.

On warm afternoons Jack drags the pirate ship into the baking-hot glasshouse, pronounces himself Captain Sparrow and Charlie as Smee, and they are shipwrecked in the Caribbean. Jack explains this all seriously and what Charlie doesn't understand, he makes up for with enthusiasm. Jack strips off his t-shirt, Charlie does too, and then they are rolling and tussling on the floor until there are yelps, accusations of a pinch or a bite, and she has to separate them. 'Stop it, boys. This is too wild,' she says, but this only delights Jack, who puffs out his chest and shouts, 'We're the Jolly Rogers and we are wild!' Charlie whoops and charges at him, and then they are wrestling on the floor again. At times like these, her boys seem more like animals than children. They are different here, she's noticed: louder, more boisterous, charging around like pups let off the lead.

She's still adjusting to the scale of this house, so much larger than their flat in London. It was a move made possible by the inheritance left by Paul's father, who said that boys should grow up with horses and fields, not buskers and buses. They needed more space, and the paddock is perfect for two young boys.

When they can afford it, she will decorate, painting over the yellowing walls with calm neutrals; she will replace the avocado bathroom suites with white sanitaryware and heated tiles. She dreams of polished walnut floors, a deep-pile velvet carpet, a marble fireplace, a hand-painted kitchen with an island and brushed-chrome appliances. At the hairdresser's, she flicks through copies of *House & Garden* and makes her wish list. For now, the house is comfortable and she doesn't mind Charlie sending the fire engine crashing into the kitchen cupboards, upending his cup and spilling juice on the worn carpet, leaving Marmite finger prints on the walls.

The lake, sheltered by trees, is as enchanting as she remembers. The soft white clouds, the pretty red-brick houses with sloping gardens, the wooden jetties and rowing boats, are all reflected in the lake like an Impressionist painting. Mallards and moorhens paddle, yellow gorse sways and a willow tree dips its boughs in the sea-blue water.

Up close, the lake is as murky as before, choked with weeds. Perhaps the clay soil, stirred up by invisible currents, is tainting the water. The rocks are coated with lichen. A person could easily slip and fall in; no one would know. She wonders if there is machinery at the bottom, abandoned by the miners, sunken like a shipwreck.

The gardens and jetties are still empty, the deckchairs unoccupied. Perhaps the people who live here come outside in the afternoons, when it's warmer.

A boy in a tracksuit and trainers is sitting on Samuel Thomas's seat. His head is bowed, he is wearing a cap and she cannot see his face. The sun comes out from behind a cloud, the lake glitters, and for a moment she is blinded. She looks away. When she looks up again, shading her face with her hand, the boy has gone.

She follows the path around the lake to the bench and sees the white chrysanthemums in cellophane left by the water's edge. It is a small bouquet, from a supermarket or petrol station. The water laps, the wind breathes and sorrow spreads like a stain.

Across the lake, she sees, or thinks she sees, a shadow moving through the trees. She wonders if it's the boy, and if he left the flowers for Samuel Thomas. Her heart aches for the lost child and those who loved him.


The front door opens and Charlie bursts in, wrapping his arms around her knees. Jack staggers behind him, carrying their bags, his raincoat flaring like a cape. Charlie seems to have lost his coat and Jack isn't wearing any socks. She kneels and holds both boys close; their faces are cold and their hair is wet. Usually, she'd be on her feet again, tidying their bags and putting away their coats and shoes, but today she can't let them go.

A car door slams and Paul comes in, stamping his boots on the mat, a newspaper in one hand and a bag of shopping in the other. He smiles down at them. He takes a tissue from his coat pocket and delicately blows his nose; there are shadows under his eyes. Paul leaves early, before they are up, and is home after they've all gone to bed. He is working too hard, as usual.

Charlie wriggles out of her arms, takes off her slippers and tries to put them on over his shoes.

'How was swimming?' Sarah asks.

Jack sits up. 'Good. Daddy let me go in the front and we listened to rock music and there was an old Doris driving too

29

slowly and Daddy said a word, something like shift,' he says all in one breath. He glances sideways at Paul.

'You don't miss a trick,' Paul says, gently cuffing Jack on the ear. 'Hope you don't grass up your mates at school.'

Sarah can always rely on Jack for a full report. 'Oh well,' she says lightly, thinking she must speak to Paul about his language. He sometimes seems to forget that Jack is a child. 'What did you buy at the shops?'

'Brunch,' Paul says, putting down the bag of shopping and taking off his coat. Charlie abandons Sarah's slippers, sits down beside the bag and unpacks a loaf of bread, bacon and a bottle of brown sauce. He holds up a carton of eggs and Sarah quickly says, 'Thanks, poppet. I'll take those.' She doesn't tell Paul that they already have these things; too much food isn't a problem in a house full of boys.

In the kitchen, Paul turns on the radio and hums while he fries bacon and whisks eggs. Jack is dribbling a ball around the table, while Charlie shrieks and chases after him. There will be a bumped head or knee; it's inevitable if this carries on. The sun has come out; Sarah opens the back door and the boys run outside. She watches them play in the garden and unpacks the wet contents of their swimming bags. She discovers Charlie's missing coat, damp from being wound up in his towel, and hangs it up to dry, but finds only one of Jack's socks. She piles everything else into the washing machine that is always on. She unloads the tumble drier and folds the clean clothes ready for ironing, putting aside a school jumper that has a hole and needs mending.

In the kitchen, the worktops are scattered with bread-crumbs, a gooey spatula and mixing bowl, discarded spoons and forks; a frying pan is hissing in the sink. Paul glides past, unaware that the hob is still burning, carrying a platter of crispy bacon, toast and scrambled eggs. The warm butter-salt aroma makes her mouth water. She turns off the hob and calls the boys in from the garden. She will clear the kitchen later, for the second time. Housework is a wheel that keeps turning and she is a mouse that must run and never stop.

They are having supper in the kitchen. The garden is in soft darkness and the fairy lights, reflected in the glasshouse, shine like galaxies of stars. The boys are sleeping and the house is silent.

There are routine matters to discuss, a fence panel has given way and there's a leak in the family bathroom, but time alone together is precious and she doesn't need his advice. She's used to managing the house on her own.

She should recount an amusing anecdote or talk about an engaging drama series on television, but instead she says, 'You're working too hard. The boys hardly see you.' Even as the words leave her lips, she is surprised at the bitterness in her voice.

Paul says nothing, but his brown eyes darken.

She finds herself filling the silence. It's as if they've boarded a train with no stops until their final destination. 'You're never here,' she continues. In the mornings she wakes to the sound of the front door closing and car tyres turning on gravel; in those moments, before the boys are awake, emptiness swells inside her. She and the children often spend weekends on their own, while Paul gets ahead at the office or travels on business. She takes the boys out to the cinema or for pizza, but they are surrounded by families with fathers, and Paul's absence is even more marked.

'One of us has to work,' Paul says.

Sarah thought she would work too, but when it came to it, she couldn't bear the thought of someone else bringing up her children. She knows that she's lucky – not all mothers have a choice – but it isn't easy looking after Jack and Charlie on her own. She's not convinced that Paul needs to work as hard as he does. 'We've been through this before,' she says.

'Yes, we have,' Paul says. 'And you do a great job with the boys and the house.'

He's trying to make peace, but somehow it sounds like a pep talk for a flagging member of staff. 'I'm not your house-keeper,' she says. 'And for the record, nor will I ever don a pinny and bake cakes while you read the paper.'

Paul is smiling, she is too, and the spell is broken. He reaches across the table and takes her hand. 'Understood. I'm sorry. It's a bad patch. I'll try to be at home more.'

'Yes,' she says, but she's heard this before. She knows that Paul will never change, no matter what he promises.

Paul tops up their glasses with wine. She sips, feeling the warmth of the wine in her stomach, and looks out at the garden. The palm tree shivers, the apple trees sway, and there is a rushing sound as the wind blows through the woodland.

'There's a lake, not far from here,' she says. 'It won't be long before Jack and Charlie are off in the woods exploring.'

'So they should,' Paul says. 'This is why we've come here.'

'Yes, but what about the lake? It's dangerous.'

'I'm sure they'd be sensible. We can't wrap them up in cotton wool.'

This is exactly what Sarah would like to do, but she says, 'What if there was an accident? What if one of them fell in?'

Paul considers this for a moment. 'Jack's a fish in the water and Charlie's coming along too. Don't worry. The boys will be strong swimmers.'

'Yes,' she says, but telling a mother not to worry is like telling the rain not to fall.

That night, she lies in their bed awake while Paul sleeps beside her. The ceiling creaks, as if someone is walking in the loft, and in the garden a fox cries. She tries to empty her mind, but it keeps sifting through her to-do list, sorting and reordering, like a tireless but dysfunctional robot. Then at last she is drifting, falling, sinking into sleep.

She wakes, her nightdress sticking to her skin and her heart pounding. The dark dream is fading, disappearing faster than she can make sense of it. It is gone. There are only shadows and a low, dull ache in her stomach. She reaches for Paul, but he has already left for the office.

She swings her legs out of bed, wraps a dressing gown around herself, and draws the curtains. Streaks of pink are lengthening in the sky and the trees are silhouettes. Charlie is calling. She goes to his room, gets into his bed and holds him close. His little body is as warm as a hot-water bottle and the ache in her stomach eases.

Charlie closes his eyes, she does too, and then the room is full of light and Jack is climbing in. The boys giggle and Charlie's feet drum against her thighs like little hooves. She untangles herself from both of them and the morning routine begins.

# Flavia

*Surrey, 1958*

The cropped fields are behind them, bathed in the light of the setting sun. Beyond, the path curves into the shadowed woods. Jim rolls up his sleeves. He loosens his tie. Flavia catches the compressed, stale scent of the commuter train, the washing powder used to launder his shirts, the pint she'd poured him before finishing her shift and, beneath it, a distilled green note that could be the countryside or his cologne.

She smooths her black skirt, which has ridden up, and finds a run in her stockings; another pair ruined by this walk through the fields that they choose more for the privacy than the pastoral surroundings. Not far from here is his wife in the white farmhouse, a woman she's glimpsed from time to time in the village but can't bear to name. Flavia imagines Jim's wife preparing supper, tucking the children into bed, and feels a stabbing pain; guilt, shame, and then a quivering moment of triumph that he is here, with her.

A breeze blows and a few leaves, stained crimson, are swirling around them. Jim turns to her and strokes the hair back from her face. 'You're beautiful,' he murmurs. He moves closer, as if to kiss her, then draws away. They are still in the open here. She longs to pull him to her; she loves this man and wants the world to know. The hopelessness of it is almost enough to extinguish the joy of being with him.

She follows him into the woods. The trees enclose them, hiding them with their branches, and the foliage shelters them. It is quiet. A woman could be murdered and no one would know. He leads her away from the path. In the knotted nests of brambles, blackberries are ripening. The sycamore trees release their seeds and the forest floor is scattered with acorns and the spiky skins of conkers. Clusters of bruised-purple grapes are hanging from a wild, sinuous vine.

He pushes her up against the spine of a tree and although she could slip through his arms and run away, she lets him imprison her once again. His fingers are in her hair, her blouse, his mouth pressed to hers, and then he's pulling up her skirt. Her body ignites and she can't deny him. They are one, moving together, and her conscience forsakes her; this is a dark art, this torture-pleasure.

He leans against her for a moment, his stubble grazing her face, his breath slowing, then pulls away. She buttons her blouse, rearranges her skirt, adjusts her torn stockings. Through the trees a grey haze shimmers, like mist.

She walks towards it, as if in a trance. The woods fall away and she is in a clearing, standing at the edge of a sheer drop. An enormous abyss unfolds beneath her. In the dying light, the barren rock glows like a moonscape. At the base of the crater, there is water, murky and still. She was a child during the war, but if she imagined the aftermath of a bomb, the devastation, it would be like this.

She takes a step backwards. A person could easily stumble, slip and fall in.

'The old quarry,' Jim says softly, behind her. 'They used to mine clay here for bricks.'

This is not what she'd expected, but now that she knows, she can see the signs of it, the trails carved by machinery. In the shadows, a small wooden hut with a pitched roof is attached to a rusting metal structure that looks like a climbing frame. 'What will become of it?' she asks. It seems suddenly important.

The ghost of a moon hangs in the crepuscular sky. The temperature is dropping and she shivers, folding her arms.

'I don't know,' Jim says. He pushes his hand through his hair. 'It's getting late. I should walk you home.'

That night she dreams that she is in the woods again, standing alone beside the abandoned quarry, gazing into its rocky depths. Pillaged, laid waste; it is a lonely, desolate place that troubles her, and yet she is also drawn to it. She senses secrets in this grave.


The water has risen in the old quarry since they were last here. It's been several weeks and they've had heavy rain. She can't see the wooden hut any more, or the metal frame. Another week, or perhaps even days, and it will be completely flooded. She wonders if someone has come to collect the old machinery, but it seems improbable. More likely it has been submerged, completely hidden, and the thought of this makes her feel uneasy, although she doesn't know why.

The pool is a silvery painting of reflected clouds. Lichen is softening the exposed rock. Birds are gathering in the dusky copse and, in the distance, there is the mating cry of a female fox.

She hears footsteps and then Jim is putting his arms around her. She leans into him, his radiating warmth, the pulse of his heart.

'It's a lake,' she says.

'Yes,' he says. 'I hear it's a conservation project. In a few years, no one will guess this was once a clay pit.'

She sees the woods grow, enfolding the old quarry in a sylvan embrace. There will be reeds and fish, and water birds will come. People will bring their children and their dogs, and perhaps even sail here. Butterflies will flit among the trees. In time, this raped, wounded land will heal. No one will remember the old quarry.

'It will be beautiful,' she says. She doesn't understand why her throat aches.

The sky darkens and the water turns to ink. 'Take me home,' she says, wishing it was home for both of them, knowing that he will leave her there, just as he has left her before and perhaps always will.

# Sarah

## *Spring 2010*

Charlie sits in his pushchair, his blond hair lit up by the sun, kicking his legs and observing passing pedestrians. Sarah has finished her errands on the high street – the supermarket, the dry cleaner's – and procured a birthday present for one of Jack's classmates in the toyshop. They needn't hurry back to the car. Jack won't need collecting from school until the afternoon.

Time plays tricks and she is a girl again, skipping in her sandals between her mother and Grandma Maggie, her cotton skirt lifting and falling around her bare legs. Her mother's high heels click on the pavement, but Grandma Maggie's flats make her as silent as a cat. They will stop at the fishmonger's, as it's Friday, then the greengrocer's. Sarah will ask to go to Williams & Son; she is hoping for a comic and a bag of sweets to pass the time while her mother tries on clothes on sale in Mary-Jane.

She could spend all day in Williams & Son: there are racks of glossy magazines, aisles of notebooks and pens, a huge fridge-freezer with fizzy drinks and ice creams, an entire aisle of chocolates and pick 'n' mix sweets. She's never seen a newsagent's with a fitted carpet, or displays of cigars behind the till. Outside, the shop is painted hunter-green, it has gables and a green-and-white-striped awning, and Williams & Son is inscribed in gold letters. Mr Williams, a stout man with a pen behind his ear, always has a kind word for Grandma Maggie.

A man coming out of Williams & Son is holding the door open and looking at her expectantly. She's been thinking about the past and somehow ended up here. She thanks the man and goes in, tilting Charlie's pushchair up and over the threshold. Twenty years on and the shop hasn't changed: the fitted carpet, the glass-box display of cigars, the aisles of sweets, even the smell of sharpened pencils is the same. Mr Williams has retired and his nephew now runs the shop; it is one of the few in the village to survive the soaring rents.

Mark Williams stands behind the till, folding newspapers into bags for his customers. He is a slim and energetic man, nothing like his portly uncle, but there's something about him that reminds her of old Mr Williams; it's his voice, perhaps, or the pen tucked behind his ear. She flicks through a magazine, waiting for the morning rush to clear. Now that she is here, she will ask Mark about the lake; the Williams family have been in Littlefold for generations. Charlie is wriggling out of his straps, trying to break free, and she gives him a packet of chocolate buttons. These days, it's she who does the bribing.

The door swings shut and the shop is quiet.

'Good morning,' Mark says. 'You look like you're enjoying those buttons, little man.'

Charlie beams, offering a sticky button.

'I'll let you have that one,' Mark says. 'How's the new place?' he asks Sarah. 'All settled in?'

'Yes. Just a few boxes left in the garage.'

'Good. Your mother keeping well? Still living in the big smoke?'

'Mum's well, thanks. She works in Paris now.'

Mark considers this. 'Ah, well,' he says. 'Perhaps she'll visit.'

'Yes,' Sarah says, but she isn't sure. When she'd announced they were moving here, her mother was noticeably cool. 'I'd choose the city over suburbia any day, but it's up to you,' she'd said. Sarah wished her mother would be more encouraging, but she wasn't surprised. Vivien always said that Littlefold was too small, and she'd left as soon as she was able.

'It's wonderful to have fields on our doorstep,' Sarah says, guiding the conversation away from her family. 'I've been doing some exploring. I came across that lovely lake in the woods. The old quarry. I thought I'd take Charlie there.'

Mark is quiet for a moment. 'I wouldn't if I were you,' he says. 'That lake's deep. No good for swimming. No good for kids. That poor lad, Samuel Thomas. Perhaps you didn't hear about it in London.'

He's about to go on, but a man who has been browsing through the magazines is approaching the till with a copy of *The Spectator*. The shop door opens and a woman in a quilted jacket, wellington boots, and with a Labrador on a lead comes in. Sarah wants to hear more about Samuel Thomas, but the opportunity for a quiet conversation with Mark Williams is gone. She looks in her purse for change to pay for the chocolate.

Mark waves a hand. 'It's on us.'

'Thanks. See you soon,' Sarah says.

She walks back along the high street. So Samuel Thomas drowned in the lake; this must be what Mark was trying to tell her. She wonders about the boy who left the chrysanthemums. Perhaps he was a brother or a friend.

*

At home, she feels the pull of the lake. In the garden, watching the boys kick a ball, she thinks of white swans gliding on glittering water. Standing at the sink, her hands wash dishes while her mind flits through the woods. At dusk, when the sun brushes the field with gold and the willow tree glows, the birds seem to be calling her. It rains, pattering on the roof of the glasshouse, and she sees tears falling silently into the grey pool.

# Vivien

*Surrey, 1958*

It's the summer holidays, and Vivien is ploughing through bacon and eggs and thick slices of buttered toast. Michael, who is always hungry, is on his second helping. Mummy is writing a shopping list, with a cup of tea beside her. She won't let them leave the table until their plates are empty; growing children need good breakfasts, she says.

They are sitting in the kitchen, looking out at the sunlit garden and the misty fields. It's washing day and Mummy will tell her and Michael to play outside while she soaps and rinses clothes and wrings them out with the mangle. At least the clothes can be pegged on the line outside; in the winter, wet clothes steam by the hearth and take ages to dry.

Her mother is always washing and ironing, cleaning and shopping. Vivien is ten and old enough to help, but Mummy says the best help is to mind Michael. Vivien is secretly relieved. She'd rather climb trees with her brother than turn the mangle. Sometimes she runs errands for her mother, pedalling her bicycle to the corner shop to buy sugar or eggs.

She and Michael have finished and they help clear the table, stacking the dishes next to the sink. Mummy is wearing an apron and her dark hair is pinned up. Vivien wishes she had brown hair too, but Mummy says Vivien is lucky to have auburn hair like her grandmother. Vivien isn't sure. In the mirror her hair is the colour of carrots, and the portrait of the grandmother she's never met shows a heavy, stern-looking woman with reddish-brown hair scraped into a bun. She's never met Daddy's mother either – she lives in France – but she might this summer. Aunt Edith often goes to France, taking Catherine and Harry, and she's going to ask if Vivien can come. Daddy will say yes – he always does to Aunt Edith – but she's not sure about her mother. And if Mummy doesn't like the idea, there will be a row.

Her parents argue all the time. They think she's asleep, but she can hear them shouting. She lies awake, wishing they'd stop, and then Michael comes in and climbs into her bed. She puts her arms around him and sings softly, and they wait for it to be quiet again. In the morning, her mother looks pale and her father leaves without saying goodbye. She doesn't know why her parents fight. She wonders if her father has been naughty, the way Michael is sometimes, and Mummy has to tell him off.

Aunt Edith is kind to Vivien, taking her out for tea and giving her presents, but it seems to make Mummy cross. Maybe it's because her mother would like to take Vivien out too, but hasn't got time. She doesn't have a housekeeper, like Aunt Edith. Vivien loves her mother, but she can't help admiring Aunt Edith, who is so glamorous in her dresses, pearls and high heels. When she grows up, she wants to be like her aunt, not like her mother, who is always tired.

Vivien climbs over the garden fence and the breeze blows back her hair. She turns to help Michael, who has caught his foot, and sees the white brick farmhouse. It looks peaceful in the morning sun. She and Michael race across the field to the copse, where they climb trees and build dens.

Lunch is a picnic in the garden. Vivien and Michael sit in the shade of the chestnut tree, eating cold beef sandwiches. The sun is high and it is hot. Bees are playing hide and seek in the clover, and the ponies in the field swish their tails. After they've finished their sandwiches, they lie down and look up at the blue sky, and make up stories about the slow-moving clouds.

After a while she sits up. She picks a buttercup, holds it beneath Michael's chin and his skin glows. 'You like butter,' she says, and he smiles.

They gather daisies, weave chains and adorn each other with floral crowns. Prince Michael rides off on his steed to fight battles in the copse and Vivien invites her dolls to a royal garden party.

The sun softens, the shadows of the trees lengthen across the lawn, and Mummy calls them in for tea.

'What have we here? A flower fairy and a woodland sprite,' she says. She takes out her hanky and dabs at a smudge on Michael's cheek. 'A few bumps to tend to, I see.' Michael has a splinter in his finger and Vivien has scraped her knee, but neither of them can remember how it happened. Mummy cleans and dresses Vivien's knee, and uses tweezers to take out Michael's splinter. They don't fuss. Mummy used to be a nurse, she's careful, and it doesn't hurt. They are sent to wash their hands and the cold water makes Vivien shiver.

Tea is shepherd's pie, which she hates on account of the mashed potato. When her mother isn't looking, she spoons the sticky sludge onto Michael's plate. Pudding is gooseberry crumble and a jug of cream. She dips her finger in the cream, paints a dot on her nose and Michael laughs. They have seconds and aren't allowed any more. 'You'll have tummy ache and there won't be any left for Daddy's supper,' Mummy says.

At bedtime, her mother comes to tuck her in. She's tidied her hair and changed into a clean dress, and her eyes are sparkling. 'You look pretty,' Vivien says.

Her mother smiles. She strokes Vivien's cheek. 'Sweet dreams,' she says, closing the door gently behind her.

Vivien sleeps and then is suddenly awake. Her room is dark and the house is quiet. Her throat feels dry. She slips out of bed and goes downstairs.

Her mother is sitting at the kitchen table, which is set for two. The chair where her father should be is empty. Two plates are covered with foil.

'What is it, Vivien?' Her mother sounds hoarse. Her eyes are red.

'I'm thirsty. Where's Daddy?'

Her mother looks away. 'The war was easier,' she says, and her voice breaks.

Vivien doesn't understand. She moves closer to her mother. 'Mummy?'

Her mother gathers Vivien in her arms, holding her tight, and Vivien can't see her face. After a moment, she pulls away. She pours Vivien a glass of water. 'Daddy will be home soon. Off to bed now, darling. It's late.'

Vivien goes back to bed and lies awake for a long time, listening for her father's key in the lock, but all she hears is the hoot of an owl and the wind whispering in the garden.

# Sarah

*Easter 2010*

It is Easter and the boys are hers for three weeks. Sarah feels a weight lift on the last day of term; no uniform or homework, no rushing in the mornings to get to school. By the end of the holidays, Jack and Charlie will be bickering, the novelty of being together at home will have worn off, but for now the weather is fine and they spend their days outdoors.

She is standing in the sunny paddock, watching Jack and Charlie hunt for caterpillars and snails. Jack turns stones over and studies leaves; Charlie follows, waving his stick like a sword. The willow tree floats as if in water.

The field is dotted with earthy hills. When they'd first moved in, she and Paul had wanted to trap the mole and roll the field, but she's grown fond of this shy, industrious animal and wouldn't want him to be gone. None of them have ever seen the mole, and this adds to his mystery and intrigue.

Jack is sitting on top of the gate, swinging his legs, the breeze lifting his fine, dark hair. Charlie crouches in the long grass, holding a worm in his palm, talking to it in his own made-up language. At times like these, she half expects to see Grandpa Jim setting up croquet on the lawn and Grandma Maggie carrying out a tray with tea and freshly baked scones. She hadn't realised how disjointed it would feel living in Littlefold without them.

Sarah wonders if the people who reside by the lake are sitting in their gardens or untethering their boats. She won't be able to go there again until the holidays are over. Jack would enjoy a walk through the woods, but Charlie's little legs wouldn't manage it and he's too heavy to carry.

They stay at home and the world melts away. It's just her and the boys, their garden and the field, and the creatures that inhabit it.

Sarah is up early. Paul's car turning out of the gravelled drive woke her and she's given up trying to sleep. In another hour, the boys will be up, but for now the house is quiet.

She stands in the kitchen, warming her hands around a mug of tea, looking out at the frost-covered lawn. Mist wreathes the paddock and makes a blanket for the willow tree. The woods are in shadow.

A dark shape is leaping through the mist. At first, she thinks a dog has got into the field, but it's moving too gracefully.

A roe deer, with liquid eyes and tapering ears, is standing beside the gate. It is watching her. She longs to touch its velvet coat. She doesn't move, anxious not to startle this beautiful, delicate creature. Perhaps it is lost. Suddenly, the deer freezes, it's body tensing, bracing to run. She wonders if it's a neighbour, out walking their dog. When she looks back at the deer, it is gone. There is only the mist in the paddock, the woods beyond.

The unseasonable frost signals a change and a gale rolls down through the woods. The willow tree lifts as if it might

47

take flight, the oak trees bend and the wind throws petals on the wet lawn. The bright sunny days that they've been enjoying are over. The last week of the holidays will be spent indoors.

Charlie's nose starts to run and Jack goes hoarse. Colds are routine, but then Sarah is woken one night by crying. She wraps a dressing gown around herself and finds Charlie standing at the gate to the nursery, shuffling in his sleeping bag, tears on his flushed cheeks.

She carries him downstairs, takes his temperature and gives him infant paracetamol, which he dislikes; he spits some of it out, leaving a sticky pink stain on his pyjama top. He wrinkles his nose at a beaker of water, but eventually she persuades him to drink. She takes him back upstairs.

A fever is always a worry, but there is no sign of a rash. He is tugging his ear and she wonders if he has an infection. She changes his top and tries to put him back to bed, but he won't lie down. His bottom lip juts out the way it does when he's truly miserable.

The night passes slowly with Charlie lying in her arms. He is more comfortable with his head raised and she thinks it must be his ear that is troubling him. He is heavy against her shoulder and her arm aches from holding him. Paul is away on business – he's never here when the boys are unwell; it seems to be an unwritten rule, along with children falling ill in the middle of the night. She listens to rain pattering against the window, and drifts in and out of sleep.

'Mummy!' Jack has jumped onto the bed and is wriggling under the duvet. 'What's Charlie doing here?' he asks, but before she can answer, he says, 'Can I have a croissant for breakfast? And can I dress up? I want to be a crocodile.'

Sarah almost smiles, but her head feels like lead and her mouth is dry. She glances at the clock on the bedside table: it's just gone six. She pulls Jack close with her other arm. His warm feet brush hers and his body feels long and lanky; his legs seem to have grown overnight. 'Charlie isn't well. Yes, you can have a croissant and dress up, but Charlie needs to sleep and so do I. Could you be a big, helpful boy and play quietly in your room until it's seven o'clock?'

'Poor Charlie,' Jack says, stroking his brother's cheek. 'He'll have to have medicine. At least he can watch TV.' Jack knows the routine. 'I'll make him a card.'

Jack is a caring child; at times like this he seems older than his six years. He's always helped her with Charlie, right from the beginning, passing her nappies and trying to make Charlie laugh when he cried in the bath. She sometimes wonders how she'd manage without Jack, which is a peculiar thought to have about a child. She can imagine him grown-up, always looking out for her and Charlie, but she doesn't want him to feel it's his job.

'I'm sure he'd love that, but why don't you play with your Lego now and make him a card later?' Jack doesn't often get his Lego down; the tiny pieces are a worry with Charlie, who puts everything in his mouth.

'OK.' Jack climbs out of bed and then she can hear him in his room, dragging a chair over to the shelf where his Lego is. She drifts off again, but then Charlie is stirring; he tries to sit up and accidentally smacks her face with the back of his hand. She swings her legs down from the bed, wishing already that she could get back in.

The doctor has prescribed antibiotics for Charlie's ear infection, and Sarah takes the boys to the pharmacy and the supermarket while it buckets down rain. They are home at last, the boys are watching television, and she is wondering how to persuade Charlie to swallow his medicine, which looks like glue and smells like liquorice.

49

The dishwasher lights are flickering in an odd way. She switches it off, empties it and then loads it with the breakfast plates, scraping flakes of croissant and jam into the bin. She tries to switch it on, but nothing happens. The machine beeps, as if transmitting a coded message. She turns it off, then on again; still nothing. She will have to wash the dishes up in the sink and call out an engineer.

Sarah is always surprised at the speed at which domestic life unravels. First a sick child, then the dishwasher breaks; there will be something else – like buses, it always comes in threes. It could be worse, Paul will say later when he rings from his hotel with a view over the Côte d'Azur, and although this is true, she will have to resist the urge to put down the phone. Cocktails and canapés for him this evening; a sleepless night for her. She doesn't want to be a complaining housewife, but she can see how it happens. It's a slow, almost imperceptible change, brought by a life revolving around the school run and the supermarket, household chores that are never done, the constant demands of children. She'd go back to the office, but she wouldn't trust anyone else with her boys while they are little; by the time they are older, it will be too late – a keen and unencumbered graduate will have taken her place.

'Hello Mummy.' Jack is standing in the kitchen.

'What is it, poppet? Would you like a drink?'

Jack opens the fridge, hopping on one foot while he scans the shelves, and takes out a pot of yoghurt. 'I can hop twenty times without stopping. It's a record,' he says, peeling off the plastic lid and licking it. 'Someone's at the door. And Charlie's got your handbag.'

Sarah hurries into the hall and finds Charlie sitting on the floor next to her unzipped bag; her keys, tissues, a packet of raisins and crumpled receipts are carefully arranged around it.

He looks up at her and smiles, offering a lipstick. She quickly repacks her handbag and opens the front door.

A man with dark silvered hair and navy overalls is standing on her doorstep. His sleeves are rolled up, and his tanned arms look capable and strong. Sarah's hand flies up to smooth her hair. Charlie is hiding behind her, holding her knees. The man smiles warmly at her, then Charlie.

'Beautiful bambino,' he says, in a rich, lyrical voice. Sarah feels disoriented, as if she's found herself in an opera.

'Hello,' she says, finding her voice. 'Can I help you?'

The man holds out a business card. 'Do you need a gardener? I look after Mr and Mrs Joneses' garden. I am here every week, working with two others.'

The card is black, with elegant silver script: *Nico Saunders. Landscape Gardening and Maintenance*. Mr and Mrs Jones are the retired couple who live next door. She has heard a van turn into their driveway every week, the unloading of machinery, the rumble of a lawnmower. The Joneses' lawn is striped, the flowerbeds are neat and the hedge is pruned. Their own garden could do with attention, the beds have weeds and the grass is long, but Paul wouldn't agree to a gardener; he likes to do it himself, although he doesn't have the time.

Sarah looks at the card again. Saunders is an English name, but this man doesn't sound like he's grown up in Surrey.

'I could look at your garden now, if you like. Give you a quote.'

She knows she can't hire him, but she says, 'Yes. Thank you.'

He doesn't ask to come in. Instead he goes through the side gate and she meets him outside.

It is still blustery, but the rain has stopped. The wind blows Nico Saunders' dark hair back from his face. He stands on the patio, feet apart, arms folded, quietly surveying the garden. Charlie sails past on his scooter, first one way, then the other. It's hard to believe that he had a fever last night.

'What are you doing?' Jack is leaning out of the glasshouse door, staring at Nico.

'Come and say hello. This nice man is looking at our garden.'

Jack doesn't move. 'Why?'

His question is ambiguous and Sarah chooses the more polite interpretation. 'He's a gardener. Why don't you put on your shoes and come and play with Charlie?'

'I don't know where they are,' Jack says contrarily, although they both know that he does.

Sarah gives up and turns back to Nico, who says, 'Your garden is very nice, but it needs work. The field, it is yours?'

'Yes,' Sarah says.

Nico's gaze drifts over the woods. He says something, but his voice is too low to catch the words. He shakes his head, as if to clear his thoughts, and turns to her. His dark eyes seem to see through her, right to the heart of her, and suddenly she has a terrible feeling that she might cry. She looks away, trying to compose herself. She is tired, that is all.

'I will give you a quote. I will write to you. Yes?'

He sounds concerned. She must look dreadful.

She tries to smile. 'Thank you,' she says. It is a waste of his time, but she doesn't know what else to do.

Later, she takes the rubbish out to the bins, and finds that the leaning sycamore tree has fallen across and blocked their driveway. That's three, she thinks, and goes inside to call the council.

# Edith

*Surrey, 1961*

Edith is sitting at the kitchen table, making a guest list for George's fortieth birthday party. Anna is ironing, her long hair falling over her shoulders; she hums softly, gliding the iron over the board, and the creases vanish. The house is quiet. Catherine and Harry are at school, and George is at work.

'I'm nearly at a hundred. We'll need a marquee,' Edith says, thinking aloud, tapping her pencil against her leather-bound notebook.

Anna slips one of George's shirts over a hanger. It is perfectly pressed. 'It will be lovely to have a party at home,' she says thoughtfully, arranging Harry's school shorts on the ironing board.

Edith looks out at the garden, the large wrap-around limestone terrace and the manicured lawn with its scalloped borders sloping down to the rose garden and the orchard of white-blossomed apple trees. It will be beautiful in the autumn, a fiesta of gold and crimson leaves; perfect for a party. She will speak to the gardener about outdoor lighting and George would love fireworks. Of course, October can be cold and wet; a heated marquee would be prudent.

Once the guest list is done, she will have invitations printed, book the caterers, choose the menu and finalise the seating plan. George is busy at the office, but he can leave it to her. She likes to be busy. There's nothing worse than watching the minutes tick by until it's time to collect the children. There are times when she envies George: his career, his freedom, his life beyond Littlefold. She'd have liked to work, she did well at school, but mothers were expected to stay at home. The world has changed, but it's too late for her. Still, she is grateful. She has a loving husband, two happy children and a beautiful home. They have their health and don't need to worry about money. She knows that help at home is a luxury, but she can't imagine life now without Anna, and the nanny was a godsend when the children were little. She doesn't know how women with young families, like her sister-in-law, manage on their own.

The doorbell is ringing. She isn't expecting visitors. Anna puts down the iron and disappears into the hall. There are voices, too low to hear the words, then the sound of footsteps advancing. She closes her notebook. She smooths her hair.

It's her brother. His face looks bloodless. His eyes are as dark as slate.

'Jim,' she says, standing up. He's wearing a suit, but it's too late for him to be going to the office. It doesn't look like he's brushed his hair. His tie is askew. 'What's happened?' she asks, desperate to know, dreading his answer. 'Are the children all right? Is Maggie?'

Jim nods, but doesn't speak. Edith breathes out the air that she didn't know she was holding inside her. Her brother's arm moves, very slightly, and she notices the folded letter in his hand. She wonders what news it brings: the death of a friend, a court case, bankruptcy . . .

Anna has put the kettle on and is opening cupboards, placing cups and saucers on a tray. 'Anna, please bring the tea to the sitting room,' she says. She will drink the tea, but her brother needs a brandy.

Jim seems to sleepwalk into the sitting room, then sits down on the blue velvet armchair that was left to Edith by their mother. Edith sits opposite him, on the new Parker Knoll sofa, the glass-topped coffee table between them. Jim's hand, still gripping the letter, is trembling. He drinks down the inch of brandy she pours for him, but still doesn't say a word.

'Darling, what's the matter? Please tell me,' she says.

He leans forward and gives her the letter. She unfolds it and quickly reads the brief lines of inky-blue, flowing script.

Dear Jim,

I am expecting a baby. Our child.
    I haven't told anyone. I do not wish to cause pain.
    If you want to know your child, you may.

                                            Yours always,
                                            Flavia

She carefully folds the letter and gives it back to her brother. He tucks it into his jacket pocket. Flavia is the Italian barmaid at the Anchor. She's an attractive young woman: long dark hair, black eyes, skin as smooth as butter. She has the curves that men like.

A few years ago, she saw a spark between Jim and the Italian girl. She tried to warn Maggie, but her sister-in-law wouldn't listen; it was pride or, more likely, denial. Perhaps the affair has been going on all this time. She doesn't approve, but she isn't surprised that Jim has strayed. She never understood why he married Maggie. It was very sudden, during the war. The family hadn't been able to go to the wedding. It had upset them all, at the time. Before the war Jim had been courting Elizabeth Page, the daughter of a local property developer. It would have been a fine match. She and Elizabeth went to school together; they were friends. Maggie is different. She never lets down her guard. She doesn't give anything away. It's as if she's behind an invisible shield that no one can penetrate. This must be what happens when a girl loses her mother, or a woman is a nurse in the war. It's easy to admire Maggie, who is so capable and strong, but perhaps she didn't show Jim enough affection. No doubt she was overstretched, doing all the housework and looking after the children.

She wonders if her brother loves Flavia. If he does, he might leave Maggie and go with Flavia to Italy. Vivien and Michael would lose their father. The thought of Jim leaving makes her throat ache. She almost lost him once, when he left for the war. She can't risk losing him again.

Anna comes in carrying a tray with a teapot, a small jug of milk, a sugar bowl, and two cups and saucers. She puts the tray down on the glass-topped table, then leaves, closing the door quietly behind her.

Edith waits for a moment, then says, 'Do you love her?'

'Yes. I don't know.' Jim looks away. 'The past few years have been difficult. Maggie and I drifted apart. We weren't getting along. Flavia was kind ...' His voice is tight. He is starting to cough, the way he used to as a child.

'Do you still love Maggie?'

'She's my wife. She was my angel—' He breaks off, interrupted by a coughing fit. Suddenly, Edith is eight years old again, woken in the night by her little brother's cries and the sound of her mother's quick footsteps on the stairs. She stands beside his cot, shivering in her nightdress, talking softly to him while her mother boils water to steam his room. He coughed so hard, he was sick.

She pours him a cup of tea. 'Here,' she says, gently. 'This will help.'

Jim takes a sip of tea. His coughing subsides. 'She'll never forgive me,' he says.

Edith isn't sure if he's referring to Flavia or Maggie. Perhaps he doesn't know. There will be pain, no matter which way he turns. If he stays with Maggie, it will be better for Vivien and Michael. If he leaves, there is a risk that he'll leave them all. And she isn't certain that Jim will be able to choose. If he loves them both, and it seems that he does, it will be impossible. A baby will bind Jim more tightly to Flavia. The affair will carry on.

Regardless of her intentions, Flavia will confide in someone. One person is all it takes: all of Littlefold will be humming with the news. Jim Howard and a barmaid! Poor Maggie. Mind you, that'll bring the Howards down a peg. She can already hear the whispers behind hands, see the sideways glances. She can't bear the thought of the family being gossiped about. It won't be fair on Maggie and the children. It will be horrid for all of them.

'Don't tell Maggie. It would only hurt her,' Edith says. She's quiet for a moment, thinking. 'Perhaps Flavia should have the baby in Italy,' she says. 'She'll have her family to help her. It will give you both time to think.'

Jim shakes his head. 'I don't know. I'm not sure she'll listen to me.'

No one would blame Flavia if she didn't. Men don't understand about childbirth or babies. Perhaps it would be better coming from a woman. 'I could try speaking to her, if you like.'

'I couldn't ask you to do that,' Jim says, but his voice lifts.

2B Hawthorn Road is a fifties semi-detached house on the outskirts of Littlefold, near the old brickworks and quarry pit. Edith has heard that the council is transforming the pit into a nature reserve, but it's an ambitious project and whether it's successful remains to be seen. This is a neighbourhood of tradesmen; the vans of builders, plumbers and electricians are parked on the paved driveways. Net curtains are twitching and she regrets bringing the new Jag. She should have come in the Audi, but her mind had been rehearsing what she'd say to Flavia, and the Jag's keys were in her handbag.

Flavia lives here with her uncle and aunt. When Edith telephoned, Flavia invited her for coffee. Edith unfolds her compact mirror and applies lipstick. She carefully steps out of the car, smoothing her shift dress. She's too formal, but it can't be helped. She has a charity lunch and there won't be time to go home and change.

She stands on the doorstep, listening to the bell ring inside. These boxy pebble-dashed semis are unappealing, but 2B is neat and cheerful, with clipped grass and clean windows, and hanging baskets of peonies.

The door opens and Flavia says, 'Please, come in.' She smiles, but her voice wavers. Her black hair falls loosely around her shoulders. Her skin is glowing. She steps aside, cradling her swollen stomach with her hand. Edith feels a twinge of envy; her own pregnancies left her pale and exhausted, but Flavia looks radiant and womanly. She wonders, fleetingly, what the baby will be like. Jim's child. She pushes the thought out of her mind.

They sit opposite each other on paisley sofas in the pink-carpeted lounge. Edith sips the dark coffee that is too strong and accepts a biscotti that she doesn't touch. The ceilings are low and unsoftened by coving, but the large windows make the lounge airy and bright. The house is silent. Flavia's aunt and uncle must have gone out. A menu from a restaurant she hasn't heard of, La Trattoria, has been left on the coffee table. Caponata, arancina, granita; she doesn't know the dishes, but the words are lyrical and exotic, and make her think of summer holidays in the Mediterranean.

'La Trattoria is my uncle's restaurant,' Flavia says. 'Sicilian food. It's in Fenton.'

Fenton is a busy suburb that Edith passes through when she drives up to town. She's never had a reason to visit.

'How interesting. My husband adores cooking from the Continent. We must try it some time,' she says politely, wondering why Flavia didn't choose to work at her uncle's restaurant instead of the local pub.

'I would like to be a waitress, but there isn't a vacancy,' Flavia says, as if she's guessed Edith's thoughts. 'For now, I work at the pub.'

Waitressing will be difficult with a baby. Edith puts down her cup of coffee. She brushes a fleck of lint from her dress. 'Flavia,' she says. 'Jim has asked me to speak to you.'

'Yes,' Flavia says. She folds her hands in her lap, then inter-links her fingers.

'He is terribly worried. He has a family, a wife and two children. They don't know about you.'

'I don't want to make problems. I have written to Jim.'

'Yes. He showed me your letter,' Edith says. 'But there will be talk. It's inevitable.'

Flavia lifts her chin. 'I will not talk.'

'No,' Edith says. She tries again. 'Your aunt and uncle

must be very busy with the restaurant. Looking after a baby will be tiring. Does your mother still live in Italy? Have you considered going home to have the child?'

Flavia is quiet for a moment. She looks away. When she looks back at Edith, her eyes are shining. 'Yes, I have been thinking about this. I will go back to Sicily. My mother will help me.'

Relief rolls over Edith like a wave. 'That sounds very sensible.' She opens her handbag and takes out an envelope. Jim would be furious if he knew, but George thought it was worth a try. 'Please, take this.' She places the envelope on the coffee table.

Flavia looks at the envelope, then at Edith. Her back seems to stiffen. 'Thank you, but I don't need money,' she says, quietly. She stands. 'My aunt and uncle will be home soon.'

Edith had come prepared to dislike Flavia – she disapproves of adultery – but this young woman is gracious and dignified, and she can see why Jim has fallen in love with her. She thinks again of the unborn child, cocooned inside, and feels a pang. The child will grow up without a father. No good will come of this line of thought, she tells herself. A child can't miss what he's never had. It would be worse for Vivien and Michael. She picks up her handbag and puts the envelope back into it. 'I understand. I wish you all the best.'

'Thank you. Goodbye,' Flavia says.

Edith drives away from Hawthorn Road, leaving the pebble-dashed semis and the old brickworks behind. So Flavia will go to Italy. Whether she stays there is another matter, but there is no need to think of that now.

# Sarah

*Late Spring 2010*

The Easter holidays are over and the boys are back at school. It's been a month since Sarah was here. The dry leaves are gone, swept or blown away, and her footsteps fall silently on the woodland path. A soft, greenish light filters through the thick canopy of trees. Toadstools are sprouting out of tree stumps and the mildewed crevices of coppiced logs.

At the top of the hill, she stands in long grass, looking out at the shimmering fields, the distant border of leafy trees. An aeroplane draws a white arc in the blue sky. The sun seems to pulse. A rabbit stands, motionless, then drops to all fours and runs away. She lifts her arms above her head and stretches, then walks on, trying not to touch the verges of overgrown nettles.

She climbs over the stile, crosses the field where the two mares are grazing, and she's into the woods again. The path drops and the ivy-clad trees seem even taller than she remembers. White feathers, caught in the undergrowth, flutter like tiny flags. There is holly with blood-red berries, and delicate, draping ferns. Someone has woven branches into a den.

The trees muffle sound. Soft noises, the rustling of a bird or rabbit, seem magnified. A twig snaps and she looks around, but there is no one. She wonders if it is foolish to walk in the woods on her own. Surrey isn't the safe place it once was; the days of children being turned outside to play are gone. Perhaps Aunt Edith was right, she should not be here, but the path is levelling out and here is the wooden plank bridge.

The lake sparkles like a turquoise sea. Birds are singing, butterflies flit and bees flock to drifts of bluebells. It is warm and still, and the anxiety she'd felt in the woods evaporates.

For the first time, there are people in the sloping gardens. An elderly couple is sitting at a picnic table, drinking tea, on chairs positioned for the afternoon sun. The woman, as tanned as leather, is wearing a kaftan and oversized sunglasses. The man, reading a newspaper, is also very brown; his face is shaded by a panama hat, and he is in a polo shirt and shorts. Sarah wonders if they've spent the winter on a cruise ship, touring tropical islands. A young woman in a sundress is lying on a jetty, one hand holding a book, the other trailing in the water.

Sarah sits on Samuel Thomas's bench. The sun warms her face. Gadwalls paddle in the shade of the willow tree's green veils and her thoughts are drifting like the ripples.

Someone is sitting down beside her. Her neck prickles and the tiny hairs on her arms rise. She hears the strike and fizz of a match, then glances sideways and sees a boy, his cap pulled down low, lighting a cigarette. He is in a hooded tracksuit and trainers, regulation clothing for teenage boys. He leans away, rummaging in a bag, and takes out a can of lager. She wonders if he's the boy she saw here before.

He takes off his cap and runs his fingers through his tufted blond hair. He's young, perhaps sixteen, but his face doesn't have the awkward proportions of an adolescent. His skin is smooth, like honey. He's tall, even sitting down, and has the broad shoulders of a boy who rows or swims.

He breathes smoke out slowly, then jabs his cigarette in the direction of the elderly couple and the woman sunbathing. 'Look at them,' he says disapprovingly, even though he's the one drinking and smoking on a school day. He takes a swig from the can and she wonders if it's his first beer today. He stands up, swaying a little. 'This isn't the fucking Costa del Sol, you pretentious twats,' he shouts across the lake. The couple flinch, then quickly look away. The woman doesn't move and the book hides her face. They know him, Sarah thinks.

The boy sits down. He takes another drag from his cigarette. 'Idiots,' he mutters.

He doesn't seem to expect her to respond, but at the same time, it's impossible to act as if nothing has happened. She feels uneasy sitting next to him. She wishes that she hadn't come. She pretends to study her watch, then swings her bag over her shoulder.

'Going, are you?' His grey eyes pierce her.

'I have to collect my son,' she says, somehow feeling obliged to offer an excuse.

'You don't look old enough to have a kid.'

She's not sure if this is a compliment or an insult. 'I've got two.' And then, because she says it so often, 'Both boys. A six-year-old and a toddler.'

He taps ash from his cigarette. He smiles. 'I thought you were an artist, looking for something to paint.'

She feels the blood rush to her face. 'No. I like to walk, that's all.'

He reminds her of someone, those eyes, that smile, but she can't think who it is. Perhaps it's an actor from a film. 'You're new round here, I can tell,' he says.

She can't decide if he's mocking her, or trying to chat her up. 'I'm not that new. My mother's a Howard and my family's been in Littlefold for generations.' She knows that she sounds pompous. 'I must go.'

He starts to say something, but then seems to change his mind.

She walks away without looking back. The nape of her neck tingles and she knows he's watching her.

# Vivien

*Surrey, 1961*

Vivien is crouching in the fruit and vegetable patch, picking raspberries. She is thirteen years old. The fruit is soft and delicate, and her fingers are stained with juice that looks like blood. Daddy is picking gooseberries, which is tricky because of the prickles, so he's wearing gloves. Gooseberries need to be baked in a crumble and sprinkled with sugar before she or Michael will eat them.

She sits back on her heels. It is hot and the sun simmers like an egg broken into the blue sky. There are hay bales in the fields beyond and two ponies are resting in the shade of the copse. Michael is also supposed to be picking raspberries, but his bucket is only a quarter full.

'You'd better not have any more. You'll get tummy ache,' Vivien says.

'I won't,' Michael says. 'You've had as much as me.'

'I have not,' Vivien says. Her bucket is nearly full.

'You have,' Michael insists. 'You've been pinching mine.'

There was a time when Vivien would rise to this, but

she's a teenager now, nearly an adult. She decides to take no notice.

Her father tosses a handful of gooseberries into his pail, stands up and takes off his gardening gloves. He has a smudge of dirt on his cheek and his blonde hair is tousled. Drops of sweat have gathered by his temples. If he's heard their bickering, he shows no sign of it. He's been quiet like this for days. His eyes seem to look past them and his answers to their questions often don't make sense. He's rummaging in his trouser pockets. 'I must have left my keys in my jacket,' he says. 'Vivi, can you run inside and have a look for them upstairs? I want to get the sprinkler out of the garage.'

After the bright sun in the garden, the house is as cool and dark as a church. She runs the tap in the kitchen sink and fills a glass. She drinks down the cold water and fills the glass again. It is quiet. Mummy has cycled to the corner shop to buy sugar and butter for the crumble.

Her parents' bedroom is large and airy, but the wooden beams make it cosy. Through the window, her father is still toiling in the fruit and vegetable patch. Michael is turning cartwheels on the lawn, kicking his bare legs into the sky. He'll be sick after all those raspberries.

Her father's jacket is draped across the dressing-table stool. Vivien bends to pick up the jacket and sees her reflection in the glass. Her hair is darkening, just like Mummy said it would; glossy and deep red, like wine. She wonders when she'll be allowed to pierce her ears. She'd choose pearls, like the ones Aunt Edith wears.

She empties the pockets of her father's jacket: coins, mints, a train ticket and the keys. There is also a letter, folded into a small square. Inky-blue cursive script has stained the thin tissue-like paper. This isn't one of her mother's shopping

66

lists. She unfolds the letter once, then twice. She sits down on the stool.

There is the sound of footsteps, running up the stairs, and then her father is in the doorway, looking flushed and out of breath. She has already folded the letter and is slipping it back into his jacket, but it's too late. He knows what she's seen.

He takes his jacket from her. 'You shouldn't read other people's letters,' he says, softly.

She can't speak. Her face flames. She wishes she could go back in time, to that moment when she first saw the letter. She would never have opened it if she'd known. She can't make sense of it.

Her father kneels and takes her hands in his. His eyes are watery and the thought that he might cry is terrifying. 'It's all right,' he says, but his voice breaks. He looks away. He's swallowing and swallowing, as if something's stuck in his throat. Eventually he says, 'You mustn't tell anyone.' He tightens his grip on her hands. 'Please, Vivi. Promise me.'

'Yes,' she says. It's her fault for reading the letter.

Her father breathes out slowly. He releases her hands and stands up. 'Good,' he says. He runs his fingers through his hair. 'Right. Let's get the sprinkler.'

Aunt Edith has suggested that she go up to Catherine's old room, to see if there are any books she'd like to borrow, while she and Daddy have a cup of tea. Vivien envies Catherine, who is eighteen and on holiday in Spain with friends from university. She runs her fingers along the spines of the books gathering dust on the shelf: *Ballet Shoes*, *Anne of Green Gables*, *Little House on the Prairie* – she's fond of these stories, but she read them all years ago.

Arranged on the dressing table is a blue plastic brush, a framed photograph of Catherine with a group of giggling school friends, an old Max Factor lipstick and a bottle of Estée Lauder's Youth Dew. Two coats and a few dresses that Catherine has grown out of are hanging in the wardrobe. This room is a museum to Catherine's childhood; closed up, bereft. She goes downstairs.

In the drawing room, her father and her aunt are sitting close together on the sofa, talking in low voices. There's something complicit about the way Aunt Edith touches her father's arm, the way he leans towards her. His face mirrors her expressions; he speaks, adopting her tone and cadence. They look up and she sees how similar they are: fair hair, handsome, angular faces, variable grey eyes. Aunt Edith is elegant, with her blow-dried bob, carefully applied make-up and shift dress. Her father is lean and boyish, in his polo shirt and trousers, with ruffled hair. It's as if they've both been cut from the same rock, but her aunt is more polished.

'Vivien, there you are. Come and sit with us,' Aunt Edith says brightly, as if she's forgotten that it was her idea for Vivien to go up to Catherine's room.

Vivien sits down opposite them on the velvet armchair with a high back that makes her think of a throne. Aunt Edith leans forward, balancing on the edge of the sofa, her silk-stockinged knees pressed together, and pours Vivien a cup of tea.

'Have a biscuit,' her father says, pointing to a plate of custard creams, chocolate bourbons and ginger nuts – no doubt left over from one of her aunt's coffee mornings.

Vivien is trying to watch her weight, but she can't resist a chocolate bourbon. The biscuit crumbles and melts in her mouth.

'Your father and I were just talking about how grown-up you are,' Aunt Edith says. 'It seems like only yesterday that you were a little girl, and here you are, a teenager.' Vivien

68

sees the swiftest exchange of glances between her father and aunt; if you blinked, you'd miss it.

Her father ties a shoelace that has come loose. He stands up, brushing lint or dirt that isn't there from his chinos. 'Right,' he says. 'I've just got to . . .' He gestures vaguely in the direction of the hall, and Vivien has no idea if he's referring to the cloakroom or the telephone, or something else. Perhaps he isn't sure himself. He walks out of the room, closing the door behind him.

Aunt Edith smooths her skirt and carries on. 'Yes, you've got so much to look forward to. It won't be long before you're learning to drive and choosing a dress for your first dance,' she says. 'Of course, being a teenager can be confusing sometimes.' She's quiet for a moment, then leans forward. She clears her throat. 'Darling, Daddy has told me what happened. It's terribly important that you don't tell anyone about that letter. Your mother would be so upset. And Michael's too little to understand.'

'Yes,' Vivien says, suddenly wishing that she was little like Michael.

'I know it feels wrong to keep this from Mummy, but it's just for a while, until things settle down. You won't say anything, will you?'

She wants to believe her aunt, who has always been kind to her. She wouldn't want her mother to be upset. 'No. I won't,' she says.

Aunt Edith pats her hand. 'Good. I knew you would understand.'

Vivien doesn't understand. She has no idea who Flavia is, or why her father would be interested in a baby when he already has two children. Perhaps her father will love the baby more than he loves them. Thinking about it makes her burn inside until she feels that she might explode. She wants to scream or break something. Alone in her bedroom at home, she kicks off a shoe and it flies up, hitting the ceiling. Her shoe leaves dirt on the paint. No one else notices, but the mark makes her feel ashamed. She wishes that she could wipe it away, but it's too high to reach.

Her aunt doesn't speak to Vivien about the letter again, and nor does her father. The days pass, then weeks, and the months turn into a year. No one mentions the woman called Flavia or the baby, but Vivien can't forget them. The secret sits like a stone in her stomach. She feels like a traitor; her mother's smile, touch, her kind words, stab her. There was a time when she told Mummy everything, but words are now as deadly as knives. She sees the confusion in her mother's eyes and the distance grows between them.

She reads alone in her room. *Rebecca*, *Désirée*, *Gone with the Wind*; the heroines in these books become her friends. Michael knocks on the door, asking her to play, but she doesn't answer and eventually he goes away.

The secret grows, like a tumour. She is a girl with porcelain skin and long auburn hair, but inside she is grotesque. Lying on her bed, she watches aeroplanes travelling across the sky. One day, she will leave this place, and with every step the secret will lighten, until it's as small and soft as a feather, and float away.

# Sarah

*Early Summer 2010*

Sarah is following a narrow trail, through long feathery grass. Hay bales are like sculptures on golden fields. Charlie had clung to her legs when he'd heard the tractors. 'Noise,' he said, covering his ears. 'Gee-gaw,' she told him, using his language, and he'd brightened; vehicles fascinate him.

The grass is so long that it reaches her waist and she imagines lions stalking prey. The trail leads to the main road, and in the distance, she can hear the rumble of cars. She will walk to the high street, buy milk and a newspaper, and circle back home. The sun feels hot on her neck and shoulders. She takes off her cardigan and ties it around her hips.

She doesn't see the boy coming towards her until they are almost on top of each other. They collide, her knees buckle and she is falling. He catches her arm and they stagger together, then collapse on the ground. She hears laughter and looks into hazel-flecked grey eyes. She gets up, brushing grass off her trousers. Her arms are prickling, but she doesn't know if it's the nettles or the shock of touching him.

'You should look where you're going,' she says.

He stays sitting down. His jeans are ripped at the knees, but they were probably like that to start with. 'You were going the wrong way,' he says, shading his face with his hand.

'I wasn't going to the lake.' Her cardigan has slipped and she ties it again.

'Perhaps you're on your way to a mothers' meeting.' He smiles.

She bristles. Does this boy ever go to school? 'I have errands to run. Unlike some, I can't do as I please.' She knows that she sounds prim and old-fashioned.

He stands up slowly, as if time is not important. 'That's too bad. It's going to rain tomorrow.' He's silent for a moment, then says, 'I'm sorry about the other day. I'd had too much to drink.'

She hadn't expected an apology.

'Can't your errands wait?'

She thinks of the bustle of the high street, the queues in the supermarket, the routine conversations. Perhaps he's right; it would be a shame to waste a day like this.

He runs his fingers through his messy blond hair. His eyes glisten and she sees the lake where they met. And although she knows it's not quite proper for her and the boy to be alone together, she goes with him, unable to resist.

The woods are full of rhododendrons, sprinkling their purple petals on the path. She thinks of the families visiting parks to see the rhododendrons, and here they are in secret abundance. Vines of frothy white wisteria perfume the air and the leaves of the trees make lacy green patterns. A squirrel darts in front of them and disappears into the bracken.

The path is wide enough for them to walk side by side. It's different, being here with the boy. In some ways she's more relaxed, it's reassuring to have company, but when his arm

72

brushes hers, she feels a jolt like electricity. He is quiet and she finds herself filling the silence.

'I expect you know these woods like the back of your hand. Paul and I want our boys to be like you, growing up here.' She has woven her family in deliberately, delineating a boundary, but he doesn't seem to notice. She's not even sure he's listening. His mind seems to be somewhere else.

The wooden bridge is dusty and redundant: the stream has evaporated or drained away, and plants with huge boat-shaped leaves are growing out of the sandy black soil. A strange, sharp scent catches in her throat.

She follows him down to the water. There, hidden beneath the boughs of the willow tree, white lilies are floating like constellations.

'They're lovely,' she says.

'Yes,' he says. He looks away.

They sit together on the bench, watching the breeze ruffle the shining lake. They don't speak. The water isn't only grey today, but pink and green and blue, as if an artist has been painting. Two swans float past, as white as the clouds drifting across the sky. The lake, the houses, the gardens and the jetties are all bathed in golden light. This place is damaged, but it is beautiful.

A heatwave has descended and the high street looks like the South of France. Women in long floating dresses and flip-flops sit at small tables outside cafés, sipping iced drinks; men who don't need to work arrive in top-down sports cars; the hardware shop has sold out of fans.

Sarah has drawn the curtains and closed off the oven-hot conservatory, but the heat seeps into the house. It will be cooler in the woods, she thinks. It's been a few weeks since she was last there, with the boy. Various matters have required

73

her attention: a blocked drain, a fault with the car, school open mornings. She wonders if he'll be there today.

The woods don't provide the relief she'd hoped for. The trees seem to trap the heat and the air swarms with midges. Limp shrubs brush against her arms and there is a putrid smell of slow-rotting things. The fields are bleached, the path is a threadbare rug of trampled grass, and the verges are tangled with nettles. She toils through thick, heavy air. The soles of her flip-flops beat her heels and send up clouds of dust. The rhododendrons have wilted.

On one side, the lake is green, as if the trees have melted into the water. From the other side, it is steel-grey, swirling with currents; she imagines a sea monster turning, the water streaming over its muscled back. Up close, the water is littered with scum and leaves. A shoal of tiny fish dart beneath the surface and a Canada goose lands, beating its wings. Electric-blue dragonflies hover like tiny planes. The lawns of the neighbouring houses are striped yellow and brown. A drop of sweat slides down her neck.

The lilies are still here, hidden beneath the boughs of the weeping willow tree. More have opened their delicate petals, showing their pink-jewelled hearts. She wonders where the boy is, if he's at school, what he's doing. She knows it's wrong to think about him, but she can't seem to help it.

She imagines dipping her feet in the cool water, slipping into its silvery depths. The heat makes men mad, they say. She turns away. She walks home.

# Anna

## *Surrey, 1972*

The Smiths have moved to a larger house and the three hours that Anna is there on a Tuesday isn't enough. Mrs Smith has four children under seven and hardly has time to brush her hair, so Anna's put an ad in the post office.

*Cleaning lady required for family in Littlefold. Tuesday after-noons, working alongside the family's housekeeper. Candidate must have experience, good references and like children.*

Anna's had two phone calls, one from a sixteen-year-old girl who hadn't read the ad properly, and another from a bossy-sounding woman who would walk all over young Mrs Smith. She will have to keep looking.

On Saturday afternoon, Anna is pegging washing on the line when Jeff opens the back door. 'Mum! Phone,' he calls. She puts down the pegs and the basket of damp school shirts and overalls, and goes inside. Jeff is shouldering on his denim jacket. His new cologne is overpowering; he's put too much on. 'Are you off out, then?' she asks.

'Quick pint. Back later,' he says, dropping his keys into his pocket. It's hard to believe that he was once a chatterbox. The older he gets, the less he tells her.

'All right, darling. Have a nice time,' she says, picking up the phone, wondering how her son can be seventeen. He's a head taller than her and his trainers are huge. Mattie is ten and still holds her hand when they cross the road, but another year or two and that will be gone. For a moment, she feels light-headed; it's the cologne, or the thought of time marching on. She runs her fingers over the spirals of the telephone cord. 'Hello?'

'I'm calling about the ad. Is the job still available?' The woman's voice is like music. She sounds foreign, but Anna can't place the accent.

'Yes, it is,' Anna says, watching Jeff swagger down the street, pushing up his sleeves. She hopes the girl he's trying to impress isn't one of the school dropouts who hang around the Bear, smoking and getting up to no good. 'Do you have experience?'

'I worked for five years as a housekeeper in my country. It was a big house and I did all the cleaning and ironing. I also did babysitting. I have good references.'

This woman sounds capable and warm, and Mrs Smith could do with some help with the children. 'You speak good English. Where are you from?'

'Thank you. I am from Italy, but I have worked in England before.'

Anna can't help being impressed by this woman who seems so worldly. She'd love to travel, but they haven't the money for holidays. The income from her cleaning and Mike's decorating covers their mortgage and the bills, and anything left over is squirrelled away. 'We'd be working as a team. Is that OK?' she says.

'Yes, of course.'

They agree to meet at Mrs Smith's at two o'clock on Tuesday. It will be a trial, to see how they get on.

'I'm Anna, by the way. What's your name?'

'Flavia.'

It's an interesting name. Anna's come across it before, but she can't remember where. 'Thank you, Flavia. See you next week.'

On Tuesday, Flavia arrives at two o'clock on the dot. She's overweight, but her face is beautiful – dark eyes, flawless skin, a warm smile. Her black hair is pulled into a ponytail. She ties on an apron and gets straight to it, mopping the kitchen floor and tidying the playroom.

She sings softly while she works, and two-year-old Alfie Smith follows her from room to room, trailing his blanky. She's light on her feet with the vacuum, and wields the iron and board like a bow and cello. She doesn't need direction. She seems to know instinctively what to do.

They are dusting upstairs when Mrs Smith comes out of the master bedroom in a dressing gown, the sleeping baby draped over her shoulder like a stole. Her strawberry-blonde hair is tangled and there are shadows under her pale blue eyes.

'Hello, you must be Flavia. I'm so sorry. I didn't realise the time,' she says. 'Toby's still not sleeping through the night.'

'Mummy!' Alfie is running out of his bedroom, waving a duster like a flag. He launches himself at his mother, wrapping his arms around her knees. 'Hello darling,' she says, stroking his dark hair. 'Thank you for watching Alfie. I hope he didn't get in the way,' she says.

'He was fine,' Anna says. 'He helped Flavia with the vacuuming.'

'Sweet boy,' Flavia says, softly.

'Jenny and Lizzie will be back from school soon and it will be pandemonium,' Mrs Smith says. Late-afternoon sunlight is filtering through the windows. She hides a yawn behind her hand. 'Excuse me. Would you like a cup of tea?'

'Don't worry about us,' Anna says. 'You put your feet up while you can.'

Anna and Flavia finish upstairs, then pack up the cleaning equipment. They find Mrs Smith in the kitchen, buttering toast. Toby has been transferred to a travel cot and is still fast asleep. Alfie is in his high chair, picking at a bowl of corn-flakes. It looks more like breakfast than teatime.

'Everything is spick and span,' Mrs Smith says. 'I have a nap and the entire house is done. You are clever.'

'Flavia's a great help,' Anna says.

'I hope you'll come back next week,' Mrs Smith says to Flavia.

Flavia smiles. She lowers her eyes. 'Yes. Thank you,' she says.


Anna is shopping in the village. It is raining and she has forgotten her umbrella. She goes to the bank to pay in cheques, then to Williams & Son for a birthday card. At the post office, a queue of men and women in raincoats are shifting from foot to foot, their umbrellas dripping onto the vinyl floor. She joins the queue, squeezing in by the door, and the woman in front of her glances over her shoulder. It is Flavia, holding a parcel wrapped in brown paper.

'Anna!' Flavia kisses her on both cheeks. Her skin is warm and her hair smells of lemons. 'You are wet.'

'Miserable, isn't it?' Anna pushes her damp hair back from her face; it's gone limp and is starting to frizz. 'It's that time of year.' She says it automatically, but it's early September and it shouldn't be as wet as this. 'I expect it's still warm in Sicily.'

Flavia runs her fingers over the parcel. 'Yes. My son is still swimming in the sea.'

'How lovely,' Anna says, taking this in. 'I didn't know you had a son.'

'He is ten next week. This is his present. Lego.'

Anna can't imagine living away from Jeff and Mattie. Flavia must miss her little boy very much. 'My Mattie likes Lego, too,' she says. She wonders who looks after Flavia's son; perhaps it's grandparents, if Flavia and the boy's dad have split up. 'Will you go back to Italy soon, to see him?' The question is out before she can stop it.

Flavia looks away. 'Perhaps. I am very busy. I am waitressing now, too.' She shrugs, as if shaking a thought away. 'I am lucky to have so much work. I can send money home.'

Before Anna can speak, someone calls out, 'Next.' They've been busy talking and haven't noticed the queue moving along.

'Bye, Anna. See you on Tuesday,' Flavia says. She goes up to the window and places the parcel carefully on the scales. 'To Sicily, please.'

Anna hadn't realised that Flavia was working as a waitress as well as cleaning. She wonders if she'd have the strength to do what Flavia does: live away from home, working all hours, while someone else brings up her son.

# Anna

*Surrey, 1977*

Flavia switches off the vacuum, unplugs it and winds the cord up. They are in the sitting room and Anna is cleaning the windows. The garden beyond is a playground: a swing set, a climbing frame, bikes and scooters, a trampoline. No children, though. They are all at school.

Anna carefully dusts the framed family portraits arranged on the mantelpiece. There's a sweet one of Alfie when he was little, holding his blanky. It's hard to believe that Alfie is now seven and baby Toby is five. Anna doesn't know where the years have gone. The proof is there, in the children, and the grey hairs in her fringe. Her own boys have grown up.

'I have some news,' Flavia says, and Anna is whisked out of her thoughts. 'Phil has asked me to marry him.'

Anna puts down her duster. 'Flavia! Tell me you said yes.'

Flavia smiles, shyly. 'Yes.'

They hug tightly and Anna feels Flavia's heart thudding. 'You deserve every happiness,' she says.

Flavia's eyes are shining. 'Thank you. Phil wants to bring

my son here. He is fifteen now. He can learn English and help Phil with his work.'

Flavia will be reunited with her son at last. Anna doesn't know how her friend has endured the years of separation. Phil's a good, kind man.

Anna is dusting in George's study. She tries not to look at the papers on his desk, it's none of her business, but it's impossible not to see the red letters under the glass-domed paperweight. She rarely sees George, he's usually at the office, but last week he was at home. He looked unwell, but it wasn't just the cold. He'd put on weight and the lines on his forehead had deepened. When their paths crossed on the landing or in the kitchen, he didn't make his usual polite enquiries.

Edith hasn't said anything, but her voice is too bright and she seems distracted. A bottle of pills has appeared on her bedside table. Edith is always entertaining, but Anna can't remember the last dinner party or charity lunch. It isn't her place to ask, but she can't help wondering. It's the business, perhaps, or George's health. She is in every morning these days, and she's come to know Edith and George in a way that no one else would. Cleaning is intimate work.

Edith is particular, every possession has its place, but George is untidy like most men, leaving his clothes on the bathroom floor. George is fastidious about his teeth, his side of the bathroom sink cluttered with mouthwash, dental floss and different types of toothpaste. Edith drinks a cup of tea in bed; in the mornings, Anna wipes away the brown ring on the glass-topped bedside table. Now and then, George bathes in oils that leave the bath slippery and aromatic. The only fragrance that Edith wears is Chanel No 5. Edith sometimes chews her fingernails, putting most in the bin but missing one or two slivers that Anna notices while vacuuming. Anna sees

81

all this and more, but she wouldn't dream of discussing it. Her clients entrust her with the minutiae of their lives.

In the houses where she works, she is witness to important family events: births, weddings, deaths. She feels the tides of their secrets; the hushed voices, the closed doors. Some people look down on cleaning, but she can spot the chips on their shoulders a mile off and wouldn't work for them. She isn't one of those girls who cleans and goes. She tries to be useful, reporting any leaks or loose floorboards. She's handy with a screwdriver, and does her best to repair broken drawers and cupboard doors. She likes Edith and George's house the most: the lofty ceilings, the original Georgian fireplaces, the double-aspect sitting room – it's a world apart from the glitzy mansions that are springing up like mushrooms.

She carries her cleaning caddy into the kitchen. She runs hot water into the sink, pours in Fairy Liquid and puts the kettle on. Edith comes in, carrying the morning post.

'Cup of tea?' Anna says. She opens a cupboard and takes out two mugs, one with polka dots that she always uses, and the tall one with roses that Edith likes.

'Thank you. Yes please,' Edith says. She leafs through the envelopes, but doesn't open anything. She puts the post down on the granite worktop. 'Any plans this weekend? It looks like it will be nice.'

Anna drops a teabag in each mug and looks in the fridge for milk. 'We're off to a wedding. My friend, Flavia, is getting married.'

Edith doesn't speak. Anna turns, holding the bottle of milk. Edith is looking at her, blankly.

'Have I not mentioned Flavia before? She helps me with cleaning at the Smith's.'

Edith runs her fingers through her hair. 'No, I don't think you have,' she says. 'Flavia is an interesting name. Italian?'

'Yes. She's from Sicily.'

Edith is quiet for a moment, then says, 'Years ago, there was a barmaid at the Anchor called Flavia. She was very attractive.'

Anna stirs milk into the tea and gives Edith the mug with the roses. 'She's never mentioned it.'

'No,' Edith says. She turns to look out at the garden. She sips her tea.

Anna dips a sponge in the sink and wipes the worktops. Flavia doesn't speak much about those early years in Littlefold. She's told Anna that she waitressed at her uncle's restaurant, but her mother became unwell and she returned to Italy. She's never mentioned the Anchor, but Anna wouldn't be surprised; Flavia's a hardworking, resourceful woman.

Later, at home, loading the washing machine with cleaning rags, a long-ago memory comes to her, like a piece of wreckage surfacing on an ocean. Edith, all dressed up, rushing out of the front door – 'I must dash. I've got a lunch for the hospice.' The scent of Chanel No 5 in the hall. The Jag rumbles and there's the sound of tyres on gravel. Anna glances at the clock on the kitchen wall. It is ten o'clock, too early for lunch, but perhaps Edith has some shopping to do in the village. She plugs in the hoover, sees a piece of notepaper on the floor and picks it up. A few words jotted down in Edith's slanting handwriting. *Flavia – 10.30 – cheque*. Flavia is a beautiful, unusual name. Perhaps a foreign lady wants to make a donation to the hospice. Anna puts the note on the worktop and starts vacuuming.

# Sarah

*Summer 2010*

At the weekend, Paul suggests they go out for dinner. Sarah reserves a table for two at the the Anchor and Anna agrees to babysit.

It's years since she was last here. The beer-stained carpet, the overflowing ashtrays and the wooden benches have gone; the floor is polished oak, there are white tablecloths and silver cutlery, and the leather-bound menu lists fillet steaks and pork belly. It's a warm evening, the pub is busy, and she's glad that she booked.

Paul is studying the wine list. 'I'll have the steak, please. Medium rare. And a glass of Malbec,' he says to the waitress.

'I'll have the same. Thank you,' Sarah says. The waitress scribbles on her pad, then hurries away to another table.

'This is a good find,' Paul says, taking off his glasses and polishing them. 'Interesting wine list.'

He looks cool and clean, in his pressed chinos and shirt. His nose is pink; he spent the day with the boys in the garden and caught the sun.

'Good,' Sarah says. It's difficult to impress Paul, who is accustomed to entertaining clients at Michelin-starred restaurants. She smooths her dress over her knees. The dress is cornflower blue, with straps, and the material feels silky against her bare legs. She's wearing heels and lipstick, and has blow-dried her hair. 'I used to come here as a child. It wasn't as smart as it is now, but the garden was lovely.'

The pretty walled garden hasn't changed, with its curving herbaceous borders, climbing roses and mature apple and pear trees. Beyond the low brick wall, the view of fields and hedgerows is the same; it's protected land, liable to flooding, and can't be developed.

Her mother would bring her here for an early supper before heading back to Balham. Her grandparents never came with them; pub food was too heavy, they said, and they preferred to be comfortable at home.

'It's nicely fitted out,' Paul says. 'I like the paint. It would look good in our dining room.'

The stone colour is attractive, but Sarah has grown fond of their dining room's traditional red walls, and the cracks in the paintwork don't irritate her the way they used to. 'It's very modern. I'm not sure,' she says.

'Yes. Well, there's plenty of time to decide about paint. Still, we ought to get on with the kitchen. We could do with a decent range oven and one of those American-style fridges. Why don't we go round a few showrooms?'

Traipsing round busy showrooms with a bored Jack and an inquisitive Charlie in tow while they try to discuss kitchen plans and choose appliances isn't appealing.

The waitress puts two glasses of red wine down on the table in front of them. Sarah takes a sip and feels the warmth in her stomach. 'I've been thinking. Do we have to renovate the house? You're busy at work and I've got my hands full with the children. Why don't we wait? We needn't hurry.'

Paul puts down his glass. 'I thought you wanted to renovate.'

'Yes, of course I do,' she says, but the truth is, she's stopped purchasing *House & Garden*, and hasn't thought about paint or tiles for weeks. 'I'm trying to be practical. I'm not sure that the timing is right.'

Paul is quiet for a moment. The lines on his forehead deepen. 'I think we should press on. It might be tricky, but we'll manage. When it's finished, we'll have a beautiful home that we can enjoy for years. I'd like to have people round, but the house isn't ready.'

'We can have people round. Our friends won't mind and you can carry on entertaining clients in town.'

'Yes,' Paul says, but he doesn't sound convinced. 'I thought you'd be keen on a project, now that Charlie's at nursery and you have more time.'

Sarah feels the tendons in her neck rise. She's tried to explain before, but Paul just doesn't understand what day-to-day life with young children is like. There isn't any superfluous time. If they renovate the house, she will have to oversee the building works – it will be her, not Paul, as she's the one at home. She and the boys will have to live through it, endure the noise and disruption, while Paul escapes to his office.

She's become attached to the house. The shabby décor no longer troubles her, the way it did before. The house harks to the past, a simpler time without the internet or mobile phones, when the pace of life was slow and quiet, and she was a child. There's a dignified beauty in old, weathered things.

And although they purchased the house for its potential, it was her – not Paul – who was keen to renovate. She wonders

86

why he's developed this sudden interest, and if he's really worried about what his colleagues think. She can't help feeling disappointed. She thought he was above one-upmanship.

She could ask, but it's unlikely to resolve anything. It would be a pity to ruin their first night out together in weeks.

'I don't have as much time as I'd hoped,' she says. 'Let's not talk about this now.'

Paul's eyes flicker. 'All right,' he says evenly, and changes the subject.

The evening passes pleasantly enough, but something between them has changed; the underlying discord niggles, like a muscle that has been strained.

When they leave, Paul holds open the pub door and she nearly trips over the step; she's not used to wearing high heels and the wine has gone to her head. The lane is silvery in the moonlight, the vast black sky is scattered with stars, and the houses and the common are cloaked in darkness. She breathes in the soft, cool night air. She can't remember the last time she was out this late.

Paul's hand is resting lightly on her waist, beneath the shawl draped around her shoulders. 'Neither of us can drive. Let's leave the car. I'll collect it in the morning,' he says.

'I don't mind walking. I've brought my flats,' she says. It's one of the benefits of having a large handbag, which is usually full of snacks and sippy cups and spare clothes for Charlie. 'What about Anna? We don't want to keep her waiting.'

Paul glances at his watch. 'It's nearly midnight. I'll ask about a taxi.' He goes back inside.

She sits down on a bench and takes out her flats from her handbag. Her high heels are too tight, pinching the sides of her feet, and her arches are aching; even if they don't walk home, it will be a relief to take them off.

In the illuminated beer garden, twenty-somethings are

sitting close together at tables beneath gas heaters, drinking and chatting. Now and then, there is laughter. She slips on her flats, which are even more comfortable than she'd imagined, and tucks her high heels into her handbag. She used to wear high heels every day, climbing up and down stairs at the office, and jumping on and off buses and the Tube; it never troubled her. Motherhood has altered her in so many ways, but she never expected it to affect her feet. She stands up, adjusting her shawl.

The pub door opens and she looks up, expecting to see Paul, but it's not him. It's the boy. He is coming towards her.

'Sarah,' he says, softly. He's in a slim-fitting black t-shirt and dark jeans. His arms look tanned and strong. His hair isn't as messy as usual; it's been styled, with wax or gel.

Before she can speak, the door opens again and this time it's Paul. The boy follows her gaze. He shifts from one foot to the other and suddenly seems unsure. He hesitates for a moment, then turns, walks over to one of the tables and sits down. Another boy, who looks older, slides a pint in front of him. The boy strikes a match, leans across the table to light the cigarette of a dark-haired girl, then lights one for himself. The girl lifts her chin, blows smoke out slowly, and flicks her eyes at Sarah. Her neck is slender, smooth and swan-white.

'No luck, I'm afraid. We'll have to walk,' Paul says. And then, lightly, with only a trace of curiosity, 'Who was that?'

'I see him walking in the woods sometimes.' Her stomach flutters. It's not as if there's anything to hide, she tells herself. 'I don't know his name,' she says, and wonders how the boy knows hers. She's certain that she hasn't told him. Perhaps he's asked someone about the Howard family and pieced it together. It wouldn't be difficult, if he knew who to ask. She can see Mark Williams, his pencil tucked behind his ear, saying 'Yes, the Howards lived at the old farmhouse.

Lovely spot, although it was a shame about the motorway. Their granddaughter, Sarah, moved here from London not long ago. She bought one of those big houses by the woods. Yes, it's good to have one of the old families back ...' Mark Williams would have been a mine of information.

The boy has been asking about her. The thought of it, or perhaps it's the cool night air, makes her shiver. Paul puts his arm around her, drawing her close, and his familiar warmth steadies her. They walk together along the dark lanes, past palatial homes set behind wrought-iron gates, guided by the pale moon and the pools of light floating beneath the street lamps.

# Flavia

*Surrey, 1977*

Flavia is standing at arrivals, scanning the passengers streaming through customs. She places her hand on the barrier, as if to still the fluttering inside her. Phil has taken the day off work to accompany her, and although she said there was no need, she's glad he did. It makes it different from those other times, when she was here alone.

Like a cat, she's lived many lives. She is a young girl, arriving in England for the first time, weary from the journey but excited, eager to learn new things. Three years later, she leaves broken-hearted, resolved never to return. In Sicily, her mother holds her close, but her disappointment is worse than anger. Flavia is still a girl, but she is also a mother of a small boy with dark eyes and black hair. He bears no resemblance to the English man who gave him life but does not want him. Her son grows up believing his father is Italian and she doesn't contradict him. When he asks, she says that his father abandoned them before he was born.

Time passes and her resolve weakens. It is her love for

Nicolas that makes her turn again to England: she can earn more money there for his books and lessons. She doesn't want to go back to Littlefold, but her uncle offers her well-paid work at La Trattoria and it's too good an opportunity to let go. 'It's just for a while,' she says to Nicolas, wiping away his tears and hers when it is time to leave. 'Nonna will take good care of you.' Soon, she will send for him. He is ten years old.

Being away from Nicolas is even worse than she'd imagined. Every boy with dark hair is him. She sees mothers shopping in the village with their children and she aches for him. Hard work will numb the pain, she thinks. She accepts all the jobs she is offered and looks for more. Every floor she scrubs, every restaurant table she clears, every hour of overtime, is for Nicolas. Her hands, once soft and smooth, become red and chapped. At night, her legs feel as heavy as lead, but her mind flies to Sicily; the salt sea, cresting white, the olive groves, and a boy with golden skin kicking a ball in the village square. In her letters to Nicolas, she doesn't talk about her work or missing him; instead, she describes games of cricket in green fields, and the bright lights and shops of London.

She wonders about Jim from time to time, worrying about what to do and say if they meet. They move in different circles, but it seems inevitable that their paths will cross; a question of when, not if. One morning, while shopping in the village, she sees him. She is going into Williams & Son and he is waiting by the door, a folded newspaper in his hand. He sees her and stands completely still, as if frozen. She goes inside, closes her umbrella and pretends to look for something in her bag. She's hoping that he'll leave, but when she turns, he is still there. It has been ten years. She thought he might be fatter, with grey or receding hair, but he hasn't changed.

His face is softer, with fine lines; that is all. She is trembling inside, it's the shock of seeing him, and she wonders if he senses it.

'Flavia,' he says. His voice is almost a whisper. He touches her arm, as if he can't believe she's real.

She flinches, as if she's been burned. 'Excuse me,' she says, trying to move past him.

'Wait. Please. I've been trying to find you.'

Another lie. 'No,' she says. She walks away from him, down an aisle of greeting cards. He is not hot-blooded, like the men from her country. He will not make a scene.

The following week, she sees him again, at the supermarket. The week after, it's the post office. It's no coincidence. He's coming into the village on the day that he knows she will be there. This is how it begins: little by little, he comes into her life – a chance meeting, a kind word, a gift. He pursues her and eventually she gives in.

It was wrong of her to love a married man all those years ago, but he'd said that his marriage was broken and she believed him. He kept finding reasons for not leaving his wife: it was her health, or it would jeopardise his career, or the children were too young. Flavia said it couldn't go on. The separation lasted a month. He came looking for her in the pub and waited until she'd finished work. He told her he was sorry. He said he loved her. This time, he'd leave his wife. But he didn't, of course, and so it went on. He lied to her for years. Worse, she lied to herself.

If he'd wanted to leave Maggie, he would have. Perhaps he'd loved Flavia too, but it wasn't enough. Eventually, he had to decide: a baby cannot be hidden. He chose his wife.

It was a long time ago and that was another life. She is a different woman now: stronger, wiser, with a child to think of. The next time they meet in the village, he trails her to the car park. She spins on her heel, anger flaring inside her. 'Stop following me,' she says.

His face crumples. He holds out his hands, as if in surrender. 'Please, Flavia. You left so suddenly. Is there a child?'

A lump swells in her throat and she swallows it down. He could have found her if he'd wanted to. He could have talked to her, instead of sending his sister to dispatch her to Italy. He doesn't deserve to know. 'No,' she says. 'Leave me alone.'

She doesn't see him again. She keeps herself busy, fitting in as much cleaning as she can around her shifts at her uncle's restaurant. She takes on a new job, with the Jeffries family, whose housekeeper has retired. The Jeffries are converting their double garage into an annexe and there are always one or two trade vans parked in the driveway when she arrives. One morning, Mrs Jeffries asks her to make Phil, the electrician, a cup of tea. 'Milk, no sugar. He's sweet enough,' Mrs Jeffries says with a smile, before disappearing into the study. Phil is a tall, broad-shouldered man with the build of a rugby player but the long, tapering fingers of an artist. He carefully washes up his mug instead of leaving it by the sink.

He wears spectacles while he works and the delicate frames make him look bookish. His toolbox is immaculate. At lunchtime, he sits in his van, eating a sandwich and reading the paper. The following week, she feels his eyes on her while she hoovers. He lingers in the kitchen long after he's drunk his tea and asks her out. She declines – she doesn't want to get involved with another English man, but he asks her every week and eventually she agrees.

Phil is different. He's strong and honest, where Jim was fickle and weak. He's quick to introduce her to his friends and family, and when they go out, he puts his arm around her, as if he wants the world to see. She tests him, telling him about her son, but it doesn't unnerve him. Instead, he asks her to marry him; together they make plans for Nicolas to come to England.

Her uncle and aunt move to Fenton, to be closer to La Trattoria, and give Flavia and Phil money to help buy their house on Hawthorn Road. Number 2B is semi-detached, with three bedrooms and a small but neat garden. It is near the old quarry, which is now beautiful woodland and a lake, although she doesn't often go there, as it brings back memories of Jim. Their neighbours are plumbers, electricians and decorators; people like themselves, who tend to the large households of Littlefold. At last, she has a home of her own. A place for a new life with Phil and Nicolas.

The past swirls like mist as she stands here at arrivals, but Phil's hand is warm and steady on her shoulder. Suddenly she sees him, emerging from the crowds of passengers. He is walking towards them. He is here. She holds him tightly. It has been two years. He is taller than her now, and his body feels lean and muscular. He is fifteen, nearly a man. 'Mama,' he says softly. He has a beautiful smile. Then he's shaking hands with Phil, who is clapping him on the back and beaming like a schoolboy. Her heart will burst from too much happiness.

# Sarah

### *Summer 2010*

Sarah takes Charlie onto the trampoline in the field, to be out of the way while Nico Saunders and two dark-haired men attend to the garden. She has agreed to a trial visit; the quote was reasonable and Paul hasn't got the time.

Nico strides around the lawn in his navy overalls and boots, wielding his strimmer as gracefully as a baton; the stocky younger man pushes a heavy-looking lawnmower; the wiry older one with thinning hair is weeding and turning over the flowerbeds.

Charlie likes to bounce, but today he stands quietly with his nose pressed against the netting, watching the gardeners. It's mid-morning, but already hot, and she and Charlie are in shorts and t-shirts. She lies down, feeling the sun on her face, her arms, her legs. She closes her eyes and sees a spectrum of glowing colours behind her eyelids.

A breeze lifts the hair from her face and the boy slips into her thoughts. It was awkward, seeing him at the Anchor. She could have told Paul about him, but she didn't know what to say. He's a boy half her age; they met at the lake; they've gone for a walk. She doesn't even know his name. Another image she can't shake is the boy leaning across the table, lighting that girl's cigarette. There was something deliberate about it. She wonders if he was trying to make her jealous, but that couldn't be right. The dark-haired girl, glancing at her and then away, was proof: Sarah wasn't competition.

She hears laughter, the springs beneath her contract, and Charlie lands on top of her. The sudden weight of him takes her breath. He climbs her as if she's a mountain, his feet digging into her thighs, his ragged toenails scratching her skin. He burrows into her neck and presses his lips to her cheek so hard that she feels his teeth. She gently pushes him away. He rolls on to his back, kicks his legs into the sky and laughs again. His canines look like fangs. This place is changing him. He's not the placid child he was in London. She could leave him in the woods and he'd be raised by foxes; she sees him, dirty and barefoot, tussling with the cubs.

She lifts his t-shirt and tickles his smooth, milky stomach. She thinks he's had enough and stops, but he lifts up his t-shirt. 'More,' he demands. She tickles his neck, his feet, his back. He is getting so big; it's hard to believe he once fitted inside her. He'll soon be into Jack's next set of hand-me-downs. She won't miss the tantrums that arrive as suddenly as April showers, but it will never again be so easy to delight him. She buries her face in his neck, breathing in his butter-Marmite smell, and he wraps his legs around her waist.

There is movement, a shift of light and shade among the trees, and a twig breaks. Someone is walking along the footpath beside the field. She sits up, taking Charlie with her. Neighbours with dogs sometimes use the path to cross up and into the woods. The tall trees and brambles behind the split wooden fence make it feel as if their field is screened, but this is an illusion. Passers-by can easily see in. She looks closely at the gaps in the trees and sees – or thinks she sees, someone standing in the shadows. There is no sign of a dog. The tiny hairs on her arms rise and she draws Charlie closer. She glances back at the garden, where Nico Saunders and his men are working. She and Charlie aren't alone; there is no need to worry. When she looks back at the path, the shadow has gone, and she wonders if she imagined it. She unzips the netting, climbs out of the trampoline and lifts Charlie down.

Nico Saunders and his men are packing away their tools. The lawn is striped, the flowerbeds are neat and the bamboo has been tamed. It is a different garden.

Charlie slips his hand out of hers and runs towards the men. He stands in front of them, smiling hopefully. The young stocky man pats Charlie on the head in a friendly way and finds him a stick to play with; the older one carries on tidying the tools and takes no notice.

Nico has removed his t-shirt from beneath his overalls. His tanned, strong arms glisten and his hair is damp with sweat. He gestures at the garden, as if he is a conductor cueing an orchestra. 'It is OK?'

'Yes,' Sarah says. 'It's wonderful.'

He smiles, and she sees the pride he takes in his work. 'Good,' he says.

'It's so hot. Would you all like a drink?'

'Yes. Thank you,' he says.

Charlie follows her inside. Sarah runs the tap until it's cold and fills three glasses with water. She carries the glasses into the garden, but the men have disappeared.

'Gone,' Charlie says, disappointed.

They find the men in the driveway. Nico is raking the gravel, the older man is sweeping the doorstep and the younger one is loading the van. Sarah wonders if she should have asked the names of Nico's assistants, but they seem content to let Nico do the talking. Perhaps they don't speak much English.

The three men drink down the water in gulps, then carefully put the empty glasses on the doorstep, to one side. 'Thank you,' Nico says. 'Would you like us to come next week?'

'Yes please,' she says.

Charlie waves as the van reverses in the drive, then howls when it turns into the lane. Sarah carries him into the house, kicking and bucking in her arms, wondering how she is going to tell Paul that they now have a team of gardeners.

# Edith

*Surrey, 1980*

The removals men are coming tomorrow, and Edith has been sorting and decluttering for weeks. The Laurels, the new house, is a smaller property. She's agonised over paintings and ornaments, lamps and china plates, and delivered boxes of donations to charity shops. Larger items – the Georgian dining table and chairs, Catherine and Harry's old beds and desks, the oversized sofa set, have been sent for auction. She doesn't expect to make much, but every bit helps.

It's been a year since George's heart attack and she's still adjusting. She frequently makes two cups of tea and has to pour one down the sink. In the evenings, just after seven, when the packed train from Waterloo pulls into the crepuscular station and men in suits with briefcases spill out of the carriages and flow over the pedestrian bridge, she half expects him to arrive at the door in his coat, holding a folded copy of *The Times* and enquiring about supper. The floorboards creak and she wonders if it's George, moving around upstairs.

Sometimes, she catches the scent of him, a trace of sandalwood and black pepper, lingering in the air.

This is not why she's leaving. The reminders of her husband are comforting and she isn't interested in a fresh start. If it were up to her, she'd stay, but she doesn't have a choice. George's airline business had been struggling for several years before he died, and the liquidation and payment of debts took all their savings. The house has to be sold. It has nothing to do with downsizing or its isolated position, although this is what she says when she's asked. It is vulgar to talk about money.

The Laurels is a pretty three-bedroomed red-brick thirties house in a gated estate. The décor is tired, but the kitchen has recently been refurbished and has all the mod cons. The south-facing garden is large and beautiful, with beds of lavender and roses, and mature trees and shrubs. The location is excellent: a ten-minute walk to the village. It's a wrench to leave her home, the place she'd imagined growing old in, but she knows it could be worse.

The doorbell rings. It must be Jim. She's asked him to come and have a look through some books that she's kept mainly for sentimental reasons: classics and biographies that once belonged to their parents. She's hoping that he'll take one or two. The rest will go to Oxfam.

Jim sits at the kitchen table, flicking through a yellowing copy of *Peter Pan*. 'Can I have this one, for Sarah?'

Edith puts the kettle on and drops teabags into two mugs. 'Of course,' she says. Her brother looks too young to be a grandfather. He's in his late fifties, but tennis twice a week keeps him fit and his fair hair hasn't thinned. He's wearing a shirt with a jumper knotted loosely around his shoulders, as is the fashion these days with the younger men. The baby must be about six months old by now. 'How are Vivien and little Sarah?' she asks.

'Sarah's fine, but Vivi's tired. Maggie's driven to Balham today to give her a hand.'

'Babies are sweet, but exhausting,' Edith says. She envies Jim and Maggie, having a grandchild near. The pain she'd felt when Catherine left, taking two-year-old Alice and four-year-old Rose, hasn't eased with the years. Australia is a better life, Catherine said, but the seaside is what holidays are for; it's no substitute for family and home. She hasn't seen Alice and Rose for three years and there's no sign of a visit. Catherine has suggested that Edith go out and stay with them, but she doesn't like flying and it wasn't her decision to move to Sydney. She'll never understand why Catherine left. She's asked Harry, but he didn't know or wouldn't say. Yes, she and Catherine had their differences, but all mothers and daughters have their ups and downs. And getting along with Catherine wasn't easy. If Edith offered advice or made a suggestion, Catherine would invariably take offence. She'd tell Edith to stop interfering, but a mother's duty is to help her children. She only ever wanted the best for them.

Edith doesn't know if there will be more grandchildren. Harry and Jane work hard and play hard, and a two-seater sports car doesn't seem compatible with raising a family. They've recently acquired a pedigree cat.

She never thought she'd long for grandchildren. She's not one to make a fuss over babies. When her own children were little, she found it difficult and tiring, but when Alice and Rose came it was different. She could just enjoy them. Catherine sends photographs and they speak on the phone, but it isn't the same.

She wonders why Jim hasn't gone with Maggie. 'I hope you haven't stayed on my account. The removals men are coming and Anna will help with the unpacking.'

'I knew you'd have it all organised,' Jim says. 'I'll pop by in the morning to keep you company. We both know I'd be useless in Balham. Babies are Maggie's department.'

'Yes,' she says, wondering if there's another reason why Jim's stayed. She carries the mugs of tea to the table. She sits down. 'Is everything all right?'

Jim sips his tea, then says, 'Lawrence and Vivi aren't getting along. Maggie thinks he's got a drinking problem. She wants Vivien and the baby to come home. She's going to talk to her about it today.'

'Poor Vivien. I'm sorry. I had no idea.' Edith has never warmed to Lawrence; the few times they met, she found him arrogant and condescending. Vivien is a clever girl, but she made a mistake, marrying this man. She should have focused on her career. She's a beautiful woman, with her willowy figure and auburn hair. She could have had her pick of husbands.

'I didn't want to trouble you. I'm sure it will be all right.' Jim smiles, as if he must reassure her, but she can tell that he's worried.

'Yes,' she says. It will be difficult to persuade Vivien to come back. She traded Littlefold for London as soon as she was able. Surrey was too provincial, she said, but Edith knows the truth: the burden of keeping Jim's secret had tainted this place.

Her brother's secret, and her own part in it, troubles her. She wakes in the middle of the night, her heart racing, wondering if Maggie should have been told. If Maggie had known about the affair, Vivien would have been spared, but then Maggie might have left Jim or driven him away. He would have gone to Flavia, perhaps to Italy, and been lost to them all. Edith agonises over it, but there are no answers. At the time, she did what she thought was best. There is one last secret. She knows she should tell him, but her fear of the past stops the words.

'I'm sure you'll soon have the Laurels shipshape,' Jim says. 'Sometimes, I wish I could move too.' He is quiet for a moment. 'Flavia has come back. I've seen her in the village.'

So he knows. She wonders if he knows everything. 'Yes, Anna told me. She and Flavia clean houses together. Flavia is married now.' Jim's eyes flicker, with regret or interest, she cannot tell. 'I don't think Anna knows about you,' she adds.

'Flavia won't speak to me. She won't talk about the child.'

She can't put off telling him any more. It's his right to know. 'Anna says that Flavia has a son. A teenager. His name is Nicholas.'

Jim stares. 'Nicholas,' he says softly. 'He's here.'

'I wanted to tell you before, but I . . .' She looks down at her hands, folded in her lap. They are trembling very slightly, betraying the turbulence inside her. 'I should have told you. I'm sorry.'

'It's not your fault,' he says. He stands up. 'I should go.'

'Yes, of course.' She says nothing more. This time, she will not interfere.

# Sarah

## *Summer 2010*

Sarah is sitting on a school chair that belongs to Year 1, her knees drawn up high, listening to Miss Heath discuss Jack's progress. She feels like a child again, sent to see the form teacher, and butterflies swirl inside her. Paul looks uncomfortable. He keeps shifting and doesn't seem to know what to do with his legs. If Miss Heath has noticed, she doesn't show it. She seems to have no problem at all balancing on a tiny chair, even though she's wearing a pencil skirt and high heels. She's young, probably in her twenties, and has the supple figure of a girl.

'Jack is a bright, inquisitive child. His reading is strong, as is his maths,' Miss Heath says.

'That's good,' Sarah says.

Paul nods, but doesn't comment. He'd expect nothing less.

'Yes,' Miss Heath says. She glances at her notes.

'Has he settled in?' Sarah says. 'He doesn't talk much about the other children.'

Miss Heath is quiet for a moment. 'Jack's a creative child.

He enjoys imaginary games.' She licks her lips. She leans forward. 'You're aware, of course, about Finn.'

Paul has been studying the children's work, displayed on the classroom walls and suspended from the ceiling, but now he looks back at Miss Heath.

'Finn,' Sarah says, her voice lifting like a question. Jack's never mentioned a friend called Finn. Perhaps it's a boy from another class. She hopes that Jack hasn't befriended a troublemaker.

'Yes,' Miss Heath says. 'Jack talks about Finn a great deal. He pretends to play with Finn at break.'

It takes a moment for Sarah to understand what Miss Heath is telling them.

Paul says nothing. A tiny muscle in his neck quivers.

Miss Heath gives them a bright, reassuring smile. 'It's not unusual for children to have imaginary friends. I only mention it because this may be why Jack hasn't yet made a close friend at school.' She pauses, but neither Sarah nor Paul speak. 'Perhaps inviting a few children round would help.' This suggestion is directed at Sarah.

'Yes, of course,' Sarah says, finding her voice. 'Who does he get on with in class?'

Miss Heath considers this. 'He's often partners with Emma Winters,' she says.

'Emma?' Paul is unable to hide his surprise.

'Yes,' Miss Heath says. 'Jack's an intellectual child. Boys can be very physical.'

'Jack has a brother,' Paul says. 'There's plenty of rough and tumble at home.'

Miss Heath looks past them, towards the door, where the next set of parents is hovering. 'Boys will be boys,' she says vaguely. She puts down her pen, signalling a close to their meeting. They all shake hands and Sarah follows Paul out of the classroom.

She arrives at Paul's Aston Martin without any memory of walking to it. Jack's never talked about an imaginary friend. He's happy and energetic at home, always ready to indulge Charlie in wrestling. It's as if Miss Heath has been describing a different child.

Paul is quiet in the car, then says, 'Jack's never had a problem making friends before.' He says it as if it's an accusation and she feels her shoulders tense.

'He's the only new boy. It takes time to settle in. Anyway, he has made a friend.'

'That's another thing,' Paul says, driving too close to the kerb. She presses her arms into her ribs, as if she can compress herself, somehow protect herself from a collision. 'Jack's always been a boy's boy.'

They don't hit the kerb, the lane straightens, and she places her hands on the leather seat. 'Yes, but he's in a co-ed school now,' she says, her voice sounding calmer than she feels.

Paul carries on, as if he hasn't heard. 'Let's get some of the young lads in his class round. Some time with the boys is what he needs.'

The tightness in her shoulders is spreading up her neck. 'You're right. Jack does need more boy time. He needs you, but you're never here.' The words are out before she can stop them.

Paul grips the wheel. 'So it's my fault. It's my job. But someone has to pay the mortgage.' He speaks through gritted teeth.

This is true, but she's come to understand that the real reason Paul works so hard is because he's ambitious. *If we won the lottery, you'd still spend all the hours that God sends in the office,* she wants to say, but that would only add to the argument. 'Yes,' she says. 'But this isn't my fault, either.'

He says nothing, but his grip on the wheel relaxes.

'I think we should follow Miss Heath's advice and have Emma round. This imaginary friend is probably just a phase,' she says.

Paul's mobile phone is ringing and he glances down at the screen. 'Yes,' he says. She isn't sure that he's heard or is even speaking to her. His thoughts have swung back to the office.

Jessica Winters is enthusiastic about arranging for Jack and Emma to play together. 'Emma adores Jack! Yes, we must do a play date. Wonderful idea,' she gushes over the phone.

Sarah feels herself shrink inside; a 'play date' sounds so formal. She was going to suggest that Emma come over at the weekend, when Paul is around to help with Charlie, but Jessica says, 'I'll collect Jack after school on Tuesday, if that suits. We can catch up over coffee when you come to collect him, say around six?' Sarah finds herself agreeing, although the timing will be awkward: Charlie will be tired, and Jack is likely to be overexcited and refuse to leave.

On Tuesday, Charlie wakes up early from his afternoon nap and barely touches his tea. By quarter to six, he's rubbing his eyes. Sarah straps him into his car seat, already knowing that he will fall asleep; she has a packet of chocolate biscuits in her pocket, as he's likely to cry when he's woken up. She puts the car key into the ignition, then opens the sun-visor mirror and applies lipstick. Charlie is looking blankly out of the window.

She stands on the Winters' doorstep, Charlie on her hip, while the doorbell rings. Charlie was furious at being woken and it's taken several biscuits to placate him. His eyes are red from crying and there is a chocolate stain on his t-shirt. The enormous house, rendered smooth white and with a grey-tiled roof, looms above them. The huge black door, adorned with nickel, is flanked by columns and box topiary in heavy granite urns. She dabs ineffectually at Charlie's chocolate stain with a tissue. She smooths his hair, but it springs back as tufted as ever.

The door opens, light spills onto the stone doorstep, and Sarah feels as if she's on a stage in the spotlight. 'Darling, come in,' Jessica says, brushing her cheek airily against Sarah's. 'The children are just finishing their tea. They've had a lovely afternoon.'

At least it's gone well, Sarah thinks. Like all first dates, one never knows.

Jessica seems to float in a cloud of scent. Her blonde hair is sleek and highlighted, her fitted white shirt shows off her tiny waist, and her beige trousers are spotless. She doesn't look like she's ever cooked or cleaned, or played with her children.

Inside, the house drips new money: veined marble floors, tiered crystal chandeliers, floor-to-ceiling canvases of nudes and bulls. Jessica glides through the cavernous hall, past a glass pedestal table with a vase of long-stemmed artificial red roses. Sarah imagines a girl falling from the third floor, lanced mid-air by the shards of the chandelier, blood spreading on the polished stone.

The kitchen is painted grey cabinets, creamy granite, a wooden-topped island and integrated brushed-steel appliances. There's a wine cooler, four ovens and a huge American-style fridge. A small woman with dark eyes and black hair is washing up.

Jack and Emma are perched on leather chairs pulled up to a glass table, eating ice-cream sundaes drenched in chocolate sauce and scattered with sprinkles.

'Hello Jack,' Sarah says.

Jack licks his spoon. 'Hello Mummy,' he says. He seems at ease, not at all intimidated by his palatial surroundings.

Hundreds and thousands are scattered on the floor around

the table. 'These sprinkles get everywhere,' Jessica says. She strokes Emma's long golden hair, fingering it like silk. The small dark-haired woman appears with a dustpan and brush, and silently sweeps up the sprinkles.

Charlie has been quiet, leaning his head against Sarah's shoulder, but now he's twisting in her arms. She puts him down and in an instant, he is climbing on a chair and dragging himself, commando style, across the table. 'Mine,' he says, reaching for the container of sprinkles, his sticky fingers smearing the glass.

'Coffee?' Jessica says, pretending not to notice. Her right eyelid, carefully dusted in shades of brown, twitches.

Sarah scoops Charlie up, but he yelps and writhes, and it's impossible to restrain him. She is rummaging in her pocket for sweets or keys – anything that might be a distraction, when Jack gets down from his chair and, in a voice that adults reserve for children, says, 'Charlie, would you like to come to the playroom? There are lots of cars and diggers.'

The words are like a spell. Charlie immediately quietens and allows himself to be led away by Jack and Emma.

'Our children are precious,' Jessica says, dreamily. She places a hand lightly on Sarah's arm. 'How do you like your coffee, hon?'

'Just milk, please. Thank you.'

'Cappuccino? Latte? Espresso?'

'Oh,' Sarah says. 'Whatever's easiest.'

Jessica waves a hand in the direction of the coffee machine and her bracelets jangle like manacles. 'It's all easy.' She smiles, showing rows of pearly teeth; her forehead is as smooth as a doll's.

They sit together at the table, which has been cleared and wiped, sipping cappuccinos. Jessica's nails are long and polished taupe, and her wedding finger displays a collection of glittering rings. She leans forward, as if she's about to divulge a secret. 'I've been hoping to catch you at school, but it's manic at pick-up,' she says. 'I'm so sorry. It must be tough. You've got enough on your plate, with your little one.'

Sarah has no idea what Jessica is referring to. She says nothing, and Jessica carries on. 'Don't take any notice of the other mums. Jack's a good boy. There's nothing wrong with him.'

'Wrong?' Sarah says, and her voice seems to echo.

'So he's a bit left of centre. Most bright kids are, these days.'

It's as if Jessica is speaking in code. Sarah wonders if this is to do with Jack's imaginary friend. 'I'm sorry. I don't understand.'

There's a glint in Jessica's eyes, as if she's won a game that Sarah didn't know they were playing. 'Jack's top of the class. You know how it is. Mothers can be terribly competitive.'

The thought of the other mothers spreading rumours about Jack, to somehow sabotage him, is unsettling. Perhaps this is why he's struggled to make friends. She wonders how Jessica knows more about Jack's progress at school than she does. Miss Heath didn't mention ranking and it hadn't occurred to her to ask.

Jessica gives her a knowing smile. 'My Emma tells me everything,' she says.

Extricating herself and the boys from the Winters' house is almost impossible. The playroom is as well stocked as a toy-shop; her suggestions to the boys that they leave become pleas, then bribes, and finally, whispered threats. It seems to take an eternity to track down their clothes – they've been dressing up – and put on their coats and shoes. All the while Jessica hovers, dispensing lollipops to the children and entreating Sarah to stay for a glass of wine. Jessica doesn't seem concerned about homework or bath time. By the time Sarah has buckled the boys into the car and they've exchanged more kisses than she's seen among families parting at airports, it is eight o'clock.

Collecting Jack from the play date is exhausting, but coming home revives her. She can breathe again. She chivvies the boys through the evening routine at double speed: bath, pyjamas, teeth, bed. Jack's homework can wait until morning.

The boys are sleeping and the house is quiet. She makes a cup of tea, stirring milk into the tinted water, breathing in the soothing aroma. Jessica Winters' house was glamorous, but she could never live there; shining glass and polished stone, airless and artificial, it felt more like a cage than a home. Her own house may look tired and dilapidated to others – this is how she'd felt at first – but now she sees it differently. More and more, she finds comfort in its imperfections; the crumbling glasshouse, the creaking floorboards, the moss blanketing the roof. In a village that prides itself on state-of-the-art mansions, her house stands apart; seasoned and beautiful, it's her portal to the past.

She delights in the secret wildness of her home. Ivy tendrils snake through the gaps of the French doors. Birds beat their wings and squirrels gambol in the loft. In the mornings, she finds sinuous, iridescent trails on the rugs. Clusters of ladybirds congregate in the cornices and spiders festoon the Georgian-barred windows with glittering webs. Darkness falls and dogs let off the lead haunt the woods.

She imagines the house disappearing, pulled by creepers into the rich dank soil; an underground lair, hidden by a cloak of ivy. She and the boys would sleep undisturbed in the day, and at night, come out like the foxes and roam the fields and the groves.

In the moonlit garden, the trees are swaying in the wind. She sees the boy sitting beside the lake, reflected in the silvery water. He comes into her mind when she least expects it. Perhaps this is what it's like to have an imaginary friend.

# Flavia

*Surrey, 1980*

Flavia sits on the sofa sifting through the morning post, discarding the circulars and making a pile of correspondence and bills on the coffee table. Specks of dust float in the shafts of sunlight slanting through the windows. The pink carpet needs vacuuming. It is Saturday, and she will clean and tidy her own house, dusting and hoovering, changing the beds, mopping the tiled bathroom floors and wiping the Formica countertops in the kitchen.

She and Phil would like to update the house – the sixties decor that her aunt and uncle chose is looking tired – install a new boiler and rewire, but Phil hasn't got the time to work on it himself and they can't afford a contractor. She doesn't mind waiting. They are lucky to have a house with so much potential. The garden is small, but Nico has filled the borders with hydrangeas and camellias, asters and roses; daffodils and lilacs for colour and scent in the spring. He's planted a crab-apple tree for its white blossoms and the birds. The clay soil is a challenge, he tells her; in the winter, the earth soaks up rain like a sponge, but in the summer it cracks and hardens. Anna says he has green fingers.

It's hard to believe that her son is eighteen. It seems only a moment ago that she was cupping his small face in her hands. He's a handsome young man; olive skin, black wavy hair, dark eyes that seem wise beyond his years. He goes by Nico these days, preferring the Italian diminutive to Nicholas, the English version of his name. It brings an Italian element to Saunders. It was a pragmatic decision of Nico's, to take Phil's name, but it seemed to bring them closer together. Phil knows that he'll never be Nico's father, but they have become good friends and respect each other.

The boys left early this morning in the van. There's a new build that's on a tight deadline, the team is working overtime, and Phil said they could use Nico's help. Flavia isn't sure that Nico is suited to electrics and building, but it's good of Phil to give him work while he decides what to do. By the time the boys are back, the house will be spick and span, and a casserole of meatballs in tomato sauce will be simmering in the oven.

When they first married, she and Phil thought they might have a child together, but it never happened and she was secretly relieved. That part of her life, when she was young with a baby, is behind her. She worried that Phil might be disappointed, but he said, 'Don't worry, my love. I have you and Nico, and that's all I need.'

It's been three years since Nico arrived in England and he has settled in well. He still speaks with an accent, but his English has improved. He never talks about going back to Sicily. There are more opportunities for him here, and now there is Maria, he has even more reason to stay. Maria, the pretty, dark-eyed daughter of her uncle's neighbour in Fenton; a good, Italian family. They are young, only

113

eighteen, but Flavia can see the love between them. Maria works in a boutique in Littlefold, selling designer dresses to wealthy housewives. Flavia can't believe how much women pay for these clothes, which they discard the following year to make room for the new season. Maria is good at her work. She is charming and attentive, and her slim figure shows off the boutique's clothes. If they marry, Flavia knows that she will gain a daughter. Family is everything in Italy.

An envelope is addressed to her in small, almost illegible handwriting that she hasn't seen for years but instantly recognises. Dread seeps into her, chilling her veins. The blood drains from her stomach. She should tear it up, throw the letter away, but instead she opens the envelope and reads the words on the expensive cream notepaper.

Dear Flavia,

I know you wish to forget what happened between us. I don't want to intrude on your happiness, but I understand you have a son. If I can offer support, if Nicholas would like to know his father, you need only ask. I am truly sorry for the pain I have caused.

Jim

Flavia wonders how paper can be so light and yet carry so much weight. She's never told Nico the truth about his father. She didn't want to unsettle him; nor does she have any desire to revisit her past and the mistakes she made. Although Jim lives in the same village, they might as well be in different countries; they lead parallel lives and their paths rarely cross. She'd hoped they could carry on like this, but she also knew that it was only a matter of time before Jim found out

114

about Nico. In his letter he sounds regretful; he is hoping for redemption perhaps, but it's too late. Nico isn't a child any more. Jim is hinting about money, hoping it will entice her, but it didn't all those years ago and it won't now. She and Phil will never be wealthy, but they are comfortable and happy. Nico doesn't want for anything.

She can't help wondering if Jim is trying to find a way back into her life. She's married now, but wedding vows didn't stop him then. Perhaps he thinks that Nico binds them together. The life she's made with Phil, her little family of three, is too precious to risk. It isn't that she's still in love with Jim, but he has this power to draw her in. The truth is, even after all these years, she doesn't trust herself to resist. She strikes a match and holds it to the letter. The paper shrinks and blackens, and his words vanish in the flames.

# Sarah

## *Summer 2010*

Charlie is lying on the carpet in the playroom, sucking his t-shirt and watching cartoons. His bottle of milk has rolled under the sofa. Sarah is on her knees retrieving it and discovers Lego, a remote control for a car and a Playmobil pirate. She puts the bottle of milk next to Charlie and tidies the toys into the toy chest.

In the kitchen, Jack is sitting at the table, chewing a pencil and kicking his legs, a maths worksheet in front of him. His fringe is long and he keeps flicking it. She collects the breakfast plates and carries them to the sink. She loads the dishwasher and looks out at the sunny garden. Paul is away on business and the weekend stretches ahead like a path winding up a mountain. At least the weather is fine and the boys can play outside. She misses Paul most in the evenings, when the house is quiet, but in some ways the days are easier on her own. She and the boys have a routine, but Paul has different ideas; he often forgets that children need regular meals and bedtimes.

The boys are more boisterous when Paul is around; a week

apart must seem a long time to young children. Jack doesn't complain and Charlie's too little to articulate it, but when Paul comes downstairs on Saturday morning in his dressing gown, it's as if Father Christmas has appeared. Jack shouts 'Daddy!' and Charlie jumps up and down, and then they charge at Paul and pull him to his knees. Paul plays along, crawling around and growling, while Jack climbs onto his back and Charlie clings to him upside down. They each claim him, like explorers with new territories, and inevitably there is a battle. Paul doesn't reprimand them. At times like these he seems more like a playmate than their parent, but she wouldn't want to tell the boys off either if she hadn't seen them all week.

'Finished,' Jack says, putting down his pencil. He's disappearing into the hall, headed for the playroom, when Sarah says, 'Wait a minute.'

Jack slowly reappears. He lingers by the door, chewing a fingernail.

She ruffles his hair. 'You need to go to the barber. Daddy can take you next weekend.' As the words leave her lips, she's already regretting mentioning Paul. Jack visibly slumps. She pulls him close and kisses the top of his head. 'I know you miss Daddy, but the week will fly by.' She tries to be cheerful, but her words sound hollow. An outing to the cinema would cheer him up. She will see if Anna can look after Charlie. 'Sit with me for a minute,' she says. 'I'd like to talk to you.'

They sit together at the table. Jack's face is changing, losing its childish roundness; he is leaner, angular, more defined. He has Paul's steady brown eyes. She sees a glimpse of the man he will become and her feelings are tangled; pride, but also grief for the boy.

'Miss Heath says you're doing well at school. Daddy and I are proud of you.'

Jack nods, picking at the edges of a sticker that Charlie has stuck to the table. He's a modest child, not one to dwell on praise. The sticker is of a teddy bear and says 'Brilliant'. 'Did Charlie get this at nursery?' he asks.

'Yes. It's for wearing grown-up pants, like you.'

'A sticker for wearing pants? That's outrageous.'

She can't help smiling. 'Yes. Well, not exactly.' The conversation has drifted, as it often does with Jack. 'Miss Heath told us that you have an imaginary friend. Is that right?'

'Finn,' Jack says, matter of fact. 'He lives in my cupboard. He goes to school with me.'

'I see,' she says, carefully. 'Is he nice?'

'Most of the time. If he's naughty, he has to stay in the cupboard.'

The thought of a naughty boy in a cupboard would have unsettled Sarah as a child. 'I hope that doesn't worry you.'

Jack looks puzzled. 'No. He's only pretend.'

A weight lifts from her. 'Yes, of course. Good. What about Emma? Do you still play with her?'

'Yes. Can she come to our house? She'd love our trampoline and I want to show her my toys.'

It's difficult to see what Jack and Emma have in common, but he seems keen and it's their turn to reciprocate. 'I don't see why not. I'll ask her mummy.'

The thought of another encounter with Jessica Winters isn't appealing, but Jack is beaming and she can't disappoint him. He pushes his chair back from the table. 'Can I watch TV with Charlie now?'

'Yes – just one more thing. Do you know anyone else called Finn?' She's been wondering how he came up with the name. She's imagined a boy in another class at school or a character in a TV programme.

Jack is quiet for a moment. 'There's a big boy called Finn. He said hello once, when I was playing in the field.'

'When was this? Where was I?'

'I can't remember. I think you were making supper.'

Shock and guilt collide inside her. 'You shouldn't talk to strangers. Why didn't you tell me?'

'I don't know. He was nice. He said he liked my trainers.' Jack's ears have gone pink and he's mumbling the way he does when he's in trouble.

'I see,' she says, in a softer voice. 'What did he look like?'

'He was tall. He had yellow hair. He said he'd see me around, but I didn't see him again.'

It's not a lot of detail, but she has a feeling it's the boy. The name, Finn, would suit him. She wonders if he's been following her home. 'If you see him again, come and tell me.'

'OK,' Jack says. He's biting his lip. 'I'm sorry I didn't tell you before.'

'That's all right. I'm sorry I was cross. You mustn't talk to strangers, however nice they seem. You know that, don't you?'

'Yes,' he says.

She pulls him close and kisses him. In the playroom, the theme song for Jack's favourite TV programme is starting up. 'You don't like *Dennis the Menace*, do you?' she teases.

Jack nods, smiling. He goes off to the playroom.

The other day in the field, when the gardeners were here, she had a feeling that she was being watched. There was someone in the shadows. The boy has been asking about her, following her, talking to her son . . . it's intriguing. Her stomach lurches, as if she's edging closer and closer to a precipice.

The end of term brings its fanfare of sports days and speech days, and the summer holidays begin. The days are warm and easy: a sprinkler and a paddling pool is all they need. Picnics in the garden; makeshift camps made by draping sheets over garden furniture; ice lollies. Charlie goes brown and even Jack has colour in his cheeks. Other parents will be tutoring their children, but she prefers to let Jack be free. Play is more important than times tables. There will be plenty of time for slogging later on. She and Jack take turns reading in the afternoons – picture books, chapter books, whatever takes his fancy, but that's all.

It's a relief not to be at school. She'd felt a coolness from the other mothers that she didn't understand, but after the play date at the Winters', it became clear: Jack was precocious and she was to blame. Once she knew, she noticed it more: the hushed conversations, the sideways glances, the tight smiles. She came to dread the school gates and often arrived late. Jessica Winters was an unlikely ally, but at least she was a friendly face. She seemed keen to nurture Emma and Jack's friendship. 'Girls can be mean. There are some right little madams in our class,' she confided. So Emma was excluded too. Sarah didn't comment; she didn't trust Jessica not to repeat what she said. With two older children, Jessica had more experience with playground politics. 'Don't worry, hon. There will be new kids next year and it will be someone else's turn,' she said, before she and her family retired to their villa in Spain.

Sarah hasn't seen the boy, Finn. She asks Jack from time to time, but he hasn't seen him again either. Charlie's still too little for the walk to the lake. Sometimes her mind plays tricks and the boy's voice comes floating into their garden, but then there's the rumble of a lawnmower and an exchange in Italian; it's Nico Saunders and his men, working next door. The gardeners come once a week, after they've finished with the Joneses' garden. Paul grumbled at first, but he appreciates it now that it's summer and the grass grows as fast as it's cut. She wonders what the boy is doing, where he is. If he was following her before, he isn't any more. It's for the best, she tells herself, burying the disappointment that blooms inside her.

The other boy, the one who died, is also on her mind. One evening, when the children are in bed, she searches on the computer and eventually finds an archived *Littlefold Advertiser* news report. Samuel Thomas drowned when a boat capsized on the old quarry lake. A friend was with him. The friend, who survived, isn't named. She wonders if it's the boy Finn and if this is why he comes to the lake. It would explain the turmoil she senses in him: his volatile behaviour, the absences from school. The news report is brief and leaves her dissatisfied. It doesn't explain how the boat capsized. She imagines the boys playing dares or getting into a fight. Or it could have been an accident; a fault with the boat. She knows it's morbid, but she can't stop thinking about it. Perhaps it's because she has two boys of her own who might one day be tempted to take a boat out on the lake.

Samuel Thomas is gone, nothing can bring him back, but what happened that day also shattered the childhood of his friend. There is no mention in the news report of that. She wouldn't expect there to be.

The fine weather holds and the summer passes pleasantly. One weekend, after lunch, Paul suggests a walk through the woods. 'Let's go to that lovely lake you told me about.'

It seems a long time since she and Paul spoke about the lake. It isn't that she doesn't want to go there with him, but the lake has become her place, somewhere she goes on her own. 'What about Charlie?' she says. 'He'll get tired and I can't carry him.'

'He can have a shoulder ride,' Paul says.

The lake is as idyllic as she knew it would be: an expanse

of sparkling water, an oasis, in the midst of green woodland. It isn't quiet, the way it is during the week. There are more people walking their dogs, a few families with children, an elderly couple out for a constitutional stroll. It occurs to her that she's never seen a boat on the water. No rowing or fishing, despite the sign for the Littlefold Anglers. This was to be expected during the week, but today the boats tethered to the jetties look more decorative than real. It's because of Samuel Thomas, she thinks. No one wants to use their boats here any more.

'Nice spot,' Paul says, lifting Charlie down from his shoulders. 'I can see why you like coming here.'

They walk together around the lake, with Jack and Charlie running ahead and back to meet them, as if in a relay race. They pass the memorial bench. They don't sit down – the boys don't seem to need a rest – and Paul doesn't notice the inscription or the dates. She doesn't see the boy, but this doesn't surprise her. He's probably out with friends.

Jack and Charlie aren't as interested in the lake as she thought they'd be. There's more for them to do in the woods: finding sticks, building dens, climbing trees. The lake doesn't pull them, the way it does her, and she is relieved.

In August, Paul takes time off from the office at last, and they rent a villa with a pool in Greece. The sun, the swimming, the leisurely lunches of feta and bread and olives do them all good. A week later, they fly home. Paul goes back to work and she takes the boys to the uniform shop to get ready for the new academic year.

# Vivien

*London, 1980*

Vivien sits in an armchair beside the window, her baby in her arms, looking out onto Balham High Road, which is always congested. Four floors up, the traffic is muted to a hum. Her daughter, Sarah, slowly opens her eyes then closes them, and her breathing deepens. Another few minutes and Vivien will be able to put her in the cot. If her own mother wasn't about to appear, she'd go back to bed too. Sarah was restless last night, waking every few hours like a newborn. Vivien wonders if she's teething; her cheeks are flushed, drool pools from her mouth and her gums are swollen. She's nearly twelve months old.

The trees lining the high street are bare and puddles shine on the pavement. The drizzling rain, the cold wind, the low grey sky; this is November in the city. In Littlefold, there will be blackberries in the brambles, bonfires, a white frost. For a moment, she aches for the place where she grew up, the fields and the woods, but then it's gone. London is her home now. Her eyelids are heavy. She is drifting, sinking into dreams, but a siren wails and she surfaces with a jolt. Sarah sleeps on, undisturbed by the noise. Vivien stands, walks slowly into the bedroom and carefully places Sarah in her cot, gently tucking the blankets around.

Awake, Sarah is an angel until she's put down. Vivien can't bear to listen to her daughter cry, but it's impossible to tidy or cook, or do anything with a baby in her arms. The flat is proof: the bed is unmade, the laundry basket is overflowing, last night's dinner plates are stacked beside the sink, the carpet needs vacuuming. Her mother will be here in an hour and she hasn't even had a shower. Maggie raised two children in a spotless five-bedroomed farmhouse, and here Vivien is struggling to manage a baby and a tiny flat. Maggie's nursing was a better preparation for the life of a housewife than Vivien's literature degrees. Chaucer and Flaubert are no help when you've run out of clean clothes and there isn't any food in the fridge.

She runs the shower, getting in as soon as it's hot, soaping her skin and rinsing herself. The heat and steam revive her. She wraps a towel around, dries herself and applies cream to the fading stretch marks spun like webs across her stomach and thighs. In the mirror, her face is pale and her eyes are as dark as slate. She pulls her hair, which needs washing, into a ponytail.

In the bedroom, she opens the wardrobe and the door creaks. Sarah murmurs and turns in her cot, and for a moment Vivien thinks she's waking up, but no, it's fine. She dresses quickly, pulling on a jumper and jeans. The days when she used to try on outfits and perfect her make-up are gone. Before she had a baby, she took care over her appearance, she liked to look polished, but now she doesn't have the time. If she's clean and neat, and her baby is too, it's an achievement.

She tackles the sitting room, collecting tea-stained mugs and tidying away Sarah's cuddly animals and toys. She carries the two bottles of wine that Lawrence drained last night to the kitchen. The bin is full and there isn't time to empty it, so she hides the bottles in the cupboard below the sink. Maggie already disapproves of Lawrence; the empty bottles would give her ammunition. Vivien opens a window in the kitchen to air it, and washes up plates and mugs. Sleepless nights affect her like a drug. She moves slowly, as if wading through treacle. Her thoughts are like sparks in the fog.

London wasn't supposed to be like this. After university, where she'd studied first English and then French literature she'd hoped to work in advertising or marketing for French businesses not be at home looking after a baby and doing chores. One of her French literature tutors was Lawrence Bradshaw. Handsome and sophisticated, he seduced her with the sensuous poems of Baudelaire and the bohemian music of Aznavour. He smoked Gitanes in bed, which seemed the epitome of decadence. His French mother had given him a perfect French accent and a disdain for English cooking. He drank a bottle of wine a night; it had seemed natural at first, part of his heritage.

She finished her PhD and moved into Lawrence's flat while she looked for a job. Falling pregnant was an accident, but Lawrence was pleased and she was swept along by his enthusiasm. She'd always planned on having a family, she told herself; a career would have to wait, but perhaps she could do some teaching. She doesn't know if all babies are the same or if Sarah is particularly demanding, but she couldn't mark an essay now.

She loves her baby with an intensity that takes her breath, but she wasn't prepared for motherhood. Her world has shrunk to the flat, the high street and the Common. It astonishes her that she can be controlled by such a tiny person.

Sarah's vulnerability, her demand for only Vivien, binds them in a way that she couldn't have imagined. It is a new life and she's still adjusting.

She'd cope better if it weren't for the battles with Lawrence. In the evenings, after a few drinks, he lectures her. She's a hopeless mother, he says, a useless wife. She cooks him a casserole, but he won't touch it. 'This is tasteless,' he says coldly, pushing his plate away. He pours himself another glass of wine. 'The flat's a mess. You look terrible. What do you do all day?' She tries to explain that it's hard work looking after a baby, but he doesn't understand. 'You can't let Sarah take over like this,' he says. His words sting, but Vivien tells herself it's the drink. She says nothing, but he carries on needling until she gives him the quarrel he's after. The fight seems to be what Lawrence needs; his anger ignites, flares and is gone. Afterwards, he holds her close, stroking her hair. *'Je t'aime,'* he whispers, but he never apologises. Somehow, Sarah sleeps through their arguments.

Lawrence won't admit he's an alcoholic. He dismisses her suggestions of counselling; she's the one who needs help, he says. He twists her words until she begins to question her own sanity. He breaks her down bit by bit.

He drinks until he can't walk, until he vomits. He calls her names. *Salope*: Bitch. It doesn't shock her any more. She's numb to it. He raises his fist and she knows that one day he will hit her. And when he's through with her, he'll start on Sarah. She will not risk her daughter.

Her mother has guessed about Lawrence; no doubt she came across alcoholics while nursing. Maggie wants her to come home, but she can't go back to Littlefold. She doesn't want to be reminded of her childhood, the shame and anger buried deep inside her. She loves her father, but she can't forgive him. And there is no place for a single mother among the cliques of housewives. 'My life is in London. I'll manage somehow,' she tells her mother.

'You must do as you think best,' Maggie says, but she doesn't understand. Vivien can't explain; it would only hurt her mother, and she wouldn't know what to say. Her father never mentioned the letter again, or the woman who wrote it. It was as if the woman, Flavia, had ceased to exist. From time to time, Vivien wondered if the child was stillborn or the woman had moved away, but somehow she knew this wasn't the case. She tried to ask Aunt Edith once, but she didn't know or wouldn't say. She didn't dare ask her father, for fear of reminding him of his other child. She worried that he might leave her and Michael.

The years of silence have made her dumb. She doubts she could speak of that time now. The secret is lodged inside her.

She will move out of Lawrence's flat and find a new home, a safe place for herself and her baby. She will look for a job, or a few part-time jobs if need be. She wishes that she could apply for a position in advertising, but it will be impossible to commit to long hours while Sarah is a baby. She will have to find another way, perhaps as a secretary in a good firm, where she can bide her time until her daughter is older.

Sarah will go to nursery while she works. Vivien can't imagine how she will leave her baby to be fed and comforted by strangers, but she will do it because she has to. One day, she hopes her daughter will understand.

# Sarah

## *Autumn 2010*

The autumn term arrives like the tide, sweeping Jack and Charlie back into school and nursery. In the mornings, Jack slings his satchel over his shoulder and jumps onto the school bus; the sleeves of his new blazer are too long, his shiny black shoes look huge and he is wearing a proper tie. He waves at her and Charlie from the window, but his face looks pale through the glass. At nursery, Charlie wriggles free from her arms, takes off his coat and rummages through baskets of toys. She tries not to mind when he doesn't say goodbye.

A brisk walk is exercise and fresh air is good for everyone. This is what she tells herself as she climbs the path. She pushes her hands into her pockets and her breath comes out like smoke. She kicks up dry, brittle leaves. The wind blows and more leaves are falling, spiralling to the ground, a carpet of red, gold and brown. She collects a few conkers for Jack and Charlie.

Wild blackberries glisten in the brambles. She picks one, easing it from its stem; it is delicious, not like the blackberries in the supermarket, which are bigger but taste as bitter as lemons.

At the top of the path, she rests for a moment beside the apple tree. It is cold and there is mist on the cropped fields. Yellow-green apples are hiding in the tree's branches; some have fallen, bruised, and lie rotting on the ground. There are more blackberries here, hiding in the brambles, decaying, half-eaten by birds.

A child's book is folded over the fence. It's a book of nursery rhymes, but the pictures have faded and the pages are warped. She sees it falling out of a bag, rained on and blown about, discovered by one of the ladies who jog, carefully displayed. She's seen this before: an odd sock placed on a rock beside the lake, a handkerchief hooked onto the brambles, a penknife plunged into a tree trunk. There's something unsettling about these objects, which seem more like clues than lost possessions.

Webs shine like constellations on thickets of holly and she imagines full-bodied spiders crouching in the shadows, waiting to devour victims snared by silken threads. Red berries are like cherry tomatoes. She squashes one between her finger and thumb, the flesh splits, juice spurts and her skin stings. Small indigo globes, displayed on the ivy, could be mistaken for blueberries. A child might be tempted to taste this beautiful, no doubt poisonous fruit. Shiny red toadstools with white flecks have sprung up in the undergrowth, like the seats for woodland fairies in children's stories.

A small, still bundle is lying on the path. A mouse, tail curled around, its head resting on a leaf, one tiny paw cradling an acorn. If it weren't for the flies, she'd think it was asleep. Her throat tightens and she looks away. In London, autumn was confined to manicured parks; gold and russet trees; neat piles of leaves. Wild and beautiful, fertile and cruel, autumn here is full of mystery.

The lake is murky brown, as if the colours of the trees have bled into it. A pale sun hangs in the overcast sky. A solitary figure is sitting on Samuel Thomas's bench. He has his back to her and she cannot see his face. Her heart begins to pound.

He turns. His dark eyes seem to look through her. His skin is grey and his face sags, but then he smiles and becomes the man she knows. He stands, pushing his hands into the pockets of his overalls. 'Mrs Sarah,' he says.

'Nico,' she says. She doesn't know what else to say, so she sits down on the bench and he does too, leaving space between them.

Nico runs his fingers through his black, silvered hair. He coughs. 'I am waiting for someone.'

'Yes,' she says, but she doesn't understand.

'My son sometimes comes here instead of going to school.'

His words echo in her head. 'Yes. He sits on this bench,' she says, before she can stop herself.

'You know my boy.'

'I've seen him here. I didn't realise he was your son.'

'He doesn't look like me.'

Now that she knows, she can see the similarities: the warm smile, the strong physique, the shadows in their eyes. 'There is something,' she says.

Nico sighs. He interlinks his fingers. 'He helped me this summer. He worked hard. But he doesn't go to school.'

So she hadn't imagined it. It was the boy in the Joneses' garden. He was working with his father next door. 'I expect all teenagers skip school now and then,' she says lightly.

For an awful moment, pain twists in Nico's face, and then it's gone. 'Yes,' he says. He stands, brushing grass or dirt that isn't there from his overalls. 'He must be somewhere else

130

today. I should get back to work. Goodbye.' He walks away, into the woods.

A drake swims across the water, leaving a shining wake. Her initial shock fades. It's reassuring to know that Nico Saunders is the boy's father; he's a respectable, hard-working man. Nico didn't mention his son's name and she didn't think to ask. It must be Finn. The boy has an excuse to be near her home. The thought of this stirs her in an unexpected way; troubled, she pushes the feeling away.

She is standing beside the old apple tree, looking out across rolling fields. The sky is lightening.

She holds an apple in her hand, bruised and soft, and her fingers trace the black holes made by worms. The brambles, glistening with dew, are draped with cobwebs. Mist veils the trees.

There are footsteps in the bracken. He takes her hand. They watch the sun rise, brushing the sky with amber and gold. They don't speak.

She wakes, slowly, peacefully, but then she realises it was the boy.

He's stalking her dreams. Finn. She incants his name, like a prayer.

# Maggie

*Surrey, 1981*

Maggie's got her coat on, and is winding a woollen scarf around her neck, when the telephone rings in the hall. She picks up the receiver. 'Hello,' she says, glancing at her watch. She doesn't want to be late for her shift at the hospice shop.

'Hello Mummy.' It's Vivien. She sounds upset. 'Are you busy tomorrow?'

Maggie's supposed to be at the shop again tomorrow, helping to sort through donations. It's that time of year, when winter draws to a close, the snowdrops arrive like small miracles, and spring cleaning begins in earnest in the households of Littlefold. Playrooms will be emptied to make room for children's toys received at Christmas. Wardrobes will be purged in anticipation of the new season's collections. As the days grow longer and warmer, the garages will be aired and tidied. It will be a fruitful few weeks for the charity shops. 'What's the matter, darling?' she says.

'It's Sarah. She's got tonsillitis.' Vivien's voice breaks. 'The nursery's a germ pit. She's only just over that stomach upset.'

'Poor little thing,' Maggie says. She often collects her granddaughter from the nursery when Vivien can't get away from the office. It isn't as clean as she'd expect it to be; a nursery would have been kept spotless in her day. She doesn't like the way the girls leave the children's noses running. If it were up to her, she'd have chosen a nursery with more mature staff. Still, it's close to Vivien's flat, and what the girls lack in experience, they make up for with enthusiasm. It's a bright and cheerful place, in an old Victorian house, and Sarah is always playing happily when Maggie arrives.

'I've taken a day's holiday, but we're in the middle of a pitch. I need to be in the office,' Vivien says.

Maggie doesn't like to let the hospice down. She will ask Joan to swap shifts with her. Poor Joan lost her husband last year and likes to keep busy. They've swapped a few times before, when Vivien needed help. 'Don't worry. I'll look after Sarah tomorrow.' She'll set her alarm to avoid the morning rush. 'I can be with you by eight o'clock.'

'Thank you, Mummy,' Vivien says, but her voice wavers. She sounds like she's on the verge of tears.

It can't be easy, trying to work while looking after a sick child. She's no doubt exhausted, from a run of sleepless nights. 'Try and get some rest. Is she on antibiotics?'

There is the sound of Vivien blowing her nose. 'Sorry. Yes. It's a nightmare getting it down her.'

'Try a syringe. It's easier than a spoon. I expect the antibiotics will kick in and you'll have a better night.' Maggie wonders if she ought to drive to Balham today, so that Vivien can rest, but Joan is at a lunch and it's too late to rearrange her shift. There's no point asking Jim. He's at the club playing men's singles, but even if he was free, he wouldn't know what to do with a baby or the donations. 'I've got to dash. I'm late for the Princess Alice. I'll see you tomorrow. Lots of love.'

133

She puts on her leather gloves, pulls the front door shut and gets in the car. It's chilly and she turns the heat up. She feels the cold more these days, although she doesn't know if it comes with age or from being spoilt by central heating.

She inches slowly out of the driveway, waiting for a gap in the stream of cars. The new motorway, built less than a mile off despite fierce local opposition, has transformed what used to be a quiet country lane. Their garden isn't the peaceful place it once was. The road noise is worse in the winter when the trees are bare. Vivien lives on Balham High Road and says she'll get used to it, but Maggie isn't sure. In London, the cars are visible and she expects to hear them. At home, with a view of pastures and grazing horses, the noise jars. She drives down the winding lane, past the old farm that is now a riding school. The banks of daffodils make her think of spectators at a parade.

She turns on the radio to listen to the BBC. No doubt the news will be dominated by the royal engagement. All of England is humming with the announcement. Joan says that Lady Diana Spencer may be a commoner, but she's beautiful and refined: a natural princess. Maggie wishes the couple every happiness, but the match reminds her of her own daughter, who also married a man ten years older. She hopes it doesn't end in tears. It's not the prince – unlike Lawrence, he's a gentleman, but marriage is challenging enough without being from different generations.

There have been times when she's wished that her daughter had never set eyes on Lawrence Bradshaw, but she could never wish away Sarah. The baby's tiny hand grips her finger and her heart melts. She's petite, with delicate features and soft blue eyes that are always looking around her; clever and secretive, like her mother. Maggie knows that alcoholism is a sickness – she remembers the hold it had on her father – but she'll never forgive Lawrence for the way he treated her daughter. She's not in favour of divorce, but an abusive husband is worse. She was relieved when Vivien left him.

She tried to persuade Vivien to come home, so that she could help her, but Vivien refused. 'I can't commute. I'd hardly see Sarah,' she said.

'No, that wouldn't do,' Maggie said, remembering how little Jim saw of their children when he worked; breakfast, always rushed, and a kiss before bed. It's not easy, driving to Balham at a moment's notice, but she's proud of her daughter for pursuing a career, and she's a good mother to Sarah, even if she's not with her all day – more patient, perhaps, than if she was.

Last year, Vivien found secretarial work in an advertising firm and in January, they suddenly offered her the position of an associate, working with French businesses. It's a new firm and the female partners are keen to promote women, but Vivien says she won't get anywhere if she keeps taking time off. Maggie's often wondered what it would have been like to carry on with nursing, but it was frowned on for mothers to work after the war and she didn't have anyone to help with the children. Jim wouldn't have been keen; like most men of his generation, he preferred her to stay at home. She doesn't know how these young working mothers manage, with the house to look after as well as their children.

Vivien doesn't do any housework. She's never been tidy, preferring to bury her head in books. When Maggie's own children were little and she needed to get the chores done, she relied on the extra space in her garden; a baby could sleep in a pram beneath the trees and older children would play outside for hours. Keeping little ones occupied in a flat is difficult. To begin with, Vivien's flat was a mess, but now she's had a raise, a cleaning lady comes in once a week and tidies up. Vivien says Maggie should have a cleaning lady too, now that she's getting older, but Maggie doesn't want another woman in her house, vacuuming and dusting, and moving their things. Besides, unlike her daughter, she has the time: it's only her and Jim now, with Michael at university and Vivien in town.

When the children were young, she sometimes wondered what it would be like when they grew up and left home. She imagined going on leisurely trips with Jim, to Provence or the Dordogne, seeing the sights and staying in *chambres d'hôtes*. But Jim is as busy in his retirement as he was at the office, playing tennis three times a week and helping to manage the club. He also consults; for pocket money, he says, although they don't need the money. Every so often, he puts on a suit and spends the day in London.

Maggie's busy too, volunteering at the Princess Alice and helping to look after Sarah. She also plays tennis. To begin with, she went to the club to swim, but when Michael went to university, she decided to take lessons and now she plays doubles with Jim. Her new hobby wasn't entirely precipitated by an empty nest. After Michael left, she'd felt something change in Jim. At first, she thought he was missing his son. He seemed distant, his mind somewhere else. In the evenings, after supper, he held a book in his hands, but his eyes drifted to the garden and the fields.

It was a disturbance in him, like static. She'd felt it once before, when the children were little. They were leading separate lives, with him at the office and her so tired she could drop from the housework and the children. She knew that Jim drew the eyes of other women, and although he loved her, the romance was gone. He stayed out late at night on the pretext of client dinners, but she found lipstick on his shirt collars and his skin was scented with citrus and bergamot, a woman's perfume that wasn't hers. She thought it might be a career girl from the office, but it didn't matter who the woman was. She trusted that Jim would never leave her and the children, and the fling would fizzle out. She never spoke of it to him. It wasn't that she didn't feel hurt or jealous – she was both – but confronting him would back him into a corner and she'd risk losing everything.

The months passed, and the affair seemed to ebb and fade. Sometimes, Jim was happy and engaged; at other times, he seemed troubled and withdrawn. She kept hoping that the affair would run its course, but it was exhausting living with a man who was involved with someone else. She thinks Vivien guessed too, although they've never discussed it. Vivien was a quiet child, but she became even more introspective as a teenager. She would spend hours alone in her room, reading and doing her schoolwork. Maggie didn't interfere – adolescents needed their space and Vivien would confide in her when she was ready. She could hardly take her daughter to task for being bookish. Time passed, the distance between them grew, and she wondered if Vivien was angry with her for tolerating the affair, or if she felt torn, loyal to them both. Maggie couldn't ask in case she'd got it wrong. It was a difficult few years, and there were times when Maggie thought she couldn't carry on, but somehow she managed, and eventually Jim became more settled again. The disturbance she'd felt in him faded and then disappeared.

When Michael left for university, she felt it again. She didn't know if it was another affair, but without the children to bind them, their marriage was vulnerable. She took up tennis to find common ground, to share an interest with him that was independent of the family and the home. She'd played tennis at school and the racquet felt comfortable in her hands; she was a girl again, chasing after a lob or dashing up to the net. She and Jim made a good team. They won matches. Evenings were spent out having dinner with friends, other husband-and-wife teams from the club. It was a new life and they were spending more time together than they had in years. Slowly, she felt Jim turn back to her, like a planet towards the sun. The disturbance lingered for a while, and then it was quiet again.

# Sarah

*Autumn 2010*

Sarah wakes in the early morning dark to the soft, fluted calls of owls. She dresses quietly, puts on her coat and scarf, pulls on wellingtons and takes a torch.

The fog is heavy, like sunken cloud, and the trees are sudden apparitions. She knows these woods, but she's glad to have the torch to light her way. Her boots squelching through mud is the only sound.

The lake, wreathed in vapours, simmers like broth. Droplets sparkle on the stripped branches of the trees and solitary leaves hang from brittle stems. The brambles are barren. Trails leading down to the water are littered with trampled, discoloured leaves. The air is acrid, tainted with burnt-out bonfires. It is not the water garden it was in the summer. This is a wasteland, desolate and bereft.

A mallard comes gliding out of the fog. It eyes her, treading water. She takes the bread from her pocket and tears off a piece. Another mallard arrives, then another, and then more come. She throws the bread towards them, but they are too far to reach. She waits for a flurry, the beating of wings, but the ducks are quiet and still. They gaze at the morsels bobbing away, as if paralysed, transfixed. She throws in the rest of the bread, trying to pitch it as far as she can. A few pieces reach the ducks and are snapped up, but they do not come any closer. Perhaps they are wary of dangerous rocks, concealed beneath the cloudy surface.

She sits on Samuel Thomas's bench. Without the sun to warm it, the seat is as cold as marble. She shrinks into her coat and pushes her hands deep into her pockets.

She is here selfishly, coveting the first part of the day, some stillness before the whirlwind of her children engulfs her. Her love for them is fierce, a heat that feels primal and ancient. It would devour her if she let it: there can be no equilibrium when feelings burn like flames. Solitude has become as illicit as a drug. She feels guilty, stealing time away from her children, but without these moments alone she would be no good to them.

The fog is lifting. The sky and the water are almost colourless, as if the elements have dissolved. The ducks are drifting away.

She hears footsteps, then sees him coming towards her. It's been months since they last met. His hair has grown long, skimming his shoulders, and there is stubble on his face. He is carrying a bouquet; a fleeting thought is all it takes for the blood to rush to her face, but they are not for her. He rests the lilies on a rock beside the water. He sits down beside to her.

So he did know Samuel Thomas. She's almost certain now that he was with him on the boat that day. 'I'm sorry. I didn't know he was your friend,' she says.

The boy lights a cigarette. 'Don't be. He was an arsehole.' His words come out with smoke.

Laughter bubbles up inside her and she swallows it down.

She sees Nico Saunders standing in her garden, his gaze flicking over the dark woods; sitting alone beside the lake. 'Your father is worried about you,' she says.

'He'll get over it,' the boy says. He turns to her. His face darkens, like the sky in an approaching storm. 'Look, life is shit. So what?'

'Everyone goes through difficult times,' she says carefully, trying not to sound patronising.

'Easy for you to say, Mrs "I live in a big house with my rich husband and two kids".'

His words sting. 'You don't know anything about me,' she says.

'I know what I see.'

It was him in the shadows by the field. 'You've been watching me.'

'I was helping my dad.' He lifts his chin. His grey eyes are impenetrable.

She wants to ask why he never told her about Samuel Thomas. Instead, she says, 'Why didn't you tell me Nico Saunders was your father?'

'You didn't tell me he was your gardener.'

'Why would I? You haven't even told me your name,' she retorts. She doesn't understand how they can argue like this when they hardly know each other. She's the adult, she tells herself. She must lead by example. 'Your father's a good man,' she says. And then, because somehow it's possible to admit the truth to this boy, even though it's painful, she says, 'My dad's an alcoholic. I haven't seen him for years.'

He stubs out his cigarette. 'I'm sorry,' he says, and she can tell by his voice, the way he's looking at her, that he means it. 'I'm Finn.'

Yes, she thinks. A Huckleberry Finn, only darker, wilder. 'You're Jack's friend.'

Finn doesn't speak. He hasn't understood, perhaps.

'My son, Jack. He was in our field. You said you liked his trainers.' She laughs, although she doesn't know why.

'Right. Jack,' he says, as if it was a matter of small importance and he'd forgotten. 'I was on my way to meet my dad. He kicked a ball over the fence and asked me to throw it back.'

This doesn't square exactly with what Jack said – he'd made out that Finn initiated the conversation – but people remember things differently.

'He's a good kid,' Finn says.

He's not much more than a child himself. 'Yes, he is,' she says. She doesn't say that Jack's called his imaginary friend Finn. Jack must have admired Finn and wished they were friends. She understands how it would happen. This is a boy who draws people to him without seeming to do anything at all. It can't be easy; impossible to please everyone.

Finn looks out across the water. Something between them, as fine and delicate as a gossamer thread, breaks. He lights another cigarette, inhales, and blows out slowly. It's been years since she's smoked, but suddenly she longs to hold a cigarette again, to feel the smoke bloom inside her. If it weren't for her children, who think cigarettes are for villains, she'd ask for one.

'Sam lived next door,' Finn says, quietly. 'We grew up together. We were always larking about in these woods.'

He is silent for a moment. She doesn't dare speak. Her heart begins to pound.

'That morning, we were waiting for the school bus,' he says, as if he's beginning a story. 'It was hot. Sam said we should skip class. I'd never done that before. Back then I liked school. I was good at lessons. Anyway, we came here. No one was about so we took a boat out. The boat was old, it wasn't

142

in good nick, but it floated all right. After a while, Sam got bored. He said we should have a race.'

Finn squares his shoulders. He looks straight ahead. 'I told him, we can't. It's too deep. Too cold.' His voice is tight. It's as if he's speaking to somebody else. 'He wouldn't listen. Quick as a whip, he got out his pocketknife and stabbed it into the boat, again and again. Water started coming in.'

Finn laughs, but it's a bitter sound. 'So he got his way. We had to swim. But then he got scared. He wouldn't leave that fucking boat. I pulled him in.'

He takes another drag on his cigarette. His hand trembles. 'He couldn't swim, kept panicking. I tried to help him, but I got caught, tangled up in something. I had to let him go. When I came up again, he was gone.' His voice drops, like a sail without wind.

The lake shines like a sheet of glass. She sees a boy imprisoned in its depths. She turns so he can't see her face. 'I'm sorry,' she says, her voice catching in her throat. She feels his arm around her and then she is leaning into him. He is warm and her body melts into the shelter of his arms. He smells of cigarettes and soap, and beneath it, radiating from the centre of him, is a musky scent like the woods.

'You're lovely,' he says, softly.

She feels his breath in her hair. She pulls away. She takes a tissue out of her pocket, unfolds it and presses it to her face. The blood thuds in her head.

'I've never told anyone about the knife,' he says, carrying on as if nothing has happened and they haven't touched. He's pretending out of consideration for her, or his wounded pride perhaps. More likely it meant nothing. It was a moment, and now it's gone.

'His family thought it was an accident. I couldn't tell them . . .' His voice trails away.

'It was his fault.' She finishes his sentence.

'I told you he was an arsehole. He died and I got the blame.'

'I don't understand. Why did you get the blame?'

He shrugs. 'People talk. Some say I was the stronger swimmer, saved myself and didn't try to help him.'

She wonders how anyone could think that of a child who'd lost his dearest friend. It must be jealousy, that contemptible instinct to sabotage those who appear to have it all. 'You should tell the truth,' she says, but as the words leave her lips, doubt creeps into her head. A pocketknife wouldn't be strong enough to damage a boat, even if it was old and dilapidated. And this isn't a place where things are allowed to fall into disrepair; the jetties are always swept, the gardens are immaculate and the rowing boats are stowed away or covered for the winter. He's lying, she thinks. She wonders if he feels at fault somehow. Perhaps the boys were playing dangerous dares, or drinking. An accident, but neither was entirely blameless. She understands why he might lie. The guilt, the grief would have been overwhelming.

'Telling the truth won't change anything,' he says.

Gossip is repeated until it is gospel. It must be difficult for him to come here, but he can't seem to keep away.

'He died for nothing,' he says, his voice simmering. He clenches his hands into fists.

She knows how quickly his anger flares and dissipates. She doesn't speak, and after a while he slumps against the bench. 'I don't know why I come here. There are no answers.'

'Sam's gone,' she says, softly. 'Nothing will change that.'

'What would you do?'

This question is not what she'd expected. 'Go back to school. Work hard,' she says. He shakes his head, a cynical smile playing on his lips, but she carries on, even though it makes her sound like his mother and it's not what he wants to hear. 'I know it must be difficult, people can be cruel, but it's your chance to begin again. You said yourself that you were good at school. You could go away to university, where no one knows what happened here.'

'You're telling me to run away. Isn't that weak?'

'Sometimes, it takes more strength to leave.'

They are both silent, lost in their own thoughts.

The sun is climbing into the sky and the lake is sparkling. The children will be up by now. Paul isn't the type to worry, but he'll be wondering where she is. She stands up. 'I must go.'

'Yes,' he says. He doesn't say anything more.

She feels his eyes on her as she walks away.

Alone in the woods, her body still tingles from his touch, and she feels a flush of shame. She slips through the bare trees and the lie that Finn told her about the boat stalks her. Perhaps it wasn't an accident. He's got a temper; she's witnessed it on several occasions. He's tall and strong. She sees the boys arguing, Finn bursting into a rage, pushing Sam off the boat; he tries to rescue Sam, but it's too late. He's a troubled, guilt-stricken boy playing games with her and he's tried to befriend Jack. She's been a fool, flattered by his attentions, blinded by his magnetic beauty. She resolves not see him again. No good can come of this.

She's barely inside the front door when Charlie hurtles into the hallway. He launches himself at her and she drops to her knees. He clings to her, wrapping his legs around her waist, and rubs his face against hers. 'Love you,' he murmurs into her hair, but then he says it again and it sounds more like 'Lost you.'

She holds him tight. They stay close like this for a moment, then he pulls away and runs into the kitchen. He's wearing tracksuit bottoms and his pyjama top, but no socks.

145

She takes off her coat and hangs it up in the cupboard. It feels like it should be the end of the day, not the beginning. She longs to lie down in the quiet bedroom upstairs.

In the kitchen, Paul and Jack are playing chess. Milky breakfast bowls and mugs have been pushed to one side of the table. Charlie's drained bottle has rolled into a corner of the room and his plastic table mat is scattered with Cheerios. Jack is in his pyjamas. Paul is wearing his dressing gown.

'Hello Mummy,' Jack says. 'Daddy's lost his bishop and his queen.'

Paul looks up from the chessboard. His brown eyes are full of questions. 'You were up early. The boys thought you'd gone shopping, but you didn't take the car,' he says.

She leans down to pick up Charlie's bottle, collects the bowls and mugs, and carries everything to the sink. 'The owls woke me,' she says, without looking at Paul. 'I couldn't get back to sleep so I went for a walk. There was a lot of fog. It took longer than I expected.' She's talking too much, making too much of it, she thinks, rinsing the bowls and loading the dishwasher.

'I didn't hear any owls,' Jack says. 'Did you, Daddy?'

'No, but Mummy's a light sleeper,' Paul says.

'Mummy, did you actually see any owls?' Jack asks.

'Owls?' Charlie echoes. He has climbed onto the chair next to Jack's and is quietly moving pieces around the chessboard without either Jack or Paul noticing.

Jack could be the good cop, asking the questions, while Charlie is the diversion and Paul analyses her answers. She dries her hands on a tea towel, folds it and hangs it over the oven handle. 'I didn't see the owls, but I did hear them. They sounded rather beautiful, like a recorder or a flute.'

'Oh,' Jack says, losing interest. He studies the chessboard and moves his king. 'Checkmate. I've won!'

Charlie seems to be doing gymnastics. He's leaning on the table with one hand, stretching over his head with the other, while balancing on one leg on the chair.

Paul looks at the chessboard and then at Charlie. 'Have you been helping your brother?' he says.

'Nope,' Charlie says, sweetly. He places his hand back onto the table, rights himself, and closes his fingers around the king.

'Hey, that's mine,' Jack says. 'Give it back.'

Charlie leaps from the chair, lands in a squat and runs out of the kitchen, holding the king high like a trophy. Jack races after him and there are shrieks and unbridled laughter from the playroom.

Paul packs away the chess set. He stands up. 'Right. I'll have a shower,' he says, adjusting his glasses. He looks tired.

'I hope you weren't worried,' she says. 'I'm sorry. I should have left a note.'

'It's fine,' he says. He picks up yesterday's newspaper and flicks through it. 'I didn't realise you were such a keen rambler. I'm going to get you an attack alarm. It's only sensible, if you're out alone in the woods.'

It's just like Paul to focus on the practicalities; anything to avoid talking about his feelings. His concern deepens her shame. She moves closer to him and leans against his shoulder. He puts his arm around her, still reading or pretending to read the paper. He smells like their children, of milk and Marmite, and the aftershave she gave him for Christmas.

# Sarah

## *Surrey, 1986*

Sarah is seven years old, staying in Littlefold with her grandparents during the summer holidays, while her mother works in London.

She wakes early here, in the bedroom that used to be her mother's. It's the birds gathering in the trees, which is strange, as in Balham there is more noise and it never disturbs her. Sunlight is slipping beneath the curtains, drawing patterns on the blue carpet. Royal blue, Grandma Maggie says with a smile, and Sarah imagines the Queen gliding along the same carpet in Buckingham Palace.

She lies in bed, listening to the birdsong and the silence that seems to have its own shape and sound. After a while, she gets up, draws the curtains and stands looking out at the garden: the neat borders of hydrangeas and geraniums, the row of apple trees, the greenhouse where Grandpa Jim grows raspberries and gooseberries. Beyond the split-wooden fence are fields where the ponies from the riding school are put out to graze, and a copse where her mother played when she was a child.

She wraps a dressing gown around herself. The sky is blue and it will be warm later, but her grandparents' home is chilly in the mornings. It's an old farmhouse, with low ceilings and beams, creaking floorboards, a long, carpeted staircase with amber sidelights that she slides down when no one's looking, and a small step up into the kitchen and another down into the sitting room where she sometimes trips. There's a cellar for storing dusty bottles of wine and old furniture; it's dark and musty, with spiderwebs that cling to her hair.

The door to her grandparents' bedroom is closed and she can hear her grandfather's rumbling snores. She goes downstairs, closing the kitchen door quietly behind her. The fridge is full of cling-filmed leftovers – lumps of cheese, wrinkled sausages, congealed, crazed casseroles; all brought out at lunchtime to be eaten up. Her grandparents won't throw food away. Mummy says it's because of the war. She pours herself a glass of milk, switches on the television and draws up a chair. She will watch the *Wide Awake Club* until her grandparents come downstairs for breakfast and then it will be time for camp with other children who, like her, would get square eyes if they stayed indoors. On the weekends, she goes back to Balham. Last time, she and Mummy went to the National Gallery to see an exhibition of the Impressionists and in the afternoon they queued for *42nd Street* tickets in the gods.

She loves her grandparents, and the farmhouse is as much home to her as her own, but at night she misses her mother and her stomach hurts. Grandma Maggie is kind, reading her stories and tucking her in, but she doesn't smell like Mummy or cuddle her in bed. If she can't sleep, Grandma makes her peppermint tea and gives her milk of magnesia. Sarah's had stomach ache ever since she can remember. Mummy says it started when she was a baby. The doctor says she'll grow out of it.

She'd be prettier if she didn't have tummy ache and could eat more. She's small, with mousy hair and a gap where her two front teeth used to be. If only she was more like her mother, tall and willowy, with shiny auburn hair. Her mother is beautiful – people on the Tube stare – but Sarah takes after her father. She doesn't see him very often. When they meet, he calls her *ma belle* and gives her children's books in French that she pretends to be pleased with but are too difficult for her to read. Sometimes he's cheerful, asking her about school and telling jokes, but on other days he's cross and can't speak properly, and Mummy says it's time to go. Her parents divorced when she was little. If things had been different, she might have had a brother or a sister, but her mother hasn't got time for a husband now, let alone a baby. Sarah knows that her mother has to work to earn money, but she wishes she was at home more and could look after her in the holidays.

The door to the kitchen opens and Grandma Maggie comes in. Her face is creased from sleep, but she's neatly dressed in navy trousers and a gingham shirt. 'Hello poppet,' she says. 'What would you like for breakfast? How about a boiled egg and soldiers?'

'No thanks. I'll just have cornflakes,' Sarah says. She switches off the television.

'That won't keep you going,' Grandma Maggie says. 'I made stewed apple yesterday. It's delicious with yoghurt.'

'Maybe later,' Sarah says politely. Stewed apple is slimy and the yoghurt in the fridge looks lumpy.

Grandma Maggie bites her lip but says nothing. She unloads the dishwasher, putting away plates and cutlery. Sarah helps her to set the table and takes the cornflakes out of the cupboard.

Grandpa Jim comes in. His hair is grey and thin, but he doesn't shuffle the way old men do or take pills for aches and pains. 'It's going to be a nice day,' he says, putting teabags in the teapot and filling the kettle. 'How about a game of croquet this afternoon?'

'Lovely,' Grandma Maggie says. 'Sarah and I can make scones.' She puts bread in the toaster that always burns, regardless of its setting, then carries a jar of homemade jam and a bowl of the dreaded stewed apple to the table.

The toaster pings and there is a small exhalation of smoke. Grandpa Jim lifts out the scorched slices, scrapes off the black crust with a knife and puts the toast on a plate. He carries the teapot to the table and pours two cups of tea. Sarah follows with the toast.

Grandma Maggie sips her tea, leans back in her chair and says, 'I wonder if Edith would like to pop round? It would be nice to see her.'

There is a silence and Sarah wonders if her grandfather has heard. 'Yes,' he says, at last, buttering his toast. 'She's fond of croquet. I'll ask her.' He spoons a generous portion of stewed apple on to his plate. Sarah busies herself with the cornflakes, pretending not to see, hoping she won't be entreated to try some.

She is getting ready for camp, putting on her trainers in the hall, when she hears Grandma Maggie speaking in the kitchen. 'Edith has been very good to Vivien. I don't want her to think it's gone unnoticed.'

Grandpa Jim answers, but his voice is too low for Sarah to catch the words, and then Grandma Maggie appears, her mac buttoned and belted, a handbag in one hand and a shopping list in the other. 'We'd better go or you'll be late,' she says brightly. She puts the shopping list in her handbag and picks up her car keys. 'I'll go to the supermarket after I've dropped you off. We can make a cake as well as scones. Edith is partial to a Victoria sandwich.'

Sarah likes croquet and cake, but the thought of seeing her aunt makes her want to fidget. Aunt Edith has piercing eyes and there is no escape from the onslaught of her questions and advice – Sarah should be progressing faster through the times tables, she should take ballet for deportment, her white blouse is too draining for her complexion. Sarah usually goes to see Aunt Edith with Grandpa Jim; from time to time, he takes her to the Laurels for a cup of tea and a biscuit. Aunt Edith doesn't often come to the farmhouse.

After camp, Sarah and her grandmother spend the afternoon in the kitchen, sifting flour, weighing sugar and butter, breaking eggs and using the mixer. Grandma pours the glossy batter into two sandwich tins and smooths it with a wooden spoon. She slides the tins into the oven while Sarah licks the spoon; the batter is vanilla-sweet and delicious.

Grandma Maggie dusts the wooden workbench and the rolling pin with flour and lets Sarah knead and roll out the dough for the scones. She gives Sarah a biscuit cutter. 'Try to keep them close together,' she says. 'We'll use the scraps for a second batch.' Sarah stamps out circles as carefully as she can. Grandma Maggie lifts the scones onto a baking tray and brushes them with beaten egg. 'There,' she says, clapping her hands free of flour. 'Time to tidy up.' She whisks around the kitchen, gathering bowls and spoons, then runs the tap until it's hot. She stands at the sink washing up, and Sarah dries with a stripy tea towel. 'All done,' Grandma says, untying her apron. 'We'd better go and tidy ourselves now.'

Sarah knows without asking that she should wear a dress. She chooses her favourite: primrose yellow with puffed sleeves and a silky sash that ties at her waist. She brushes her hair, slips on an Alice band and puts on white socks and sandals.

Grandma Maggie is sitting at her dressing table, fastening

her pearl earrings. She's wearing a short-sleeved floral dress. She's about to say something to Sarah, when the doorbell rings and there are voices in the hall. She quickly runs a comb through her short brown hair and stands up, smoothing her dress. She looks closely at Sarah, smiles, and gently rubs Sarah's cheek with her thumb. 'Flour,' she says. 'There. It's gone.'

Aunt Edith is in the kitchen talking to Grandpa Jim. She is tall and elegant, in a white skirt and a pale blue pussy-bow silk blouse. Her shoulder-length hair is blonde and shiny. The French doors are open and the curtains are billowing gently in the breeze. The aroma of the baking cake and scones makes Sarah's mouth water.

'Hello darling,' Aunt Edith says, kissing Grandma Maggie lightly on the cheek. 'How was camp?' she says to Sarah. 'I hear you went swimming today.'

The grown-ups all turn to her, looking at her expectantly, and Sarah feels her face grow hot. 'Yes. It was fine,' she says.

'I expect you're good at swimming. You've got the build for it,' Aunt Edith says, in an approving tone that Sarah hadn't expected. 'I enjoyed swimming too, when I was a girl.'

Sarah isn't the fastest in her class and she's never won a race, but she says nothing, not wishing to disappoint her aunt.

'It's a lovely afternoon,' Grandma Maggie says. 'Shall we go outside?'

They sit on garden chairs around a wooden table in the shade of the tall chestnut tree. Grandma Maggie pours milk into each teacup and then Earl Grey tea. 'Sugar, Edith?'

Aunt Edith waves a hand, her bracelets sparkling. 'No, thank you, darling.' She carries on with the story that she is recounting. 'I had to get rid of Joseph. It's a pity; he was reliable, but he ruined my roses.' She sighs. 'It's difficult to find good people.'

Grandma Maggie cuts the Victoria sandwich into generous pieces and, using a silver cake slice, lifts them onto china plates. She distributes the scones. 'Would you like cream?' she asks, giving Edith a plate.

'This cake looks perfect. And it's a treat to have homemade scones. I'll just have jam, if you don't mind. I'm trying to watch my cholesterol.'

Grandma Maggie's face has gone pink and Sarah wonders if it's on account of the hot weather or Aunt Edith's praise. 'Of course. Sarah helped me. We made it together.'

Grandpa Jim tucks into a large slice of Victoria sandwich, over which he's poured lashings of cream. He doesn't seem at all worried about cholesterol. 'Very good,' he says, between mouthfuls. 'Just the ticket.'

Sarah carefully balances her plate on her lap. She doesn't usually like scones – they stick to the roof of her mouth – but these are light and delicious. The cake tastes good too, but she prefers the batter that she licked from the spoon.

It is peaceful beneath the trees. The long lawn is velvet and the sky is clear blue, with the white trails of aeroplanes. A bee lands on the sticky rim of the jam jar.

'When Surrey is like this, there's nowhere else I'd rather be,' Aunt Edith says, leaning back against her chair. 'It's a pity that Vivien can't enjoy this. I suppose Balham is more convenient.'

'Yes, she finds it helpful to be near the office. She's working very hard. She's just been promoted,' Grandma Maggie says. 'And Sarah has the best of both, the countryside and the city.'

Sarah has noticed that grown-ups sometimes speak about her as if she isn't there. Perhaps they think she doesn't understand, or wouldn't know what to say.

'Indeed,' Aunt Edith says. 'Vivien is a clever girl. I always knew she'd do well.'

Beyond the garden, in the field, three ponies are standing in the shade of the copse, flicking their tails. 'What's past those trees?' Sarah asks.

Grandma Maggie turns, shading her eyes with her hand. 'Vivien and Michael were always playing up there, coming back with torn clothes and scraped knees.' She's quiet for a moment. 'I suppose if you kept walking, across the fields, you would eventually reach the woods and the railway line.'

Sarah's unlikely to find out. Grandpa Jim would rather play tennis than go for a walk, and Grandma Maggie says she gets enough exercise running up and down the farmhouse stairs. She doesn't mind; fields and woods don't sound exciting.

'I wouldn't go for a walk on my own now,' Aunt Edith says.

'No,' Grandma Maggie says. 'The world has changed.'

Grandpa Jim is gazing out over the fields and his thoughts seem far away. He sips his tea.

Grandma Maggie and Aunt Edith say nothing more, but Sarah knows they were talking about the Railway Stranglers, the men who've been attacking women and girls walking home from the station, first in London, now Surrey. The older girls at camp were speaking about it at lunch. 'After they killed that girl, they set her on fire,' one of them said, taking a bite of her cheese and tomato sandwich. Red juice dribbled down her chin and she wiped it away with her hand. 'Littlefold could be next.' Sarah isn't worried. She always travels with her mother on the train and her grandparents bring the car to collect them at the station.

After tea, when the sun is soft and the lawn is luminous, they play croquet. Aunt Edith slips off her heels and soon takes the lead, hitting accurately and with control. Grandma Maggie is her main rival, with Sarah and Grandpa Jim following close behind. Grandma hits Aunt Edith's ball, sending it into a flowerbed. 'Good shot,' Aunt Edith says, laughing.

She pivots on her stockinged feet and goes to retrieve her ball from the roses.

'Don't let that smile fool you. Edith loves to win,' Grandpa Jim says to Sarah, leaning on his mallet. 'Still, Maggie has a good eye.'

In the end, it's Grandpa Jim who wins, taking them all by surprise. 'You're a dark horse,' Aunt Edith teases. Grandpa Jim puts his arm around Grandma Maggie and kisses her, as if she's the winner, not him.

Aunt Edith goes home, Grandpa Jim waters the garden and Sarah helps her grandmother in the kitchen. She puts cups and saucers into the dishwasher, while Grandma Maggie washes up the silver cutlery and plates by hand. Grandpa Jim comes in, wiping his shoes on the mat. He sits down on the sofa and opens a copy of *The Times*. *Twenty per cent of British children are born out of wedlock* is one of the headlines on the other side. Sarah doesn't know what *out of wedlock* means, but it sounds like it might be something good, like cubs born free in the wild.

'That was a nice afternoon,' Grandma Maggie says.

Grandpa Jim looks up from his paper. 'Yes. It went well.'

There is a silence, but it isn't awkward or uncomfortable. Grandpa goes back to reading his newspaper and Grandma carries on washing up. The farmhouse creaks in a gentle, forgiving way.

It is dusk in the garden. A bat flits among the dark trees and the setting sun glows on the horizon. The sky is streaked with pink and the lawn shimmers in the last light. Sarah still misses her mother, but she also loves this peaceful, beautiful place.

# Sarah

## *January 2011*

It's January and they've had days of rain. The fields are spongy and the barren trees drip. The boys go outside for five minutes and come back soaked, with mud-splattered trousers. Sarah has given up washing their wellies. The footwells in the Volvo are caked in dirt and the back of her seat is smeared where Charlie's shoes have kicked. The car wash works its magic, leaving the Volvo clean and sparkling, but then the boys climb in and the dirt builds up again. Perhaps she ought to embrace the mud. She imagines covering her body in a thick layer, emerging with radiant and purified skin. She wonders if the lake has risen. She sees the water breaking the banks, the woodland flooded, the ducks adrift.

She tries not to think about the boy Finn – no good can come of it – but he arrives in her thoughts unbidden all the same. She hasn't seen him since that morning in the autumn when he told her about Samuel Thomas. Perhaps she over-reacted to his untruth about the pocketknife. Now that she's reflected on it, she doesn't believe it was sinister; the police were involved and it would have come out in an investigation. More than his lie, it was his touch that comforted her, shocked her, made her feel ashamed. When she's with him, she forgets that he's sixteen and she's a married mother. She is only Sarah and he is Finn. The freedom it brings is intoxicating, and this frightens her.

She hasn't been to the lake. It isn't only about Finn. It's been too wet to walk and she hasn't had the time; the autumn term was the usual whirlwind and then the boys were at home for the holidays. The end of term seemed more manageable this time, perhaps because she'd been through it once before and knew what to expect.

On New Year's Eve, Paul woke her at ten to midnight and put another log on the fire. They sat together on the sofa beneath a blanket, the fire crackling and throwing sparks on the hearth, watching the countdown on the television. At midnight, there was the whistle and bang of fireworks from a neighbour's garden, but the boys slept on undisturbed upstairs. She imagined Finn drinking beer at a party and hoped this year would be good to him. 'I'm getting a bonus,' Paul said, pouring them each a glass of champagne. 'Why don't we use it for the house? I know you're busy, but we could have a project manager and a team. It would be done in six months.'

Her heart sank. She still didn't want the disruption and inconvenience of building works, but the truth was that the house had become her sanctuary. The thought of it being gutted was upsetting. 'I'm not sure. Even a project manager will need overseeing and there are always delays. It could easily take a year,' she said. It was impossible to tell Paul how she really felt; her deep attachment to this crumbling place. He didn't know this house the way she did. He wouldn't understand. 'Well done on your bonus,' she said, but her voice sounded hollow. Every weekend in the office or away with clients had been the price to pay. There'd been a brief reprieve over Christmas, but it wouldn't be long before he was working long hours again. There was no use discussing it. He'd promise to change, and then it would be business as usual.

The rain comes in infinite variations: drizzle as fine as mist, huge, heavy drops hammering the glasshouse, sheets of rain blown across the garden or thrown like darts beneath umbrellas. The school run is even more fraught than usual: somehow, there is more traffic and the drivers are impatient, sounding their horns. At school, Charlie refuses to get out of the car; after much persuasion, he allows himself to be lifted out, then runs straight into a puddle, soaking his shoes and socks. She buys kitchen roll at the supermarket to dry Charlie's seat in the wet trolley and arrives home with dripping plastic bags of shopping. She lives in her parka, which steams on the radiator and never completely dries. The other school mothers are all in their unofficial winter uniform – black Puffa jackets belted tightly at the waist and knee-high leather boots, but her parka and slip-on trainers are comfortable and she doesn't have the time to lace up or buckle boots.

One afternoon, while hunting in the spare bedroom for an old waterproof of Jack's for Charlie, she notices a damp, musty smell. The room has a double bed, for guests that they haven't yet had, but is mainly functioning as storage for household miscellany – Jack's hand-me-downs, sports kit, old toys destined for Oxfam, lamps and paintings from their old flat that she hasn't yet rehoused. There is a stain in the corner of the ceiling where water is slowly collecting into drips. The carpet below is soggy. She dries the carpet with a towel, pressing it in to soak up the water, and places a large mixing bowl beneath the leak. Anna gives her the name of a local plumber, but he's run off his feet with urgent call-outs for broken boilers. She's to ring back next week. She doesn't tell Paul when they speak on the phone that evening; it's not important and it would only bolster his renovation campaign.

At last, one morning, there is a break in the rain. The garden is dusted white, the wooden fence shines and there are icy patterns on the windows. She waits with Jack for the bus and their breath comes out like smoke. The sun is rising, feathering the sky with fiery colours. The bright light is almost painful after days of muted grey. The school bus skids to a halt, and Jack jumps on and waves at her through the window. He seems happier about school these days. He still doesn't talk much about the boys in his class, but he's firm friends with Emma Winters. She came to play during the holidays and they spent the morning pretending to be animal rescuers, tending to an injured whale and assisting a lost turtle. They asked Charlie to be their assistant, which was kind, as he often got in the way and didn't always understand the game – Sarah had to intervene when, to Emma's dismay, Charlie insisted on 'fixing' the whale with a hammer. She's beginning to understand the bond between Emma and Jack, and she's glad they are friends.

She tidies up around the house, making beds and gathering laundry. It's Charlie's day off from nursery. He's sitting cross-legged on the sofa, watching cartoons in his pyjamas, drinking from his sippy cup. She sits with him for a moment and he pulls her close. He smells of sleep and milk, and his messy hair is like the coat of a small furry animal. Once the chores are done, she will take him for a walk. An outing in the fresh air will be good for both of them. There's a small chance of seeing Finn, but if he's taken her advice, he'll be at school. She can't sequester herself in her house for ever.

Charlie holds her gloved hand in his mittened one and they journey together across the frozen field. He looks like an astronaut in his padded jacket, hat and boots. He bends to touch a puddle that shines like glass. 'Look, my Mummy,' he says, wide-eyed. He pulls on her hand.

My Mummy. She loves the way he claims her. 'Yes,' she says. 'The water has turned to ice.' His language, hesitant to begin with, is coming on quickly now. They have little conversations and she sees the world through his eyes. He's an explorer; she's his trusted guide.

The path into the woods is easier to climb now that the mud has frozen. It is quiet and their boots make a crunching sound. At the top of the hill, the apple tree glitters, the fence is powder-white and the fields are ruffled with waves of icy grass. Everything that was bedraggled and untidy, has been made clean and beautiful. The sun pulses in the empty blue sky. Charlie tips his face to it, his skin glows and the light polishes his hair into gold. His face is losing its infant roundness, and his legs are lean and strong. He pulls off his mittens and she tucks them into his pockets. He's big enough now for the walk to the lake. They can feed the ducks and have a rest on a bench before returning home. She's come prepared, with bread for the ducks and chocolate for Charlie – it's prudent, with a small child, to have treats handy.

The walk to the lake takes much longer with Charlie. On her own, it's fifteen minutes, but Charlie has little legs and he keeps stopping to look at things – a pebble, a spiderweb, a stick. She doesn't mind; they aren't in a hurry. The path drops and they are into the woods. Charlie looks even smaller, with the trees towering above. A squirrel scampers down the path and Charlie runs after it. He is gathering momentum faster than his legs can manage. 'Stop,' she calls, running after him, but it's too late and he is falling. He lies flat on the ground, face down, his arms and legs spread out like an angel.

There is an awful silence, and then he lifts his head and

howls. She drops to her knees beside him, gathering him up, trying to comfort and inspect him at the same time. His head is fine, no bumps, and his teeth are intact. His trousers are torn and there's blood, but his knees aren't hurt. She gently uncurls his fingers and the mystery is solved. He holds his grazed palms out in front of him, as if they belong to someone else, watching the blood slowly pool and drip. 'Ma-ma,' he says, between sobs.

The graze isn't serious, but it must sting, and the blood is frightening him. She finds a tissue in her pocket and presses it to his palms. She wipes his tears away and kisses him. After a few moments, she takes the tissue away; the bleeding has stopped and the graze is smaller than she thought. 'Look,' she says. 'All better.' Charlie hiccoughs and looks doubtfully at his hands. 'Now, what about those ducks,' she says. She gets up, tucking the tissue into her pocket, then stands Charlie on his feet, brushing the dirt from his trousers.

Charlie looks past her. He frowns. She thinks he's going to refuse to walk, and she's about to produce the chocolate, when he says, 'Who's that daddy?'

She looks to where he's pointing, half-expecting to see the father of one of Jack's friends, but it's a man she doesn't know. He is standing a few paces away. He must have arrived while she was tending to Charlie, but she'd been too preoccupied to notice him. It isn't only that he's a stranger that makes her draw Charlie closer, it's the intent way he's looking at them. His face is thin and sallow, and his eyes are bloodshot. He is wearing a hooded jacket and dirty, torn jeans, and a scuffed backpack is at his feet. He doesn't have a dog and he isn't out for a jog.

He's blocking the path and there's no way past him. She feels the tiny hairs on her arms rise. Her muscles tense, ready to run, but she can't with Charlie.

'Is your boy all right?' the man says. His voice is gravelly. He has stained, yellowing teeth.

'He's fine,' she says, trying to sound calm, but feeling breathless.

'Nasty fall.' The man looks at Charlie with interest, the way a wolf might regard its prey, and she feels her heart hammer inside her.

He takes a step towards them. She moves in front of Charlie, trying to shield him.

'All alone,' the man says softly, as if talking to himself. 'No daddy.'

'Daddy at office,' Charlie volunteers, before she can stop him.

The man smiles, gently. He takes another step towards them.

The blood thuds in her head. Her body braces, ready to fight. She will kick him, punch him, claw out his eyes. She will sink her teeth into his skin and tear his flesh. She would rather kill or die than let anyone hurt her son.

The man pushes up his sleeves, revealing a large tattoo on one of his sinewed arms. The woman's hair is a writhing nest of snakes, and her eyes are angry and wild.

The terrifying beauty of the Medusa is mesmerising. Perhaps he's an escaped convict. No doubt he has a knife.

Suddenly, there are quick footsteps behind them.

'There you are.' It's Finn, looking taller and older than she remembered. The relief is overwhelming and she has to stop herself from crying out. He lifts Charlie easily, as if he weighs nothing at all. Charlie has never met Finn, but he doesn't protest. He sits quietly in the crook of Finn's arm.

'Right-o,' Finn says, loudly. 'We'd best get on. We don't want to keep everyone waiting.' He begins to walk down the path towards the man, carrying Charlie, and Sarah walks close beside him on his other side. 'Morning,' Finn says politely, but firmly. The man slowly, begrudgingly, moves aside. As they pass, she sees the shadows in his hooded eyes. A few moments later, she looks over her shoulder. He is gone. There are only the trees and the frost-white path trailing away like a ribbon.

He would have harmed her and Charlie. If Finn hadn't come ... Her legs are weak and she has to stop.

'Are you all right?' Finn says.

'Yes,' she says, but her voice is a whisper. Her chest aches.

'You shouldn't be here.' He sounds exasperated, as if she's a disobedient child.

She wonders if he's referring to the Arctic weather, perhaps the danger of slipping on ice, but he isn't the type to worry about such things. He isn't even wearing a coat. 'What do you mean?' she asks.

'Haven't you heard? A woman was assaulted yesterday by a bloke on Wickford Common. The police have told people to be careful.'

Wickford is a quiet hamlet ten minutes' drive from Littlefold. It's hard to believe that an act of violence happened there. 'No. I hadn't heard,' she says.

Finn glances around. He lowers his voice. 'The woods are a good place to hide.'

'You think it was him.'

'I don't know. He didn't look right.'

'No,' she says, remembering the way the man stared at her and Charlie. The head of the Medusa etched on his arm. She shivers.

'Come on. I'll walk you home.'

She wants to be at home where it's safe, more than anything, but the thought of meeting the stranger in the woods again makes her throat tighten. 'We'll have to pass him.'

'It's OK. I know another way.'

They set off again, with Charlie bumping along on Finn's back. 'Giddy-up,' Charlie says, and kicks his legs. Charlie can be shy with people he doesn't know, but he seems to instinctively trust Finn.

Finn leads her past the lake and it occurs to her that she's never ventured beyond it before. They turn into a narrow track. Branches swing down and scratch her face, and she steps over bleached tree roots that look like the excavated bones of a prehistoric creature. The light fades and they seem to be going deeper into the woods, but suddenly the track ends and they are in a cul-de-sac.

The red-brick houses are semi-detached, separated by picket fences, and one or two trade vans are parked on the paved driveways. A tabby cat stares at them as they pass and the net curtains of a sitting-room window twitch.

'My neighbourhood,' Finn says. He doesn't point out his house and she doesn't ask.

They come to the end of the cul-de-sac and there is a sign. Hawthorn Road. It's one of the side streets they drive past on their way up to town. She'd assumed that Finn lived nearby, but he's even closer than she thought. There's a ten-minute walk, if that, between them. He's grown up here, she thinks. He's seen it evolve over the years, the old houses and gardens bulldozed to make way for smart estates, the fall of the fishmonger and the greengrocer, the rise of the coffee chains. The new families, squeezed out of their London flats, congratulating themselves on their identikit mansions and electric gates. She too was once a child here, in the white farmhouse across the woods and the fields. She wonders if they ever passed each other in the village, perhaps when she was a teenager. He would have been a little boy then, about the same age as Charlie.

They turn into the narrow winding lane that will lead home. The frost has melted away and the birds are singing. She hasn't forgotten the stranger who frightened her in the woods, but he seems far away now, as if in another country.

A black Porsche appears from behind a corner, going too fast, and they stop for a moment while it hurtles past. Charlie wriggles on Finn's back. 'Down,' he says, as if it's a matter of urgency, and Finn carefully lowers him to the ground. Charlie rummages in his pockets and produces two Matchbox toy cars. He gives a red Ferrari to Finn and keeps his favourite, the blue Lamborghini. 'Vroom!' Charlie says, pretending to fly the little blue car down the lane. 'Race you,' Finn says gamely, following with the red one.

It's kind of Finn to humour Charlie, but she can't help wondering if it's partly for her benefit. He keeps glancing at her, as if to check she's watching. He spins around, taking Charlie by surprise, the two cars collide, and Charlie bursts into laughter. 'Again,' he pleads. Finn pushes his hand through his hair. He laughs.

They look alike, she thinks. It's the unruly blonde hair; the sudden, warm smile. She's tried to imagine, from time to time, what Charlie will look like when he's older. Perhaps he will look like Finn.

At the front door, she takes off her gloves and loosens her scarf. Finn is quiet, lingering beside the doorstep, and she wonders if he's hoping to be invited in. She can't bring him into the family home. Even a cup of tea would feel disloyal. Just standing together beside the door makes her worry. All it takes is a neighbour checking the post or a mother driving past for a rumour to start.

She will always be grateful to him. 'Thank you for walking us home,' she says. She knows she sounds too formal, but she doesn't want to encourage him. She can't think of a good excuse not to invite him in, so she says nothing more.

'That's OK,' Finn says. He shrugs, as if divesting himself of disappointment. 'I'd better go. Can't miss double maths.'

She's forgotten all about school and the blood rushes to her face. She's the one who lectured him, and here he is, missing lessons on account of her and Charlie.

'Yes, of course. You must go. I'm sorry,' she says.

He turns, and for a moment, she thinks he's going to touch her cheek, but then he looks down at Charlie and ruffles his hair. 'See you around,' he says. He walks away, into the lane.

She closes the door, sits on the floor in the hallway, gathers Charlie onto her knee and hides her face in his hair. Charlie pulls away and cups her wet cheek with his hand. 'It's the shock. It's all right,' she says, but it isn't only that. It's too much to take in or understand. Charlie wraps his arms around her and she feels his heart beating. Sunlight spills through the glass sidelights, drawing prisms on the floor.

By the time it occurs to her to call the police and report the stranger, the man who assaulted the woman in Wickford has been found. According to the radio, the suspect was apprehended in the woods near Littlefold towards midday. The timing and the generic description given of the man is a match, but it could be a coincidence. There is no need to contact the police and she can't help feeling relieved. She doesn't want anyone to know that she was with Finn. Later, when the children are in bed and she's having supper on her own in the kitchen, she wonders why Finn was in the woods that morning.

If she was unsettled before by Finn's lie, she isn't any more. She doesn't know why he invented a story about Samuel Thomas, but it no longer worries her. She doesn't believe he'd hurt anyone he cared for. If anyone's been lying, it's her, not him. The truth is, she's drawn to this boy, and it's terrifying. She's skirting a crevasse that cannot be crossed. If she did, she could lose everything. And yet the freedom in the fall lures her, pulls her, and it takes all her resolve to turn away.

# Maggie

*Surrey, 1991*

The cemetery of St Michael's, an old Norman church, is a quiet garden of headstones and leafy trees on the banks of a river winding through woodland and fields. Maggie kneels with some effort, wincing at the pain in her knee. The inscription on the headstone, a few lines from his favourite song, is already fading. The sandstone has softened, weathered by the wind and the rain. The grass has grown over his grave.

'*For All We Know*'. She can hear it now, the smooth dulcet tones of Nat King Cole drifting up from the sitting room while she held their baby daughter and rocked her to sleep. She and Jim were young then, and their love was pure and strong. The song spoke of the transience of life; now it seems even more poignant.

A year ago, Jim was ill. They thought it was the flu, but he didn't seem to get better; the diagnosis, leukaemia, was made too late. Spring arrived, indifferent to their pain, with its promise of new beginnings that couldn't be fulfilled. She'd taken daffodils cut from the farmhouse garden to the hospital; their yellow paled in the stark, white room. He was almost motionless on the bed, but he moved his fingers very slightly. His muscles had wasted away, his skin like parchment. He couldn't speak. Nurses came and went, administering morphine, making notes on the clipboard by his bed, speaking in low, sibilant voices. The room looked out over the hospital car park and the rows of vehicles seemed as resigned as the residents of this place. His eyes closed. His breathing slowed. A last shallow breath; his chest rose a fraction: a final exhalation. There was a movement in the air, a shimmering haze that she thought might be his soul, but could have been sunlight streaming in through the blinds of the window. She bowed her head, remembering the young men who died in Foggia. This time it was her soldier.

In those final days, he'd tried to tell her something. 'It doesn't matter,' she said softly, sitting beside him, holding his hand that felt as light as an autumn leaf. She knew it would be a confession. She didn't want to hear it. Not now, not here, not like this. It was a long time ago and it wasn't important any more. Everyone makes mistakes.

She should have let him tell her: this was her mistake. In his will, Jim left money to his children, Vivien and Michael, and there was a third name she'd never heard before. Nicolas Saunders. At first, she couldn't make sense of it, but then she understood.

Edith had known all along. 'He didn't want to hurt you,' she said.

'You should have told me,' Maggie said. Helping Vivien cope as a single mother had brought her and Edith closer over the years. This felt like another betrayal.

'I'm sorry,' Edith said. 'I didn't know what to do.' She hugged Maggie tightly, and her cheek was wet.

'Yes,' Maggie said, her anger fading. Edith had been in an impossible position. She wasn't to blame.

But then Vivien told her another story, about a girl finding a letter. Her own daughter, made to keep a secret from her all these years. The extent of the deception, the collusion between Edith and Jim, was almost too much to bear. At the time, she'd felt Vivien turn away from her, but she'd told herself it was adolescence. She had nothing to compare it with. She was motherless at Vivien's age.

The arrival of the baby Sarah brought Vivien back to her at last, but those years when Vivien was Maggie's little girl are gone.

Edith will have her reasons. No doubt she thought it was for the best; perhaps she even has regrets. Maggie has given up trying to understand. If she'd known, she would have made Jim take responsibility. An affair can be overlooked, even forgiven, but a child changes everything. Jim didn't want to hurt her, but he hurt Vivien and he hurt his son. This is his legacy, and his mistake ripples on ...

*Nico Saunders. Landscape Gardening and Maintenance.* Maggie saw his van last week, while on her way back from the hospice shop. She must have passed it countless times over the years without noticing. The van indicated left; this was not the way back to the farmhouse, but before she could stop herself, she followed. The van turned into Hawthorn Road, the estate near the old quarry, and parked in one of the paved driveways.

The house was semi-detached, with a clipped front lawn and pretty hanging baskets. She turned the car around at the end of the road, as if she'd made a mistake. Nico Saunders stepped out of his van. The young man was dark and handsome. He wasn't at all like Jim. Somehow, she doesn't know why, she was disappointed. The front door of the house opened, and there was a woman with dark eyes and silver hair. She'd grown old and was heavier than Maggie remembered, but her face was still beautiful. The Italian girl from the Anchor.

Maggie drove quickly past, looking straight ahead. Her chest felt tight and her throat ached. She shouldn't have come here. This woman, this young man, belonged to Jim. They were nothing to do with her.

She leaves him a posy of daffodils, the ones he planted in their garden that shine at dusk like golden stars. She gets to her feet again with difficulty, staggering a little, the cramp tightening around her knee like a tourniquet.

She walks away, down the shaded path, and the river whispers behind her. Perhaps one day the pain of missing him, the anger he's bequeathed, will fade like the epitaph on his grave.

# Sarah

*Spring 2011*

Spring is here again. Snowdrops push up through the cold earth, heralding the close of winter, then the daffodils follow, displaying their primrose hats. In the garden, Sarah can almost hear the tiny pulsing sounds of grass growing, the unfurling of new buds and leaves. The crimson camellia seems to flower overnight, then a storm comes and its petals are spilled on the lawn like drops of blood. In the field, in the shade of the willow tree, there are pools of powder-blue forget-me-nots. By May, the tall chestnut and oak trees that border the paddock are in full leaf, bringing once again a feeling of privacy that she welcomes, but knows is an illusion. The view from the house is a pastoral painting, the garden and the field brushed with shades of green. Wisteria scents the air and drowsy wasps arrive through open windows.

She longs to see the lake, it was beautiful this time last year, but she hasn't forgotten the strange man she met in the woods. She doesn't want to walk there on her own. She hasn't seen Finn since that morning. Perhaps he is working hard at his lessons. She hopes so.

It is the weekend, the weather is fine, and she and the boys are in the garden. Paul is clearing out the garage and loading the car for the tip. He's found an old red bicycle of Jack's that's the right size for Charlie now. Charlie is pedalling up and down the patio, steadied by stabilisers, while Jack does circuits around the garden on his new BMX bike. Charlie tries to follow Jack, but his bike gets stuck on the grass; his legs aren't quite strong enough and the stabilisers don't work on uneven ground.

She's sitting on the patio step, leaning back on her hands, her legs stretched out in front of her. She's put on shorts and her skin looks pasty. A vein is creeping up her thigh like a tiny blue vine. There is a greenish-brown bruise on her shin, where she bumped into the corner of the dishwasher. She feels her body soaking up the sun like a sponge.

Charlie is still marooned on the lawn. 'Mummy,' he calls. It must be frustrating sometimes, being the youngest, with an older brother who is always faster and stronger and able to do more exciting things. She gets up and pushes him around the garden once, then another time. It's harder than she thought it would be. Charlie is heavy, and the bike is low and awkward to push. Jack flies past them. 'Can't catch me,' he calls, sing-song.

'Faster,' Charlie commands over his shoulder. If he had a whip, he'd crack it. He is a young prince; she's his lackey. She does one last turn around the garden, then stops, her hands on her hips. She feels breathless and her back is aching. She can hear Aunt Edith's voice in her head; join a gym, darling, get some exercise. She hasn't seen her aunt for a few weeks. She ought to call in one morning after the school drop-off for a cup of tea.

'More,' Charlie says, sternly.

'In a minute. Mummy's tired,' she says.

Charlie folds his arms and wrinkles his nose, the way he does when he wants to look disapproving.

'How about a snack?' she says, changing tack.

He's quiet for a moment, considering the offer, then shouts, 'That'd be awesome!' The TV must be responsible for this new expression. She feels a guilty pang, wondering if he's watching too many cartoons, but it's a struggle to wean him off, and the uninterrupted half hour here and there allows her to get things done. She resolves to do more reading with him in the afternoons, when Jack's at school.

Charlie jumps off his bike, runs into the house, and she follows him inside. He opens the cupboard, scanning the shelves for the biscuit tin that she moved to the top after reading that sugar was the new evil.

'How about rice cakes or raisins?' she suggests.

'No,' Charlie says, looking mulish.

She tries again. 'Grapes? Apple slices?'

'Biscuit,' Charlie says firmly, pointing to the tin.

They are at an impasse and the doorbell is ringing. She lifts down the tin, gives Charlie a biscuit and goes into the hall. It's only one biscuit, and she will make up for it with fruit later. She opens the front door, expecting to see a delivery van and a man with a parcel, but it's Finn. He's in a black t-shirt and cargo shorts, and has gardening gloves on. His hair is shorter, thick and wavy, and it doesn't look as if he's brushed it. 'Hello,' he says, as if they saw each other yesterday, and not months ago in January. There is a smudge of dirt on his cheek, and she has to stop herself from rubbing it away with her finger. She crosses her ankles, suddenly conscious of her bare white legs.

Before she can speak, Charlie pushes past her. 'Hi dude,' he drawls.

Finn smiles. 'Hello mate. What's up?' he says.

Sarah resolves again to cut down on Charlie's TV consumption, noticing that it is not dissimilar to the way she used to resolve to cut down on cocktails before the children were born.

'Biscuit?' Charlie says, holding out the half-eaten, gooey chocolate digestive.

'No thanks. You have it,' Finn says.

Charlie marches off, swinging his arm like a soldier, no doubt headed for the playroom.

There is a silence and Finn shifts on the doorstep in his trainers. She's wondering if she could invite him in this time, this must be what he's expecting, but it would be awkward – she has no idea what she'd say to Paul – when he says, 'I'm giving Dad a hand next door. He's got your roses. I can plant them now, if you like.'

'Oh, good. Right. Yes, of course,' she says, embarrassed to have considered it would be a social visit. She and Nico spoke a few weeks ago about plants for the garden. He'd cleared the flower bed beside the paddock gate and it was looking spartan. 'Roses are beautiful in the summer,' he'd said, and she'd agreed.

Finn disappears next door and she goes back to sit on the patio step in the garden. She hadn't realised that Nico worked on the weekends. Perhaps he's got a lot more to do now that the weather is warmer. Paul is still in the garage, but he might come out for a glass of water and see Finn planting. She wonders if Paul will remember that summer's evening at the Anchor, the boy whose name she didn't know. It seems a long time ago, although it's not even a year.

Jack is practising kicky-ups with a football and Charlie is dancing around him, flapping his arms. 'My ball,' he says, but Jack pretends not to hear. Charlie hits Jack's leg with his fist once, then another time. Jack carries on, taking no notice, as if Charlie is as inconsequential as a fly.

'There's another ball in the conservatory,' she calls, but Charlie isn't interested; he only ever wants what Jack has. She can see the rage building inside him like steam, and she's about to intervene when Finn appears around the side of the house, pushing a wheelbarrow of red and pink roses.

Charlie abandons all hopes of the ball and runs towards Finn. She's about to call out – she can see a collision coming – but Finn puts down the wheelbarrow. Charlie uncurls his fingers; he's got the red and blue cars they played with the last time he saw Finn.

Jack's kicky-ups slow down and then stop. He stands quietly, watching Charlie and Finn.

'Nice wheels,' Finn says to Charlie. He takes a small trowel from the wheelbarrow. 'Want to give me a hand?'

Charlie puts the cars down on the patio and takes the trowel, carefully turning it over in his hands, feeling its weight and shape.

She stands, trying to discreetly tug down her shorts, which have ridden up her thighs. 'Are you sure? He might get in the way,' she says.

'It's fine. Won't take long. That's the one, is it?' Finn says, pointing to the empty flowerbed near the paddock gate.

'Yes,' she says.

Finn takes up the wheelbarrow again and pushes it down the garden, the handles resting lightly in his gloved hands. Sunlight flashes off the metal edges of the wheelbarrow and his forearms glisten. His black t-shirt ripples over his back and hangs loosely at his waist. Charlie follows, looking imperious, holding his trowel out in front of him like a sword. Finn unloads the roses, kneels beside the flowerbed, and starts digging with a bigger trowel. Charlie digs a hole, fills it up, and digs again.

Jack is dribbling the ball around the lawn, circling closer and closer to Finn and Charlie, pretending not to be interested in what they're doing.

Finn finishes planting the last rose and Sarah wonders if she should have ordered more. He puts down the trowel and sits back on his heels. 'Is that OK? It will look better when they've grown a bit and are in flower.' He seems different, gardening; careful, focused, calm.

'Yes, I think you're right. Thank you so much. That's brilliant.' She knows she's gushing, as giddy as a schoolgirl, but she can't seem to help it.

Finn stands, brushing dirt from his shorts. He doesn't speak, as if unsure how to respond to praise, but she can tell he's pleased. Jack circles past again and this time Finn notices. 'You've still got your ball then,' he says.

Jack immediately comes to a halt, steadying the ball with his foot. He doesn't smile or speak, but it's because he's shy, rather than unfriendly. There is a silence, and she's about to suggest they all have a cold drink, when Jack says, 'Fancy a kick-about?' in a deep voice. He's trying to sound older than he is and she has to bite her lip to suppress the smile.

'Could do,' Finn says evenly, looking at her. His eyes are more blue than grey today, as if reflecting the sky. He seems to be waiting for her to approve. Perhaps he's worried about intruding, although there's no sign of Paul.

'Well,' she says. 'If you've got time.'

'I've got five minutes. Dad's speaking to Mrs Jones about a new planting scheme,' he says. He takes off his gloves and puts them in his pockets.

Charlie is still sitting beside the flower bed. His hands are cupped to make a shelter for a worm he's found. He's speaking to the worm as if they are friends, but his voice is too soft to catch the words. He doesn't notice that Finn is taking the wheelbarrow round to the side gate, and that Jack is marking out goals with sticks.

Play begins. Jack has the ball and is travelling towards the goal. Finn follows closely, but she can see that he's holding back. Although Jack is quick and agile, good for his age, Finn could win easily if he tried. Jack scores. 'Goal,' he shouts, triumphant, and Finn gives him a high five.

Finn's got control of the ball now, and Jack is his shadow. He lets Jack take the ball off him, then wins it back. Finn's chest and shoulders, clad in black, could be sculpted from onyx. He kicks and the muscles in his legs flex. He looks like he's been at the coast, with his bleached hair and honeyed skin. It must be all that time spent outdoors, helping his father with the gardening. Or perhaps he's been in Italy, visiting family. It must be hot there by now. She wonders if he speaks Italian. There is so much about him that she doesn't know.

Finn scores a goal and glances at her, as if to check she's seen. He smiles, running his fingers through his hair. She can't help feeling, once again, that this is a performance meant for her.

Charlie comes to show her the worm. 'Lovely,' she says, although worms make her queasy. 'Maybe we should put him back now. I expect he'd like to go home.'

She's preparing for Charlie to refuse, and a protracted negotiation resulting in the worm being housed in a Tupperware box, when he says, agreeably, 'OK Mummy.' Perhaps the stormy days of toddler tantrums are behind them. He sets the worm free, watches it tunnel into the soil, then sits down beside her. The sight of his little knees and stripy socks makes her heart contract almost painfully. He leans against her, resting a small hand on her thigh, and she puts her arm around him.

The game is over. It's a draw. Jack's face is red and his dark hair is damp. Sweat beads on Finn's temples and slides down his neck.

'You boys must be thirsty,' she says.

They are sitting at the rattan table on the patio, drinking lemonade, when Paul comes out of the glasshouse. His jeans and t-shirt look dusty. He's holding his car keys.

'Daddy!' Charlie shouts, as if Paul has been away for days, rather than in the garage for a few hours. He runs towards Paul, sits on his shoes, and wraps his arms around his legs. Jack joins in, hugging Paul's waist.

'This is all very summery,' Paul says. He ruffles Jack's hair and gently untangles himself from Charlie. He adjusts his glasses.

There is a silence and then Sarah says, too quickly and all at once, 'This is Finn. His father, Nico Saunders, looks after our garden. He was just planting some roses for us. Would you like some lemonade?'

Paul's eyes are as steady as usual, but his forehead creases very slightly. 'Right. Finn,' he says. 'Good to meet you.' If he's heard her offer of lemonade, he doesn't show it.

Finn puts his glass down on the table. He stands, and for a moment she thinks he's going to shake Paul's hand, but then he seems to change his mind and pushes his hand into his pocket. He coughs. 'Yes,' he says. 'I sometimes help my dad on the weekends.'

Paul looks at the garden, as if seeing it for the first time. 'It's looking nice,' he says.

'Yes, it is, isn't it,' Sarah says. 'And now the weather is warmer, we'll be able to enjoy it. We could think about adding more plants. Camellias are lovely and do well in clay soil.' She knows that she's talking too much, but she can't seem to stop.

'Well,' Paul says. 'It's all food for thought.'

'I want another snack,' Charlie says, misunderstanding.

180

'I'm starving,' Jack says.

Sarah glances at her watch. It's midday, nearly time for lunch.

'I'd best be off,' Finn says, taking his gloves out of his pocket. 'Thanks for the lemonade.'

'You're welcome. Thank you for the roses, I mean, for planting them,' she says, stumbling over the words, laughing a little to cover up her embarrassment. Finn smiles at her, as if they're sharing a joke between themselves. She glances at Paul, but he doesn't seem to have noticed.

Finn walks around the side of the glasshouse, there is the sound of the wheelbarrow's wheels on the gravel, and he is gone.

'Daddy, can you play football with me?' Jack says.

'I'm going to the tip,' Paul says. 'Maybe later, when it's not so hot.'

'I'll get lunch ready,' she says, collecting the empty glasses. 'We can eat when you're back.'

They all go inside. Paul drives off to the tip and she finds Charlie a jigsaw to do in the playroom. Jack helps to set the table. She opens the fridge, taking out mozzarella, tomatoes and an avocado. She slices the tomatoes, then peels the avocado and cuts the green flesh into crescents. She arranges the mozzarella, tomatoes and avocado on a serving plate, drizzles over olive oil and balsamic vinegar, and decorates it with torn leaves of basil. She puts pasta on to boil for Charlie, who won't touch mozzarella or avocados, and will squish the tomatoes instead of eating them. She puts an olive ciabatta in the oven. No doubt Finn has Italian food at home. She wonders what he'd think of her attempt at a tricolore, her shop-bought pasta with pesto, the part-baked ciabatta.

'Finn's nice. I hope he comes again,' Jack says.

She carries the chopping board and knife to the sink, and

turns on the tap. In the garden, there is a glint of silver on the lawn beside the paddock gate. It's the trowel that Charlie borrowed from Finn. For a moment she wonders if Finn left it behind on purpose. The roses he planted will open soon, perfuming the air with their heady scent. 'Yes. Perhaps he will,' she says.

It is six o'clock, the boys have had their tea, the kitchen is clean and tidy, and she's opened a bottle of Chablis. She and Paul sit at the table on the patio, sipping wine and watching the boys jump on the trampoline. The garden is in shadow, but the field is sunlit and the sky is blue. The long paddock grass is flecked with buttercups, and the willow tree looks soft and feathery. Jack takes Charlie's hands, bouncing him higher. Charlie shrieks with laughter. The wine is cold on her lips, but warm in her stomach.

'This Chablis is good,' Paul says.

He is quiet for a moment, then says, 'The gardener's boy. Finn. Jack says they played football. He's not an imaginary friend.'

'No,' she says. 'I gather they met once, when Jack was in the field. I think Jack admired him and wanted to be friends. I suppose it was an imaginary friendship to begin with.'

'Yes. Well, he seems like a good lad,' Paul says. 'And they are keeping the garden neat. You were right to get a gardener. I don't have as much time as I'd hoped.'

'I'm glad you approve,' she says, pleased at this unexpected concession. Paul is in a good mood. Perhaps it's because he's finally sorted out the garage; his man-cave, he calls it.

He tops up her glass. 'Have you been to the hairdresser? You look different.'

'Oh,' she says, her hand flying up to her hair. 'No. I haven't been for weeks. Does it look dreadful?' She's been putting off going to the salon; it always seems to take up a whole after-noon and she doesn't have the time. Her hair usually skims her shoulders, but it's quite a bit longer now.

'It's nice. It makes you look young.' Paul smiles. 'Perhaps that boy, Finn, thinks you're my daughter.'

A laugh bursts from her. She looks away. 'Oh Paul. Don't be silly,' she says. Her face flames.

# Flavia

*Surrey, 1995*

Flavia finds him among the grassy graves; a tall grey head-stone, near the banks of the river. *James Edward Howard. 1917–1991.* The inscription is faint, as if penned by someone elderly and frail. In time the words will disappear completely, erased by the wind and the rain.

'*For All We Know*' ... A memory comes to her. She and Jim dancing cheek to cheek while the radio played. The voice of Nat King Cole was all around them, liquid and velvet, full of longing. For a moment, she felt Jim stiffen in her arms, then he held her more tightly and they danced on. He didn't speak, but she felt the sadness in him. She knew, without asking, that the song reminded him of Maggie. Now, though, it seems to her that the ballad could have been written about their own love affair: merely a dream, enchanting and ephemeral.

She sits down. The long grass is scattered with daisies. The sun is high, warming the leaves and the flowers, filling the air with a green, earthy scent. She didn't know that his middle name was Edward. There is so much about him that she will never know. A pair of mallards, a green-headed male and a brown female, are drifting down the river. A gull cries once and is gone. Across the water, there are pastures and horses, and a train moving swiftly through the trees.

She leans forward to place the lilies on his grave, and sees a headstone beside his that looks new. She reads the name. *Margaret Howard. 1915–1995.* And, very simply, *Beloved.* So Maggie is gone now, too. She and Jim are together again. Flavia feels a sudden twinge of envy, like a reflex, then a flush of shame. *It's a habit; it's in the past; it means nothing,* she thinks.

The last time she saw Maggie was a few years ago, just after Jim died. She heard Nico's van, went out to meet him, and there was Maggie, turning her car around. She was pretending it was a mistake, but it was clear that she'd followed Nico home. Maggie drove past them, her chin lifted, looking straight ahead. Her eyes were watering. There was a time when Flavia had been jealous of Maggie, but that had changed when she met Phil, and now that Jim was gone, it was as if a fog was lifting. Maggie was old, like Flavia. Her face was soft, with laughter lines, and her hands on the steering wheel looked capable and kind. Her hair was short and white, but Flavia remembered when it had been lustrous chestnut brown. She never meant to hurt Maggie. In another life, they could have been friends.

When Jim died, she finally told Nico about his real father. 'He was an English man. Not Italian,' she began, her voice sounding like a narrator in a film, while inside her heart was hammering. 'His name was Jim Howard.' Nico listened quietly. When she finished, he put his arm around her. 'Don't cry, Mama,' he said. 'It doesn't matter. You always did your best for me.' Her son, all grown up, with a wife and a child of his own. The baby, Finn, has sea-grey eyes and flaxen hair. His real name is Fausto, but people found it difficult to pronounce, so Nico and Maria gave him an English nickname. She wonders if one day he will look like Jim.

Nico used his inheritance to buy a house on Hawthorn Road. It wouldn't have been possible otherwise; the development of the old quarry into a nature reserve had increased the house prices. So she will have her son and grandson as neighbours. She is grateful to Jim for this.

Telling Nico lifted a weight. She told Anna too, her friend who kept house for Jim's sister. Anna didn't look as surprised as she'd expected. Perhaps she'd overheard Edith and Jim talking, and pieced it together. 'Did you guess?' Flavia asked her.

'No,' Anna said. She looked thoughtful for a moment. 'I saw a note once, in Edith's handwriting, with your name on it. I thought it was to do with cleaning. Neither of you said anything, so I thought it best not to mention it.'

Dear Anna; calm, careful, always discreet. A true English lady. Flavia told her about Edith's visit and her offer of money. 'I thought Jim had sent her to get rid of me. I went back to Italy. Sometimes, though, I wonder if he knew what she did.'

'I don't know,' Anna said, shaking her head. She was quiet for a moment. 'Edith's all alone now. Her daughter lives in Australia. Her son never visits. She's lost her husband, now her brother.'

Flavia guessed where the conversation was headed. 'It's a shame, but she's made it clear that she wants nothing to do with me or Nico.'

'Yes. I understand,' Anna said. She hugged Flavia. 'I'm sorry. It must have been very difficult for you. I wish I could have helped.'

'Don't be sorry. I couldn't ask for a better friend,' Flavia said.

Flavia unties the bouquet. She carefully places some of the

lilies on Jim's grave and the rest on Maggie's. 'Goodbye,' she says softly. She walks away.

The two mallards float down the river, through pastures and woodland and villages, travelling along the ribbon of shining water.

# Sarah

*Spring 2011*

The following weekend is hot. Paul is inside on a conference call that was supposed to take five minutes but has been going on all morning. Sarah is sitting on the patio step watching the boys do circuits on their bikes. She's in shorts and a t-shirt, and flip-flops. She applied fake tan to her legs last night, and they look a shade or two darker; it's not a dramatic change, but she was worried about putting too much on and going orange. This morning, she washed and blow-dried her hair, pulling it over a large brush until it shone like silk. She put on a new pink lipstick, 'Coquette', then rubbed most of it off.

It's eleven o'clock. The sun is climbing high into the sky, warming her legs, her arms, her shoulders. Her body aches, as if she's still numb from the winter. At ten minutes past, she hears it: the rumble of a lawnmower, the voices calling to each other in Italian. A man is singing an aria that sounds like Puccini. *La Bohème, Madame Butterfly, Tosca* ... Goosebumps sweep over her arms. A drop of sweat slides down her neck.

Her eyes are on her children circling on their bikes, but

her thoughts have slipped next door. The garden machinery jars, almost drowning the Italian song that is both beautiful and melancholy, and fills her with longing. Nico and his men are always quick in her garden – they whip around it and are gone, but the Joneses' garden seems to be taking much longer. At last the lawnmower and the leaf blowers are switched off; they must be weeding now, she thinks. It is quiet. Even the singing has stopped; perhaps the tenor felt suddenly self-conscious without the background noise of the machinery.

Jack has abandoned his bike and is running into the field. Charlie follows, the way he always does. He has to wade through the grass that now reaches his knees. A rabbit, its soft ears just visible above the forget-me-nots, scampers towards the fence and disappears into the trees. Jack pulls Charlie onto the trampoline, and they bounce together and fall down, laughing.

Paul will need to dust off the ride-on mower that's been hibernating in the shed. In another few weeks, the grass will be too long to cut. She'll have to engage a farmer with a trac-tor, which will delight the boys, but seems disproportionate for a field that is only an acre. She hadn't been concerned about the long grass – it seemed natural and the wildflowers were pretty – until Nico shook his head and said, 'Rats and snakes will come.' He'd gestured at the trampoline, an island in the green pasture. 'Not safe for children,' he said. If Paul can't spare the time, Nico could do it, but Paul will need to check that the mower is in good working order.

Suddenly, she's aware of footsteps behind her. Her neck prickles. She knows, without looking, who it is.

He sits down beside her. He smells of cut grass and earth, sweet and musky. She hugs her knees, interlacing her fingers.

'I knocked, but no one answered,' Finn says. They're so close that she can see a tiny mole on his cheek. She's grateful for her sunglasses and the part veil of her hair.

He's wearing his gardening gloves again, and holding wire and a hammer. 'Dad sent me round to pin your wisteria.'

Nico hasn't mentioned it, but the wisteria does need attention. The long vine is bowed, weighted with plumes of flowers. Inside the sitting room, the light is greenish, the view of the garden obscured by trailing tendrils.

'Yes. Good,' she says, as if it's been arranged. 'You left your trowel, by the way. I put it by the side gate.'

'Thanks,' he says, and she still doesn't know if he left it behind on purpose or not.

Finn leans a ladder against the brick wall and climbs up a few rungs. He's in overalls today, like his father. She wonders if helping out now and then is turning into a part-time job. She hopes so; the responsibility, the routine, would be good for him. He reaches into his pockets for nails, and carefully hammers them in. He's going brown, working outdoors all day in the sun. He catches her eye. He smiles. She quickly looks away, feeling the blood rush to her face.

In the field, Jack has unzipped the netting and is climbing down from the trampoline. Charlie leans forward, holds onto Jack's shoulders and leaps onto his back. Jack jogs around the paddock, his arms hooked around Charlie's legs. 'Faster,' Charlie shouts, as if he's a jockey and Jack is his horse.

Finn collapses his ladder, the metal sliding and locking into place. 'That's better,' he says. The wisteria has been tamed; a pretty border of purple flowers decorates the sitting-room windows.

'Yes, it is. Thank you,' Sarah says.

Finn's about to say something, but then Jack arrives, red-faced, and deposits Charlie at his feet. 'Hello,' he says, out of breath.

'Hello,' Finn says.

Charlie looks up at Finn. 'Piggyback?' he suggests politely, as if inviting Finn to luncheon or a round of golf.

'Go on then.' Finn kneels down and Charlie clambers on. She notices that this time he doesn't wait for her approval.

'Race you,' Jack says, and he's off, running back into the field.

Finn chases Jack through the long grass, Charlie bouncing on his back. He lets Jack lead, then overtakes him, and she can hear Charlie's delighted shrieks.

Paul comes out of the conservatory and stands beside her. 'Right, that's done. Sorry to take so long,' he says. He shades his face with his hand. 'Is that the gardener's lad?'

'Yes,' Sarah says. 'He came to pin the wisteria.'

'He's very attentive,' Paul says.

'He likes the boys,' she says lightly. She folds her arms.

'I don't think that's all he likes,' Paul says. He reaches across and pats her bottom, then laughs, like a mischievous schoolboy.

'Paul!' Her voice comes out louder than she'd expected. She doesn't know if it's the way he's touched her or what he's said, but her heart is beating like a drum. 'That's ridiculous.'

Paul smiles, looking amused. 'It's not so ridiculous.'

'I'm hot,' she says, unable to hide her irritation. 'I'm going inside.'

After the bright sun, the kitchen is dark and cool. She takes a glass from the cupboard, wondering if Finn will be back next weekend with another job for the garden. Paul doesn't seem to mind. No, on the contrary, he seems pleased, as if she's done something to be proud of. A cry breaks from her, and she covers her mouth with her hand. She leans against the worktop, waiting for the tears that don't come. The tightness inside her eases. She pours herself a glass of cold water and drinks it down in long gulps.

# Flavia

*Surrey, 1999*

'Nonna,' Finn says, slipping his small hand in hers, his voice lifting in a question as they walk away from the crowded school gates towards the car.

'What is it, *topolino*?' she says.

'After tea, can I see Sam?'

They wait at the crossing for the lights to change.

'And homework?' she says. 'Don't you have a reading book?'

'Yes, but I've nearly finished it.' He looks up at her, widening his eyes. 'After reading? Please?'

Flavia pretends to consider this, although the truth is, she loves to indulge her five-year-old grandson. 'Very well. What would you like to do with Sam, if he's free?'

Finn jumps up and down, unable to contain his excitement. 'The woods,' he says. 'We're going to hunt for bears.'

'You are brave,' she says, trying to suppress a smile. 'There are lots of wild animals in those woods. Foxes, owls, deer . . .' She lowers her voice. 'Yes, perhaps bears as well.'

It's been a while since she last went to the old quarry. The woods, the lake, are full of ghosts; it's impossible to go there without remembering Jim. It was their secret place and the heat rises to her face at the thought of how reckless she was then; young and in love, she would have done anything to be with him.

Still, she has no regrets. She can't imagine a life without Nico, and this little boy. She collects Finn every day after school, and looks after him until Maria and Nico have finished work. More and more, she sees Jim in this child; the same tall, graceful physique and unruly fair hair, those thoughtful grey eyes. And yet there is Sicily too, in his smooth, honeyed skin and sudden, generous smile.

Finn knocks on the door of the Thomases' house while Flavia waits behind him. After a moment, the door opens and Janet Thomas says, 'Hello.' She's wearing an apron and her long dark hair is pinned up. Her face is pale and thin, and already lined, although she can't yet be forty. In the background, there are shouts and yells, and raucous laughter. Sam is the youngest of four school-age children; the Thomas household is rarely quiet.

'Can Sam come on a bear hunt?' Finn says.

'We're going for a walk in the woods,' Flavia explains. 'I'd be happy to take Sam too, if he'd like to come.'

There is a huge crash from above and then howls that could be triumphant or tearful, it's difficult to tell. Janet Thomas glances up at the ceiling. She sighs. 'I'm sure he'd love to,' she says. 'Sam, love!' she calls upstairs. 'Finn and his granny are here. Would you like to go out with them?'

There's a moment of silence and then Samuel Thomas comes bounding down the stairs. He is an interesting boy. Straight black hair, as thick as thatch, brushes his dark-lashed eyes. Porcelain, nearly translucent skin. A slender, slight frame. He'd be delicate-looking if it weren't for those wiry arms and sharp elbows. It's good for Finn, who is an only child, to have a friend like Sam, although their friendship troubles Flavia sometimes. Sam's a good-natured boy, but he can be impetuous and disobedient, and has a tendency to lie. 'Careful, or you'll turn into one of those doting grannies,' Phil teases her gently, when she confides in him. 'Boys will be boys.'

Midsummer, and the woods are glorious. Honeysuckle sweetens the warm, earthy air, the trees are in full leaf and the verges are scattered with cow parsley. The lake is a shining mirror, reflecting the blue sky, puffs of cloud and the feathery boughs of the willow tree. It is peaceful, but they aren't the only ones. They pass neighbours walking their dogs, elderly couples out for an afternoon stroll, and a man who lives in one of the houses that border the lake is trimming his hedge. At other times, when she's brought Finn here, there is no one, and they don't linger.

She holds Finn by one hand, and Sam by the other. Finn's little hand is warm and padded, and makes her think of a cub's paw. Sam's fingers are slender and cool, and before she can stop him, he's slipped away and is racing down the path. 'A bear!' he shouts, over his shoulder.

'Wait,' she calls, worrying that he will trip and fall, but he doesn't listen. He runs on, hurtling around a bend and out of sight. Finn drops her hand and chases Sam, and then she is running after both of them.

She finds them at the edge of the lake, throwing stones. Finn is trying to make his stones skip across the water, and seems unaware that Sam is aiming his at the mallards and the moorhens. 'Stop it,' she says to Sam. 'That's not nice. Would you like it if someone threw stones at you?'

'It wasn't on purpose,' he protests in a soft voice, but they both know the truth.

There is a silence and they are at an impasse.

'What happened to the bear?' she says, changing the subject.

Sam considers this for a moment. He gives a coy smile. 'He died.'

'Oh well,' she says lightly, brushing it aside, not giving him the reaction he's after. 'Shall we feed the ducks? I've brought some bread.'

'Can I be first?' Sam says huskily, tugging at her handbag, trying to look inside.

Finn is still experimenting with skipping stones, his tongue sticking out the way it does when he's concentrating, so she says, 'Yes. All right.'

Sam tears pieces of bread and tosses them up into the sky where gulls are circling. The birds dive for the morsels, screaming, clashing mid-air. Sam laughs, throws more bread, and the sky becomes a battleground of beating wings and outstretched talons. The ducks tread water, looking affronted.

It often seems to happen this way; ideas don't go to plan when Sam is around.

The commotion brings Finn over. He pitches in bread for one of the mallards, who promptly snaps it up with his beak. 'Look,' he says to Sam. 'They're hungry too. Do you want to help?'

'OK,' Sam says, agreeably.

Flavia sits down behind them on a wooden bench. It's intriguing, she thinks. Finn instinctively knows how to handle Sam. He brings out the best in him. Perhaps she needn't worry.

Dragonflies hover, butterflies dance, and birds are flying among the trees. It's hard to believe that this was once a desolate, barren place. Tainted by her futile love for Jim, it used to haunt her dreams.

Time has passed and the land has healed. Water has brought life back here and made a sanctuary. And she has healed.

She isn't sorry when the boys are ready to leave. There's something unsettling about this place, regardless of its beauty, but whether it's the past or the thought of a dark abyss lurking beneath the glittering water, she doesn't know.

# Sarah

*Summer 2011*

Slipping through dreams, Sarah hears the rain drumming on the roof, pattering against the glasshouse. In the morning, the sky looks washed out. Near the paddock, where the ground dips, is now a sunken garden: a mallard floats on a pool of silvery water beneath the green boughs of the apple tree. It looks completely at ease, as if it's not at all unusual for a duck to be here. A swift dives, dipping its wings in the pool, and two rooks land on the grassy beach, scavenging for worms. The balmy days of May are over. This is summer in England, cold and wet and dreary, while all of the Continent basks in the sun.

The school bus arrives, spraying water, and Jack is dispatched in his raincoat and wellies. The bus ploughs up the flooded lane, leaving a tide in its wake. It is raining again. Inside, Charlie is parking his toy cars next to the sofa in the playroom. He loathes his raincoat, they will both be soaked by the time she's strapped him into his car seat, and the traffic is always worse when it's wet. A few hours to herself almost isn't worth the effort of taking him to nursery. However, Vivien arrives tomorrow, and this tips the balance. Sarah must prepare the spare room and if Charlie stays, she won't get anything done. She sees him jumping on the bed she's trying to make, laughing and throwing pillows; she will be tidying boxes into the garage and he will slip into the corner where Paul keeps his tools. No, Charlie must go to nursery.

An hour later, having sat in traffic listening to the news – a man has been charged with the murder of a Surrey teenager who went missing over a decade ago while walking back from the station – she's home again. She doesn't know if the world is a more sinister place now, or if its dangers are simply better publicised, but it makes her anxious. Other mothers say it's the girls they worry about, but boys are vulnerable too. She frets enough as it is about Jack and Charlie, wondering if the school gates and security would be able to stop a malevolent intruder, whether the level of supervision at swimming lessons is sufficient, if the mother collecting Jack for a play date will drive safely, whether her children will choke on grapes. She can't imagine how she will feel when they're teenagers out on their own, meeting strangers who may harbour malicious intentions, or travelling to London, where there's always the possibility of a terrorist attack. She can't remember how she felt before she had children; the years of sleep deprivation have erased all memory of it.

Her trainers are waterlogged and her hair is sopping wet. She couldn't hold an umbrella, with Charlie in one hand and his bag in the other, and her mac doesn't have a hood. In the kitchen she dries her hair with a towel and waits for the kettle to boil. The glasshouse is beaded with condensation. The mallard is still floating on the pool beneath the apple tree. She wonders if he is a scout, sent from the lake, and if

198

more are coming – female mallards with fleets of ducklings and white swans with their downy cygnets; voyagers and refugees, seeking a new abode. Perhaps the mallard has mistaken this place for a water garden.

She drops an Earl Grey teabag into a mug and pours over hot water, breathing in the soothing aroma. She lets it steep for a moment, leaking its tint, then lifts out the teabag with a spoon and stirs in milk. She only has sugar in an emergency, invariably in a plastic cup; the last time was in A & E in London, when Jack crashed his bike and needed stitches. They'd had to wait for hours to be seen. Paul's office was nearby, so he came to help. He made her tea, stirring in the sugar that he knew she'd need, and pushed Charlie in his pram along the linoleum corridors while she comforted Jack. It would be difficult for him to do that now; too long a journey. When it happens again, and with two boys it's inevitable, she will have to manage alone.

The spare room is even more untidy than usual: piles of hand-me-downs, old toys and sports kit, electric radiators and fans for the ever-changing weather, and blankets and duvets. If only there was a chute between the spare room and the garage. The morning will be spent going up and downstairs. She will make the bed, set out fresh towels, put a vase of flowers on the chest of drawers. The painted white pine furniture is too modern for this house, but it will have to do until they can source more suitable pieces. The room looks out onto the garden, the field and the woods; her mother will approve of the view, at least.

If only there wasn't that stain on the ceiling. The plumber she'd called out said the leak was coming from the roof, not the pipes. Jessica Winters gave her the number of a roofer, but he'd been tied up on another job and kept cancelling her appointment. When he finally came, two weeks late, he climbed down the loft ladder, wiped his hands on his jeans, and said, 'I've sorted it. But your insulation needs re-laying.'

'Thank you. Is it urgent?'

He shrugged. 'Needs doing before the winter.'

One more item to add to the list. The roofer agreed to send her a quote for the insulation, but it hasn't arrived yet. She wishes she didn't have to keep chasing tradesmen too busy with new builds to carry out repairs.

The ceiling can't be painted until the stain has dried out, but it doesn't look any lighter and she wonders if it's spread. Perhaps the roofer didn't manage to fix the leak, or it's to do with the inadequate insulation. She will have to call out the roofer again. She already knows what Paul will say: it's one more reason to gut the place. He hasn't yet noticed the crack in the floorboards in the dining room, zig-zagging like a fault line, the warped window in the playroom that won't close, or the ants tunnelling through the brickwork in the glasshouse. She hasn't brought them to his attention, but it's only a matter of time before he sees.

A wasp is crawling along the windowsill, its feelers quivering, the barrel of its body tapering to the sting. It's the third wasp she's found today. She wonders if there is a nest. At times like this, she feels tired. The catalogue of things she must do seems never-ending. She sees herself buried beneath a mountain of laundry or flattened by a fallen-in, waterlogged ceiling; stung by hornets and carried away by legions of ants to be feasted on by their queen.

She must get on with tidying the guest room. In two hours, it will be time to collect Charlie and then she must go to the supermarket. Bread, milk, chicken, salmon, mince, pasta, vegetables, fruit. Laundry powder, fabric conditioner, kitchen roll, Fairy Liquid. Toothpaste, tissues, dishwasher tablets, handwash. The shopping list sings in her head, faster and faster, until there's a stream of jumbled sound. Something is rising inside her, burning and sour like acid, and the carpeted floor begins to tip and slide away from beneath her feet. She sits down on the bed, places her hands on her knees, and breathes in deeply. Gradually, the nausea inside her subsides, and the floor is level again.

# Finn

*Surrey, 2004*

Finn swings his rucksack down beside a tree. It's heavy, full of schoolbooks, and he's glad to be rid of it. He is ten years old.

Sam is carrying his rucksack by one strap, slung over his shoulder. 'What've you got in there – rocks?' he says. He takes two apples from his bag, tosses one to Finn, and takes a bite out of the other one.

'Thanks,' Finn says. He holds the red apple in his hand, feeling the soft depressions of bruises on its skin. 'History and science prep. What've you got?'

'Nothing,' Sam says, as if he's proud of it. 'Bet you wish you had Mr Jameson and weren't with that bunch of swots.'

It's the first year that they aren't in the same class. Sam says the school has streamed the kids and Finn's in the academic set. Finn isn't sure. Secretly, he suspects that his parents requested the separation; they worry that Sam distracts him.

'Top in Maths, top in English. And now you're on the bloody swim squad. What's next for young Fausto?' Sam takes a mock, exaggerated bow. 'Head boy?'

'Shut up,' Finn says, giving Sam a gentle shove. 'And don't call me Fausto.'

'Don't worry, Mouse. Your secret's safe with me. Just wish I could keep up with you.'

'Rubbish. You're good at drama. Best in the year.'

Sam takes another bite of his apple, considering this. 'That's because I'm a born liar.' He grins.

Finn stretches his arms over his head. After a long day at school, it feels good to be outdoors. 'Come on. Let's find some conkers. Can't let that show-off, Philip, win again.'

The trails around the lake are scattered with brittle leaves, acorns and the slit skins of conkers. Sam's pockets are full and now he's unzipping his rucksack. 'I knew we'd find loads here. Look at this beast,' he says, polishing a large conker on his shirt. He carefully puts it in his bag.

The conkers feel smooth and polished, like gems. Finn drops one on the ground and crushes it with his shoe. The husk splits, revealing desiccated white flesh. He feels oddly ashamed and kicks the damaged conker into the nettles. Blackberries are shining like miniature baubles in the brambles. He eases a berry from its stem. He expects it to be bitter, and make his mouth water, but the blackberry tastes floral and sweet.

Sam is staring at him. He moves closer and gently touches Finn's lips with his finger, as if he's confiding a secret. 'That'll stain,' he says, softly. He picks a few blackberries and puts them in his own mouth. Juice spills from his lips and dribbles down his chin. His mouth turns purple, like a bruise.

Finn's lips are tingling from Sam's touch. Something twists inside him, like a key in a lock, that he doesn't fully comprehend. He feels his face redden. He turns away, pretending to look for more conkers, but his pockets are full and there isn't any room in his rucksack.

The lake is still and glittering, and hypnotic. He picks up

a stone and throws it across the water, watching it skip once, twice, three times, and eventually sink. He wonders how deep the lake is. Nonna says it was once an old quarry and that he must never swim here.

'Hey! There he is!' The angry shout startles Finn. A boy he doesn't know is charging towards Sam, his head down, as if he means to ram him. Another boy springs out of the bushes, running fast. They are both in the uniform of St Edward's, a local school they play matches against, and despise. Sam doesn't seem to have heard or seen them. He's got his back turned, swiping at some nettles with a long stick. The first boy reaches him, pushes him hard with his hands, and Sam falls headfirst into the nettles. There's a ragged yell and then Sam's scrambling back up, brandishing his stick. His eyes are wild. There are leaves in his black fringe. 'You bastards,' he shouts. 'Come on, then.'

The second boy from St Edward's arrives with a roar and punches Sam in the chest. Sam staggers backwards, winded, nearly falling again. He tries, ineffectually, to whip at the boys with his stick. The two boys close in on him.

Finn is running, his heart jockeying against his ribs, the blood thumping in his head. He grabs one boy by the arm and throws him to the ground. He kicks the other one in the shin. These posh boys from St Edward's are all the same; thin and pale, cruel eyes, always up to dirty tricks. They get called out for fouls in football matches. In hockey, they batter his legs with their sticks. He's sick of it and now they're picking on Sam for no reason at all.

'Stop,' Sam is saying to him, trying to hold him back. 'Enough.'

One of the St Edward's boys is crying. His bottom lip looks swollen and his arm is grazed.

The other boy is lying on the ground, moaning, clutching his leg.

Finn shakes Sam off. 'You'll leave him alone now,' he hears himself say, but his voice wavers.

The boy with the fat lip mutters something, 'divot' or 'maggot', but Finn can't make it out. Sam sets his jaw, takes Finn's arm, and guides him away.

'What did he say?' Finn asks, once they're out of earshot.

'Nothing,' Sam says. He doesn't look at Finn.

Finn turns it over in his mind. Faggot. The boy was calling them gay. He feels his face grow hot, the blush spreading down his neck. 'Why'd they go after you?' he asks.

There's a silence and then Sam starts to laugh. 'I nicked their chocolate.'

'You did what?' For a moment, Finn can't speak. 'You fucking idiot, Sam!'

Sam laughs harder. He's almost hysterical, gulping for air. 'Some temper,' he manages to get out.

Shame washes over Finn. He's never been in a fight before. It isn't like him to lose control. 'I don't know what happened.' His voice rasps in his throat. He stops for a moment, putting his hands on his knees. He's feeling sick and dizzy.

'Don't be sorry. They deserved it.' Sam chatters, trying to comfort him. 'They weren't even that badly hurt. Proper wusses, both of them, crying over a scratch.'

Finn wonders if he'll get in trouble. The boys might tell.

As if Sam has guessed his thoughts, he says, 'Don't sweat it, Mouse. No one wants to be a snitch.'

Finn takes a breath, then another, and the nausea eases. He picks up his rucksack.

'Thanks, by the way,' Sam says, quietly. 'You were ace.'

'I know,' Finn says, and Sam gently cuffs him on the arm.

They walk home together, through the woods, towards the cul-de-sac where Nonna will be making their tea. Pasta bolognese, and for afters, chocolate gelato.

# Sarah

## *Summer 2011*

The rain stops, the floods retreat; the pool beneath the apple tree shrinks, evaporating or soaking into the clay soil. There is no sign of the mallard. Perhaps he's flown back to the lake. The sun is back, shining brilliantly, the garden is a vibrant green, and the air is fresh and clean.

Sarah has swept the patio and is wiping the garden furniture with a cloth. Jack is circling the lawn on his bike, the wheels collecting white petals and leaves. Charlie straddles the broom, pretending it's a horse.

Paul has driven to the station to collect Vivien, who has taken the Eurostar from Paris to Waterloo, and a branch-line train to Littlefold. Sarah has prepared salads and a poached salmon for lunch. Later, when the garden and the field are bathed in golden light, Paul will fire up the barbecue.

She tidies away the ride-on tractor and the fire engine, parking them on the other side of the glasshouse. The house is spotless, but Jack hasn't brushed his hair and Charlie is still wearing his Batman pyjama top. 'Grandma will be here any minute. You must finish getting ready,' she says. Jack keeps cycling, as if he hasn't heard. Charlie smiles sweetly, but doesn't show any sign of putting down the broom. 'Giddap,' he says, and canters away in the opposite direction.

She finds a clean t-shirt for Charlie in the utility room. 'Arms up,' she says, peeling off his pyjama top and pulling on the t-shirt. Before he can object, it's done. She hears a car turn into the driveway, compacting the gravel, then the front door opens and there are voices in the hall. Charlie shrieks and runs into the house, skidding on the kitchen floor in his excitement. Jack brakes and sits balancing on his bike. 'Why all the fuss?' he says, nonplussed.

She wonders if he's heard anything she's said to him this morning. 'Grandma's here. Come and say hello,' she says, trying to hide her exasperation, reaching out to smooth his hair. He dodges her hand, looking mulish. It isn't that he doesn't like Vivien, but it's been a year since he's seen her and Jack takes time to warm up. Before she can insist, there are footsteps behind them and Vivien comes out of the glasshouse, carrying Charlie. She's beautifully dressed, in a pale blue linen jacket and skirt, and her bobbed auburn hair is smooth and shiny. She doesn't look at all tired from the journey.

'Hello, darling,' she says. They exchange kisses, a little awkwardly, around Charlie. 'And who is this handsome young man? You're nearly as tall as your mummy.' Jack gives an almost imperceptible nod, his eyes on the ground, and attempts a small, polite smile.

Sarah and her mother sit together at the garden table. Paul is still inside, making tea or diverted on a work call. Jack and Charlie are speeding around the patio on scooters, as if it's a dual carriageway, and she and Vivien are the roundabout. Vivien removes her jacket and carefully hangs it across the back of her chair; the jacket looks expensive – it is probably designer – and Sarah is thankful that she wiped the garden chairs. Vivien lights a cigarette and breathes out smoke. Her mother's smoked for as long as Sarah can remember, but here in Littlefold, where women take pills but would never risk being seen with a cigarette, she seems suddenly, defiantly, nonconformist.

'The Eurostar was quick, but the train from Waterloo was delayed. It seemed to take an eternity to get here. I'd forgotten how slow these branch-line trains are,' Vivien says, trying to speak over the noise of the scooters and the shrieking.

'Yes, awful,' Sarah says, vaguely. She's too distracted to concentrate on what her mother is saying. She knows how undisciplined her children must seem. 'Boys,' she says, using her loud no-nonsense voice, but she has to repeat herself several times before Jack and Charlie reluctantly come to a halt. 'This is far too noisy. I can't hear Grandma speak,' she says. 'Why don't you go on the trampoline?'

First Jack, then Charlie, throw their scooters to one side. Jack runs across the lawn and climbs over the gate, jumping down on the other side to unlatch it for Charlie. Sarah is grateful, not for the first time, to Paul for having had the foresight to purchase the trampoline. They've more than recouped their investment.

'Sorry Mummy,' she says. 'The weather's been dreadful and they've been cooped up indoors.' She wouldn't want Vivien to think that the boys are always this rowdy or that she usually raises her voice. At least they are playing nicely now.

'Your garden is lovely,' Vivien says, as if she hasn't noticed anything untoward, her gaze drifting over the field and towards the woods. 'A paddock is perfect for two boys.' She looks back at Sarah with those blue-grey eyes that have always seemed to see through her. 'You've settled in.' Her voice doesn't lift, but somehow it feels like a question.

'Yes,' Sarah says. 'It's different from London.'

'Naturally,' Vivien says, a French lilt to her voice. She's quiet for a moment. 'How is Aunt Edith? Is her Parkinson's worse? She doesn't speak about it when I phone.'

'She never complains. Her hand shakes, but Anna says the pills help. Otherwise, she seems fine. She's still on the ball.'

Vivien breathes out smoke, fanning it away with her hand. 'Oh yes, Edith's as sharp as a knife,' she says, a little too quickly. 'She's thrilled you're here. Do you see much of her?'

'I pop in with Charlie now and then. I'd like to see her more, but the days are busy. I don't have as much time as I'd like.'

'No,' Vivien says, lifting the cigarette to her lips, but she doesn't sound convinced.

Sarah understands that her mother couldn't know what day-to-day life with two young boys is like. She only had Sarah.

'I expect you'll have more time as the boys get older,' Vivien continues. 'Do you think you'll go back to work in town?'

It's hard for Sarah to imagine a surplus of time. She's heard that older children also need guidance and support, with schoolwork and dealing with peer pressure. If she was in an office in London, she'd hardly see them; a chat at bedtime, if she was lucky with the trains, and the weekends that are always taken up with children's activities and birthday parties. She'd have a snapshot of their lives. She wants the boys to grow up with her values, her advice, not that of a homesick eighteen-year-old au pair. She's determined to give the boys what she always longed for and never had: a mother at home. But she would never want to hurt Vivien, who didn't have a choice, so she says, 'I don't know. I haven't given it much thought. The boys are still little.'

Vivien stubs out her cigarette. She doesn't speak, but Sarah can tell that she's disappointed. No doubt she thinks that Sarah is throwing away her career. At least Vivien doesn't remark, as some mothers who work do, that she herself missed using her brain, as if mothers who look after their children aren't capable of intelligent thought. Anyone who has had to persuade a toddler to get dressed and brush their teeth, or motivate an older child to write a composition and memorise times tables, knows that it takes wit and grit and ingenuity; it is just as demanding, sometimes more so, than a desk-based job.

'I'm sorry I can't help you with the boys. I wish I could,' Vivien says.

An apology is not what Sarah expected. 'Oh,' she says. 'Yes, I know. Don't worry.' Perhaps her mother thinks they've overstretched with the house and can't afford childcare. 'If I decide to go back to work, we'll get a nanny. It wouldn't be difficult.'

There is a silence, she can hear the distant laughter of the boys, and then Paul comes out of the conservatory, carrying three mugs of tea.

'Milk, no sugar. Is that right?' he says, depositing the mugs of tea on the table, as if he's delivering a centrepiece. He sits down.

'Perfect. Thank you,' Vivien says, bestowing on Paul one of her gracious smiles.

'Sorry to take so long. I got stuck on a call.' Paul takes a sip of tea.

'The curse of the BlackBerry,' Vivien says. 'I know how you feel. My phone doesn't stop ringing in Paris.'

Her mother and Paul talk shop, about business in London and Paris, and Sarah is quiet, drinking her tea. A few years ago, she'd have been part of this conversation, but that was another life. The City and its concerns seem far away, as if she's emigrated to a new country. When she was pregnant with Jack, her friends with children warned that her priorities would shift; she might not want to work or do the same type of work; her life would be different. She'd nodded, thinking she understood, but having children has been a seismic change that she's only now beginning to comprehend. It isn't as simple as fine-tuning childcare or finding flexible work or needing adult conversation; it goes deeper, to the core of her. The umbilical cord was cut, the evidence is there in the little knots of flesh on their bellies, but she feels it still, invisibly binding her to Jack and Charlie. There is no way back to the woman she was before; nor would she want there to be. She must chart a new path, make a new life, while always putting her children's needs first. It isn't easy.

Contrary to the weather forecast, by late afternoon the sky is grey, a light drizzle is falling, and her visions of a leisurely barbecue in the garden fade away like the sun. They will have to do something else for supper. She decides on a roast; traditional and comforting, the perfect family meal for a rainy day.

The warm, buttery aroma of baking chicken has filled the house. To go with it, they will have roast potatoes, gravy, greens and honey-glazed carrots. Vivien has set the table. Paul is opening a bottle of the Chablis that he likes.

'Dinner's ready, boys,' Sarah calls, untying her apron. After a few moments, she hears them, thundering downstairs like a herd of wildebeests. Jack appears, wearing a superhero costume, with binoculars around his neck. Charlie follows, in a girl's pirate hat and skirt that Sarah had purchased with Emma Winters in mind. He is carrying a toy walkie-talkie.

'Let me see,' Vivien says, as if she is presiding over a

fancy-dress competition. 'Jack is Batman and Charlie is a Scottish pirate.'

Jack looks affronted. 'We're spies. In disguise.' He turns, revealing the toy gun tucked into his belt. Charlie, not to be outdone, waves his walkie-talkie. 'Spies!' he shouts.

'Of course,' Vivien says. 'Very clever.'

'I don't like carrots,' Charlie says, standing on tiptoe beside the table.

Paul is carving the chicken. Sarah lifts Charlie up onto his high chair. 'You like potatoes,' she says, putting one on his plate and cutting it into small bite-sized pieces.

'Yummy,' Jack says, jumping onto the chair next to Charlie. He reaches across the table for the roast potatoes. Before Sarah can intercept him, he's picked up two with his fingers. She's aware of her mother, standing to one side, sipping her wine. 'Spies still need to mind their manners. Use your cutlery, please,' she says. 'Mummy, do start before it gets cold,' she says to Vivien.

Vivien sits down opposite the boys; Paul helps her to slices of chicken and passes her the gravy. Sarah spoons carrots onto Jack's plate and peas onto Charlie's, pretending not to hear their complaints. Charlie asks for water; as soon as she's delivered it, Jack requests milk. Charlie knocks over his cup, spilling water, and she mops it up with a sponge. She could be participating in a relay race between the kitchen and the table. In the meantime, Paul has piled his plate high; he loves a good roast dinner. It is suddenly quiet, Paul is looking at her impatiently, and she realises that everyone is waiting for her. She helps herself, wondering why it's always up to her to meet her children's needs and then be made to feel inadequate.

She imagines stepping back, disappearing into the shadows, quietly observing from behind a screen. Paul in the eye of the storm, battling with piles of unwashed laundry and stacks of dirty plates, Charlie clinging to his legs, Jack sulking in time out, costumes to make for a play, homework to supervise, sports kits to assemble. She pours gravy over her potatoes, pitching a few fantasy curve balls at her unsuspecting husband, who is now tapping his index finger against the table as if delivering an urgent message in Morse code. The doorbell rings and a little friend arrives for a play date that had been discussed but not diarised; a mother telephones to complain about an incident involving Jack and her child in the playground; Charlie falls, may have broken his arm, and they spend six hours in A & E. She sighs. She sits down.

'Cheers,' Paul says, raising his glass. 'It's good to see you, Vivien.' Having dispensed with the pleasantries, he tucks in.

Charlie and Jack bring their cups together, like two men drinking beer in a tavern.

'It's lovely to be here,' Vivien says. 'I would have come before, but I thought you'd be up to your eyes in building works. It's a beautiful house. So much potential.'

There is a chime in Sarah's head, not unlike her morning alarm that begins gently but builds in volume until she cannot ignore it. 'I'm glad you think so. There's a lot to consider, of course. Luckily, there's no hurry,' she says. She thought she'd already explained this on the phone, but perhaps her mother hadn't understood.

'No, not unless it falls down first,' Paul says, an edge to his voice.

'It's not going to fall down,' she says, lightly.

Paul turns to Vivien, as if she is a judge hearing his claim. 'We need to redo the entire house. The wiring isn't safe and the boiler needs replacing. The kitchen and the bathrooms should be modernised,' he says, using the smooth, earnest voice that he reserves for clients. The voice of reason and

213

authority, and old-fashioned charm. 'It makes sense to do the work. It will be a good investment.'

'Yes,' Vivien says, and Sarah can see her mother falling under his spell. Paul is in his element; he's a born deal-maker and very persuasive. 'Have you had any drawings done? Have you spoken to builders?' Vivien asks. And her mother is a natural judge, Sarah thinks.

'No,' Paul says. 'Sarah's worried that the works will be disruptive.'

A point to Paul, the considerate husband, and a minus to her for blocking necessary work on the basis of sheer inconvenience.

'It is a big job,' Vivien says, thoughtfully. 'What about a project manager? A good team could blitz it. That wouldn't be too bad.' She turns to Sarah, as if appealing to a stubborn child. 'It might even be quite fun. I expect you'd enjoy getting your teeth into it, Sarah.'

Paul smiles. Sarah bristles with anger. He's playing a dangerous game, getting her mother involved. Vivien doesn't realise that she's being played like a pawn. 'Yes, that is one option that we're considering,' she says, as evenly as she can. She decides to change the subject before her mother can furnish more suggestions. 'What shall we do tomorrow? Would you like to visit Aunt Edith? Should I book somewhere nice for supper?'

Vivien glances away, as if something has caught her eye, then looks back at Sarah. 'Yes, I must call in to see Edith.' She hesitates for a moment. 'Darling, I'd love to stay for supper, but I have to catch a train back to Paris. I've got meetings first thing on Monday morning. It's a new client and I couldn't say no. I'm sorry it's a flying visit.'

Sarah knows it's not her mother's fault, but she can't help feeling disappointed. She'd assumed that Vivien would stay for at least a couple of days. This is no time at all. It doesn't seem fair on the boys, who hardly see her. In this way her mother is like Paul, unable or unwilling to be away from the office. *The years will pass with infrequent visits, the boys will grow up, and it will be too late,* she wants to say. Instead, she says, 'Yes, of course. You need to get back. I understand.' The words come so easily; she's had years of practice. It's for the best, she tells herself. A few more days, and her mother would be arranging meetings with architects and builders.

The boys are finally asleep. Her mother helped, but she was no match for Jack and Charlie, who deployed one tactic after another to string out bedtime. Sarah and Paul cleared the kitchen while the boys entreated Vivien for 'one more story' that became five; this was after lengthy negotiations about seating and who should read, which resulted in a complex compromise – Charlie sitting on Vivien's knee with Jack beside her, and Jack and Vivien sharing the reading while Charlie turned the pages. Even when her mother was at the finish line and the boys were in bed, there were requests for water, Charlie pointed out a hangnail that needed trimming, and Jack was given paracetamol for a headache.

They are sitting at the table, drinking tea. The dishwasher is humming industriously in the background. The flickering candles are wreathed in creamy tendrils of molten wax. Paul is scanning emails on his BlackBerry.

'The boys have changed,' Vivien says. 'I was impressed with Jack's reading. And Charlie isn't a baby any more. He's strong and agile.'

'Yes,' Sarah says. 'Jack's doing well at school. I think Charlie will be sporty.'

'They are growing up fast,' Vivien says.

'I suppose they are,' Sarah says, wondering if her mother is regretting the brevity of her visit.

Vivien hides a yawn behind her hand. 'I'm sorry. I think I'd better go to bed. Thank you for a lovely day.' She kisses Sarah on the cheek. 'Goodnight, sweetheart.'

'Goodnight, Mummy. See you in the morning,' Sarah says.

Paul looks up from his BlackBerry. 'Goodnight,' he says.

They hear Vivien going upstairs, the guest-room door clicks shut, and it's just the two of them.

Paul puts down his BlackBerry and pours a bourbon, swirling the amber liquid over ice. 'Would you like one?'

'All right,' Sarah says. She rarely drinks spirits, but it's been a long day. A drop of bourbon will take the edge off.

Paul gives her a tumbler and she takes a sip. The bourbon is cold, but feels like fire inside her. Her fingers tingle.

'It's nice to see your mother,' Paul says.

'Yes. It's a pity she has to hurry back to Paris,' she says.

'Business must be good,' Paul says, approvingly.

And work trumps everything, she thinks, uncharitably. 'Yes, I gather it is,' she says.

'Well,' Paul says. 'She likes the house.'

Sarah says nothing, already knowing what lies ahead.

'She thinks we should do it up.'

She wants to say, *It's not up to Vivien, it was wrong to involve her*, but instead, she says, 'Does she? I don't remember her saying that.'

'As good as,' Paul says. He puts down his empty glass. 'We can't go on like this. The house is falling to bits.'

'It's cosmetic. It's fine.'

A muscle in Paul's neck twitches. 'It's not fine. What about your mother's room? There's been a leak. The bloody ceiling could fall in.'

He's telling her off like a child. She feels her face go red. 'It's nothing that can't be fixed,' she says. 'The roofer said he'd sorted it out, but we've had a lot of rain. I'll get him round again. Once it's dry, we can touch it in with paint.' She doesn't mention the roofer's warning about the insulation.

'Touch it in?' Paul laughs, a little hysterically. 'What about the warping windows? Can those be touched in? Or the floor that's splitting apart in the sitting room? Or the dodgy wiring?' He pours himself another bourbon. 'The house needs gutting.'

A discussion fuelled by whiskey isn't going to end well. She should suggest they go to bed and speak in the morning, but instead she says, 'I don't know why you're panicking. It's routine house maintenance. And I'm just not ready to do it up.' It's no use trying to explain that she loves their home for, not in spite of, its imperfections. He wouldn't understand.

The house has earned its place among the fields and the woods. It's as rooted as the trees. She sees it stripped, hollowed out, made into something it's not: a house without a soul. She'd be lost.

Paul shakes his head. 'I work fourteen-hour days to pay for a house that's falling apart. It's our main investment. I could lose my job tomorrow. It would be much easier to sell the house if it was refurbished.'

The thought of losing this place knots her stomach. She can't imagine living somewhere else. 'Has something happened at the office?'

'Nothing's happened,' Paul says. 'It's the times we live in. We can't take anything for granted.' He's quiet for a moment. 'And I'm not convinced about living here.'

Here it is: his final card. She feels her neck and back tense. 'I see. You want us to move. Well, this is my house too, and I won't sell.' Her voice is louder than she'd intended. She's trembling inside.

'Calm down. Your mother will hear.'

He's about to carry on, but she interrupts him, propelled

by a sudden rage. 'Don't tell me to calm down,' she says. She lowers her voice. 'Don't patronise me.'

'Look,' Paul says. 'It's been over a year and Jack still doesn't fit in at school. The commute means I hardly see the boys. We haven't made any friends.'

She wants to retort that they've got plenty of friends, but the only person she can think of is Jessica Winters and Paul's never met her. She's about to say that he's never around to make any friends, but this will only give him ammunition. 'We have family,' she says, but even as the words leave her lips, she knows it sounds weak. There is only Aunt Edith.

'It's in the past,' Paul says, more gently.

'This is all very well,' she says. 'But you wanted to come here. Where do you suggest we go?' She can hear herself getting onto her high horse, but she can't seem to help it.

'I think we should go back to town. Jack will be better suited to a London prep. I'll be able to see more of you and the boys. I can take them to school sometimes and be home before they're in bed.'

She doesn't want to go back to London; the boys pacing a flat like caged animals, traffic fumes and noise, a vista of apartments and office blocks. 'The London schools are hot-houses and Jack's a sensitive boy. And as much as you'd like to see more of us, we both know that work will come first. I don't want to uproot the boys again, only to disappoint them.'

'I won't disappoint them.'

She wishes that she could believe him, but the picture he's painting is a dream. There have been too many broken promises. She's quiet for a moment, thinking. 'Let me get this straight. You want me to go through a year of building works. All that effort, and we sell up and leave. Why would I agree to that?'

Paul's face falls, but he seems more confused than guilty.

He looks into his tumbler, as if searching for an answer. 'I thought it would cover the costs of moving. Stamp duty, legal fees. I don't know. Maybe we need to give it more time.'

Frustration surges inside her. 'How much time do you need? Two years? Three? I can't live like this, knowing it could end at any moment.'

'That's life. It's transient. What difference does it make?' Paul is going philosophical, the way he does when he's had too much to drink.

The heat of the bourbon has faded away. She is exhausted. 'Maybe it's not this place. Maybe it's us.' The words are out before she can stop them.

Paul's eyes darken. The space between them feels as tangible as a magnetic force. 'I'm going to bed,' he says. He won't even dignify her confession with a response. He goes upstairs.

She carries their tumblers to the sink and washes up, sluicing away the last of the bourbon, which now smells acrid. She's drying a tumbler with a cloth when suddenly, she feels a sharp pain inside her chest. The glass falls, shattering into pieces. She leans against the sink, gripping the worktop. After a moment or two, the pain subsides. She wipes her wet face with the cloth, and puts it in the laundry basket in the utility room.

She sweeps up the larger pieces of broken glass with a dustpan and brush, wraps them in newspaper, and puts the package in the bin. She vacuums the floor and tiny fragments ping and ricochet in the nozzle. She must find every piece; Jack and Charlie are always running around in bare feet. She unplugs the hoover and winds the cord up. Her finger is bleeding. It must have been a piece of glass. She sucks it, tasting the metal in her blood. It will be better in the morning, she tells herself, as if she's comforting one of her children.

Their bedroom is dark and still. Paul is either asleep, or pretending to be. She lies on the bed, her back to him, hugging her knees. She drifts, then sinks into a dreamless sleep that leaves her dissatisfied and heavy-headed when she wakes.

# Finn

*Surrey, 2007*

Finn and Sam are thirteen years old, waiting at the corner for the school bus, just like they do every morning. It's going to be another hot day. Last night, Finn slept in his pants and with the windows open, but his room was still sweltering.

Sam is swinging his tie like a lasso. His shirt isn't tucked in and he hasn't brushed his hair. 'I can't be bothered with lessons when it's like this,' he says.

Finn shades his eyes, looking down the leafy lane. There is no sign of the bus. He's not looking forward to double maths in a stuffy classroom and Mr Martin leaning over his shoulder. He can already feel the teacher's breath on his neck. Sam will make faces to wind Finn up, and he'll pretend not to see.

'Let's bunk off,' Sam says, as if it's something they do a lot, when it would be the first time.

Finn sees his father toiling in the sun, his skin slick with sweat and grime. 'OK,' he says, before he loses his nerve. He slings his book bag over his shoulder.

They are running down the path into the woods, their bags

bumping against their legs. 'Race you,' Sam shouts. Sam's not as strong or as tall as Finn, but he's quick and agile. Already he's flying ahead, his shirt billowing like a sail.

It doesn't matter if he loses Sam. He could find the lake blindfolded. Not everyone knows the old quarry, hidden away in the woods, but it's five minutes from where they live. He and Sam are always there, playing ambush and building dens. Sam's like a brother, or at least how Finn would imagine a brother to be. The Thomas family have lived next door as long as he can remember.

The lake is shining, ruffled by a gentle breeze. Two mallards are floating in the shade of the willow tree. Rowing boats are tied to the wooden jetties and no one is in the gardens of the neighbouring houses. Sam has taken off his shoes and socks, and is sitting on the rocks, dangling his pale legs into the greenish water. Finn does the same, and sits down next to him. The water is ice cold and he shivers. Something brushes against his skin and he imagines eels winding through his legs. It is too murky to see.

Sam picks up a stone and pitches it into the lake. 'Let's take a boat out,' he says.

The gardens across the water are manicured, with pruned roses and striped lawns. Finn sees his mother bent over Papa's calloused hands, removing splinters with her tweezers, while he sits at the kitchen table doing homework. School comes easily to him, it always has, and the teachers are talking about scholarships. 'You're a good boy,' his mother says softly, when she tucks him into bed at night. Her dark eyes glisten with dreams that feel like weights on his shoulders.

Sam stands up. His black fringe is long and touches his eyes. 'Come on. It'll be a laugh.' He pushes his hair back with a hand. A slow smile plays on his lips. 'Or are you too chicken-shit?'

*

They are drifting, slowly, in the middle of the lake. The woods and the houses seem far away, and the sky is blue and infinite. Sam has taken off his shirt and is leaning against the boat, his arms folded behind his head. His chest is white and thin, and Finn can see his ribs.

Finn takes off his shirt too and the sun feels good on his skin. Water laps against the boat and a gull wheels above them. He closes his eyes. In the coloured darkness behind his eyelids, he sees Lucy glancing at him over her shoulder, her pleated grey skirt swinging around her legs; sitting at her desk, running her fingers through her long brown hair. He wants to speak to her, but his mind goes blank when she is near. He hasn't told Sam. He has a feeling that Sam wouldn't want to share him with anyone else.

'I'm boiling,' Sam says, and Finn opens his eyes. Sam is trailing his hand in the water. 'Let's go for a swim,' he says.

'You know we can't,' Finn says. Swimming at the lake is banned. The water is too cold and deep.

'You're as bad as an old woman,' Sam says, flicking his fingers, splashing Finn.

Finn leans over and slices the water, sending spray over Sam.

'You look like you've wet yourself,' Sam says, pointing at Finn's shorts. He stands up. 'Might as well go in now. I'll race you to the shore and back.'

'No,' Finn says, hearing the irritation in his voice. He'll be in enough trouble as it is for skiving.

'What's the matter? Worried you'll lose?' Sam shifts his weight from side to side, making the boat rock.

'Stop it, Sam,' Finn says. The rhythmic rocking is making him queasy.

'Stop it,' Sam needles, in a shrill voice. 'Stop it, Sam.' His dark eyes are glittering.

'Fuck you,' Finn says, but Sam just laughs, rocking the boat even harder, making it pitch and buck, as if they are at sea.

Finn feels anger boil and surge inside him. He lunges for Sam, but instead of trying to push him away, Sam grabs his arm and pulls him nearer. They are locked together, so close that Finn can feel Sam's heart beating fast and quick. And then, before he can say or do anything, Sam presses his mouth to his. Sam is kissing him, the way men and women do in films. He feels Sam's hand slip inside his shorts; it's easy, like a hand into a pocket. He should tell Sam to stop, they are brothers, this is wrong, but the heat builds inside him. He soars, flying, then resists, falling, fighting. The bliss, the agony, stalks him. Blood rushes in his head and his chest is splitting apart. His stomach heaves, a roar erupts from him and his hands push Sam hard. 'I hate you,' he shouts, knowing it's a lie. 'You fucking queer.' His words are as hollow as his heart.

Sam is falling backwards, into the lake. His eyes are wide, his arms flailing. His body crashes into the water. Finn drops to his knees and leans over the boat. The surface of the lake foams. Sam comes up, gasping, then goes under again.

Finn jumps off the boat and the water hits him like an icy fist. He dives, feeling in front of him with his hands. Fish or weeds slip through his fingers. He can't find Sam. He dives again, forcing his eyes open, but it's too murky to see. His lungs are burning, and he comes up for air. His eyes sting. The lake, the woods, the houses and the jetties are grainy and blurry, like an out-of-focus lens. Suddenly, someone grips his shoulders, leaning on him so heavily that he goes under, inhaling water. He coughs so hard that he's nearly sick. Sam's face is white, his black hair is plastered to his face, and his eyes are full of fear. He grabs Finn, clutching onto him, scrabbling, trying to climb him like a mountain, while Finn goes under again and again.

They are both sinking, clasped together. The light dims, it is even colder, and an abyss unfolds beneath them. The walls seem to be closing in, like a noose tightening. A giant orange spider with long delicate legs eyes them from a cave. Luminous fish caress their arms and a snail with undulating wings glides past. Finn brushes against something hard, a rusting metal structure and, through the gloom, sees the dark, pitched roof of a small house, as sunken as a shipwreck. Perhaps a ghost lives here; a drowned quarry miner, or a boy like him, held prisoner by the sirens. A shoal of gooseberry-shaped creatures hover in front of him, neon lights pulsing through their tiny hairs. It is a dream, he thinks, but then Sam screams, a wrenching muffled sound, and this breaks the spell. Finn swims up, chasing the fading light, pulling Sam with him. Sam is heavy – it takes all the strength he has – but somehow he manages it and they reach the surface.

Sam still clings to Finn, even though he must know they will only sink again. He seems to have forgotten how to swim. Slowly, with difficulty, Finn turns Sam onto his back, the way he was taught in swimming rescue lessons. Sam panics, floundering, but Finn holds him close, his arm cradling Sam's chest, and this calms him. It is working, he is floating, and Finn starts to swim, towing Sam behind him.

The boat doesn't look far away, but no matter how hard Finn swims, they don't get any closer. The water flows against them, firmly, steadily, pushing them away. Sam's eyes have closed and he isn't moving. He's either asleep or unconscious. Finn knows he must get Sam out of the water, but his arms are going numb. He tries to adjust his hold on Sam. He can hardly feel his own fingers. He fumbles, loses his grip, and a strong current glides between them, rippling and twisting, like a monster from the sea.

Sam is dragged away and Finn is pulled under. Tentacles or

weeds bind him and he is submerged in the dark, cavernous depths of the lake. He struggles, fights, and at last breaks free. He swims and swims, pushing himself up towards the bright surface, and air floods his aching lungs. Sunlight fractures the water. He can't see Sam. He calls to him, screaming his name, cursing him, beseeching him, but there is only silence. His brother. His nemesis. He is gone.

# Sarah

## *Summer 2011*

'It's a pity about the weather,' Aunt Edith says, her voice wavering. Her cup of tea is going cold, but she keeps her hands folded, one hand covering the other trembling one. A blanket is tucked around her knees. 'I hope it hasn't spoiled your visit.'

The rain has been falling steadily all morning. Sarah can hear it pattering against the windows and running along the gutters of her aunt's house. She wonders if the rains will bring the mallard back to her garden.

'Not at all,' Vivien says. 'I've enjoyed seeing Sarah and the boys.'

'Jack and Charlie,' Aunt Edith says, as if she's reminding herself of their names. 'Such well-behaved children. You should have brought them with you.'

A feeling of warmth rolls over Sarah like a wave. Aunt Edith rarely gives out praise. 'Paul takes the boys swimming on Saturdays,' she says. 'I'll bring them next time.'

'Swimming is excellent exercise,' Aunt Edith says, approvingly. 'I was a strong swimmer as a girl.'

'Indeed,' Sarah says. Suddenly, she's seven years old again, listening to her aunt hold forth. It isn't only that Aunt Edith is tall and beautiful, and wears expensive clothes, it's the way she stands, her authoritative voice, those bright eyes that miss nothing. Her aunt is old and frail now, her hair is white and her face is lined, but she still has that enquiring gaze that makes Sarah feel like a child.

Charlie will have had his swimming lesson by now, and it will be Jack's turn. She sees Paul doing lengths with Charlie clinging to his back, water streaming over his shoulders and tracing the imprints on his face left by his glasses. They haven't had a chance to talk about what happened last night. The morning was busy, taken up with breakfast and getting the boys ready. She and Paul spoke to each other only when necessary and were careful not to touch. Sarah's head was hurting, but whether it was the bourbon or the argument, she couldn't tell. Her hands cleared the breakfast plates and carried them to the sink. Vivien chatted as if nothing was amiss, and the boys chased each other around the house, shrieking and swinging their swim bags. Sarah wondered if her mother had overheard her and Paul arguing; perhaps Vivien had noticed the broken glass in the bin, and thought one of them had thrown it at the other. If she had guessed, she was showing no sign of it.

It is peaceful in Aunt Edith's sitting room. The sound of the rain falling and the soft grey sky is soothing. She stirs sugar into her tea; the aromatic sweetness is a balm. She won't be able to talk to Paul until this evening, when the boys are asleep in bed. Charlie wouldn't understand, but Jack has near-superhuman hearing; his ears prick up at the slightest hint of secrets or hushed conversations. She doesn't want to worry him. She knows what it's like to have parents who don't get along. In all likelihood, she and Paul won't talk about it at all. They'll both be tired and raw, and wary of another row. In a few days, Paul will pretend that he's forgotten, or that nothing happened.

She hit a nerve with him last night. She doesn't know if she has the courage to do it again, but they can't go on like this. It's only a matter of time before the same conflicts rear up again. They are just treading water.

There has been a change, but it's not this place. It was easy when it was just the two of them; equal players with parallel careers. Now they are different, made different by the children that they both wanted and love, and they must begin again. Eventually, Jack and Charlie will grow up and leave. It will come more quickly than they think. Her thoughts are interrupted by hearing her name.

'I'm sure Sarah would be happy to help,' Vivien says. She is looking at Sarah encouragingly.

'Yes, of course,' Sarah says, without any idea of what she's committing to. For all she knows, she's agreed to take Aunt Edith on holiday or have her move in with them.

'It's sweet of you, darling, but there's no need. Anna is here every morning. She does my shopping,' Aunt Edith says.

Sarah breathes an inward sigh of relief and then feels ashamed. 'If you ever need anything, or Anna is busy, just let me know. I'm always at the supermarket. It wouldn't be any trouble,' she says.

As if she has heard her name, the door to the sitting room opens and Anna comes in. 'There's a young man at the door. He's offering to help with the garden,' she says. Her cheeks look flushed and she sounds breathless. She tucks a loose strand of hair behind her ear. 'I know his family,' she adds softly, perhaps too quietly for Aunt Edith to hear. 'He's a good lad.'

Sarah sees a boy in his father's overalls. Golden hair; a smile as warm as the sun. A voice in her head whispers his name.

'Excellent,' Aunt Edith says, looking pleased. 'Yes, do ask him in.' She turns to Vivien. 'Do you mind? I can't imagine it will take long. My gardener has moved out of the area. It's difficult to find good people.'

'Not at all,' Vivien says. She sips her tea.

Anna goes to fetch the boy and the few minutes that she's gone feel like an eternity. Sarah hasn't seen Finn since he pinned the wisteria. She's been wondering when they'd meet again; she'd never have guessed it would be at her aunt's house, with her mother beside her.

Outside, the rain has eased. The sky is washed in charcoal, the trees are luminous green, and crimson rose petals are scattered like offerings on the overgrown lawn. Intricate spiderwebs cling to the tall dark hedge. The wild, wooded part of her aunt's garden is full of shifting shadows. She imagines a vixen slipping through the trees, a lugubrious ghost, the beating wings of disturbed bats. A grass snake nesting in a hill of mulching leaves. Stag beetles hiding in the hollows of coppiced logs.

She hears footsteps advancing. Her heart begins to pound. She smooths the hair back from her face.

It is Finn. His hair is damp and his skin is glowing. His denim jacket is wet. He's taken off his trainers and the sight of him in his white socks makes Sarah think of Charlie.

'This is Finn,' Anna says.

'Hello,' he says. He smiles at Sarah, looking amused. 'I didn't know I'd find you here.'

'This is my aunt's house,' Sarah says. She gestures at Vivien. 'This is my mother, Vivien.' She knows that she sounds reserved. 'Finn and his father look after our garden,' she says to her mother and Aunt Edith.

Aunt Edith doesn't speak. She lifts her hand and the other one flutters, like a freed captive bird.

'Hello,' Vivien says, but her voice sounds hollow. She's biting her lip, the way she does when she's anxious. Perhaps she's worried about Aunt Edith's Parkinson's; the shaking has worsened this past year.

Finn places a flyer on the coffee table. *Nico Saunders & Son. Garden Design and Maintenance.*

So Finn has joined Nico in his gardening business. Perhaps it's a trial, for the summer. She wonders if Finn will be responsible for the garden design; they've never spoken about it, but she can see how that type of work would suit him. Still, she hopes he isn't giving up on university. If he joins his father, he'll never leave this place. The lake, the drowned boy, will continue to haunt him.

Aunt Edith adjusts her spectacles. She picks up the flyer and the white paper agitates in her hands. She looks at Finn. 'Saunders,' she says, and her voice catches in her throat. She coughs.

'Yes,' Finn says. 'Do you know my father?'

'I knew Flavia,' Aunt Edith says.

This is not what Sarah expected.

'My grandmother,' Finn says, and he looks surprised too.

Perhaps it shouldn't be surprising; after all, Aunt Edith has lived here all her life. Sarah wonders what Finn's grandmother was like, and how Aunt Edith came to know her. Anna also knows Finn's family. In Littlefold, everyone knows each other.

'She passed away two years ago,' Finn says.

'Yes. I'm sorry,' Aunt Edith says.

There is a silence, but it doesn't feel awkward or uncomfortable. Something in the room, like a movement of air, seems to shift. Aunt Edith looks out at the garden. The trees are dripping and there are puddles on the patio. The respite from the rain looks to be brief: a band of dark cloud is approaching. 'The weather will be more settled next week,' Aunt Edith murmurs. She turns back to Finn. 'Would you like to pop by one morning? We can have a chat.'

It's as if her aunt is inviting Finn to tea, not arranging a meeting with a contractor. She wonders if this is to do with Finn's grandmother.

'Yes, of course,' Finn says. 'I can come on Monday, if that's convenient.' And it's almost funny to hear Finn sound so businesslike.

'Perfect,' Aunt Edith says. 'I'll look forward to it.'

Once again, Sarah has the distinct impression that her aunt is arranging a social visit. It can't just be about Finn's grandmother; it seems unlikely that the two women were friends. Perhaps Aunt Edith is lonely, she thinks, and feels a sudden pang. She ought to call in more.

'Right. See you then,' Finn says. He glances at Sarah, and his grey eyes slay her. She looks away.

Anna's been waiting quietly, standing to one side, but now she says to Finn, 'I'll show you out.' The kindness in Anna's voice, the protective way she's looking at Finn, makes Sarah wonder if Anna is a close family friend.

Finn follows Anna into the corridor and she closes the door gently behind them. He is gone.

Vivien sighs. She must be worried about Aunt Edith, Sarah thinks. At least their visit seems to have done their aunt good; there is colour in her face and her eyes are sparkling.

'What a nice young man,' Aunt Edith says. 'Very attractive.'

Sarah doesn't trust herself to comment.

'Yes,' Vivien says. She hesitates for a moment, then says, 'I hope it works out.'

'Nothing ventured, nothing gained,' Aunt Edith says.

Her aunt seems very taken with Finn. He seems to have this effect, drawing people in. Her mother doesn't seem as interested; perhaps her thoughts are with her work and her journey back to Paris.

Vivien stands, smoothing her skirt, and Sarah knows she was right. 'This has been lovely, but I must go,' she says. She leans down to kiss Aunt Edith. 'I'll come and see you again soon.'

Aunt Edith lightly pats Vivien's hair. '*À la prochaine*,' she says, in a perfect French accent. 'Give my love to Jack and Charlie,' she says to Sarah.

Sarah is driving Vivien to the station to catch the train to London. Her mother is quiet, holding her handbag on her knee. The wrought-iron gates and the pavements, the cars and the wooden fences, are all clean and shiny. The wet grassy verges are scattered with poppies. The sun breaks through the heavy cloud, bathing the streets and the houses in golden light, then the clouds knit together and it is dark again. This reprieve from the rain won't last long.

'It was nice to see Aunt Edith. Her Parkinson's is worse, but she seems to be managing,' Vivien says.

'She was on good form,' Sarah says.

'Yes. In some ways, she hasn't changed,' Vivien says. Before Sarah can reply, Vivien carries on. 'Life is full of surprises. When I left Littlefold, I never imagined that one day my daughter and my aunt would be neighbours here. You even share a gardener.'

If anyone else was speaking, this would sound nostalgic or pleased, but coming from her mother, it's more nuanced, laced with disappointment. 'We like it here,' Sarah says evenly, pretending not to notice. 'Paul wanted to do the gardening, but he doesn't have the time.'

'Yes,' her mother says, almost wistfully. 'They say that gardening is like therapy. Good for the soul.'

Sarah doesn't know if her mother is simply making conversation, or overheard her and Paul arguing last night, or is concerned that they've overstretched and shouldn't pay a gardener. She doesn't know what to say, so she says nothing.

There is a silence and then Vivien says, 'It will be half term soon. Why don't you bring the boys to Paris?'

Her mother makes it sound so easy. 'I'd like to, but it's difficult for Paul to take time off,' Sarah says.

'Come on your own,' Vivien says. 'I can help with the boys.'

But not with the journey. The thought of going through security at a busy airport, managing the suitcases and the pushchair, all the while keeping track of the boys, isn't appealing. A train journey involving several changes is equally daunting; two hands aren't enough.

'I'm not sure. Charlie is still little. I'll think about it,' she says. There's no point going into the logistics. Her mother, with her single carry-on, is unlikely to understand.

'You must do as you think best,' Vivien says. Sarah wonders how her mother can say one thing and mean something entirely different.

They are nearly at the end of Station Road when they meet a white Range Rover. The row of parked cars makes it impossible for either of them to pass. The Range Rover could bump up onto the kerb, but the driver, a woman with sleek black hair and huge sunglasses, grips her steering wheel and stares down at them, intractable. Her car growls menacingly, like a huge white beast.

'*Putain*,' Vivien says. She only ever swears in French, as if it's more acceptable. 'I'll miss my train.'

Reversing alongside parked cars isn't easy, and by the time they've reached a place wide enough to resolve the impasse, they are at the beginning of Station Road again.

The black-haired woman revs the engine and drives quickly past. She doesn't raise a hand in thanks.

'These suburban housewives are worse than I remember,' Vivien says.

Sarah is as annoyed as her mother, but she says, 'There are difficult people everywhere,' feeling suddenly protective of Littlefold. She drives down Station Road again, past the red-brick ticket office, and turns into the car park. 'Here we are. You'll make the train.'

In the end, the train to Waterloo is delayed by ten minutes due to flash flooding. She waits with her mother on the platform, along with families going up to town for the day, middle-aged men in rugby kit, and a group of noisy teenagers. Vivien takes a compact mirror from her handbag and applies lipstick. In her smart navy trousers and Breton-striped top, her mac belted at the waist, she doesn't look like a grandmother. Her auburn hair is as lustrous as when she was forty. Sarah tries to rub away a dirty mark on her trousers, no doubt made by Charlie's shoes when she lifted him out of the car, but the dirt smears. She doubts that she'll ever look as elegant as her mother. Even if she had the time, she doesn't have the skill or patience to assemble outfits. Vivien snaps the compact shut, closes the lipstick, and drops them both into her handbag.

She smiles at Sarah, and the fine lines by her eyes crinkle. 'It's been lovely seeing you and the boys. Let's not leave it so long next time.'

The train pulls in, brakes screeching, and the doors slide open. Sarah feels her chest constrict, the way it did when she was a child staying with her grandparents and her mother left for London. Vivien hugs her tightly. 'Lots of love,' she says. She turns into the tide of passengers getting on the train, one of the men in rugby kit helps her with her suitcase, and then she reappears, sitting beside the window. The conductor blows the whistle and her mother waves, as pale as an apparition, through the glass. The train moves along the platform, picks up speed and disappears around the tree-lined bend.

# Edith

## *Summer 2011*

The ground is soft from the rain; the grass and the leaves shine with dew. The sky is blue, it will be warm later, but for now it is cool.

The boy is here. He is walking beside her, pointing out the overgrown hedge, the dark wooded area where no grass grows, the compost mountain.

'You should reclaim your garden,' the boy is saying. 'The hedge is dead. We could remove it and plant a privet.' He gestures at the wooded area. 'Those conifers are blocking the light. We could take them out, sow grass and extend your lawn by a third.' He's quiet for a moment, considering. 'Or you could do something different. An orchard of fruit trees. A wildflower meadow.'

A new beginning, Edith thinks. 'Yes,' she says. 'These are all good ideas.'

He is very like Jim: tall and slim, cloud-grey eyes, sandy hair that he rakes through with his fingers. He has her brother's smile, his easy charm. When Anna showed him into the sitting room, it was like seeing a ghost. Now that the initial shock has faded, she can see Flavia in him; smooth olive skin and pride that he wears like armour. There is fire inside this boy. It's in his blood, bequeathed by his ancestors, the people of a volcanic island.

Finn. She knows what happened to him. It seems like only a year or so ago, but perhaps it was longer. Time has become elastic, and the past sometimes seems very close, as if she could reach across the years and touch the faces of those who are now gone. Her parents. Jim. Maggie. One by one, death comes for us all.

It is worse when it comes for the young. A sickening waste of life, of love itself. The accident was in all the local papers. It sent shock waves through the community. For weeks, there was talk of little else. Anna told Edith that the other boy on the boat, the one who survived, was Flavia's grandson. Flavia had retired from housekeeping by then, but she and Anna were still close friends. Finn Saunders, Anna said, softly. The boy was having a hard time. She turned to wipe the kitchen countertop and Edith couldn't see her face. Anna said nothing more, but Edith guessed that Flavia had told Anna about Jim.

Finn tries to hide his pain, but he is damaged, still reeling from the trauma of losing his friend. No doubt he's heard the gossip. Edith refused to listen to it. Jim was gone and she couldn't believe that a grandson of his would do anything dishonourable. She'd wanted to offer support, but Flavia had made it clear that she didn't want help, and Edith didn't dare contact Nico or Finn. The rift between the families endured; a custom, unquestioned and obeyed. When Flavia died, a sudden embolism, it was almost enough, but not quite. Each time Edith picked up a pen to write to Nico, her mind went blank. She didn't know how to begin or what to say. *It's too late,* she told herself.

238

And then he came to her, this boy, taking his strength and beauty for granted the way only the young can do. She is determined to help him. It's a chance to make amends.

'You have good specimens,' he is saying. 'The roses and lavender work well together.' He touches the plants tenderly, and says their names as if they are friends.

They have reached the side gate. Her heart clamours, knowing that in a minute he will go. Her hand is shaking even more than usual, and she pushes it deep into her pocket. She can't bear this uncontrollable agitation that makes it almost impossible to perform the simplest of tasks, like buttoning her shirt or drinking tea. She worries that it makes her look infirm.

'When can you start?' she hears herself say. Her voice breaks. She hopes that she doesn't sound as desperate as she feels.

There is a silence while he looks blankly at her. 'Don't you want a quote?' he says, at last.

She waves a hand, as if it's not important. 'Anna speaks highly of you.' She remembers Anna standing in the doorway, flushed and breathless, unable to meet her eye. She wonders if Anna encouraged Finn to come to the house. Edith won't ask or thank her; she doesn't want to embarrass Anna. They needn't speak of it at all. Anna will understand.

Finn doesn't know about Jim. One day, he will find out: it's inevitable. She hopes that he will forgive them.

He takes off his gloves and tucks them into his jeans pocket. There are callouses on his palms. 'I can start this weekend, if you like.'

So he will come back. Relief pours over her like an ablution. The garden will be a good project for him. She will pretend to oversee it, but he will have a free hand. There will be photos for a portfolio. She will endorse his work and recommend him. It isn't enough, but it's a start.

'Thank you,' she says.

His smile makes her ache inside. He turns and walks away, whistling a melody that she's heard before, perhaps from an opera or a film, and the fading notes seem to echo the longing in her heart.

# Sarah

*Summer 2011*

'Jesus Christ,' Paul says quietly, as if someone has died.

They are standing on the patio, taking in the devastation, the annihilation of Aunt Edith's garden. Ancient conifers have been felled, dismembered, and are being fed by a black-haired man to a bonfire. The flames crackle, throwing sparks, and smoke hangs over the pillaged garden. Another man wielding a chainsaw is slicing into the hedge, stripping branches, exposing the dead heart. Sarah doesn't know these men, but they look Italian and most probably work with Nico.

The lawn is littered with the carcases of trees. Charlie is climbing from stump to stump, as if he's in an adventure playground. Jack is more cautious, holding back, watching from a safe distance. Without the screen of conifers, the houses opposite are exposed, their windows staring blankly, as if in shock.

Aunt Edith is standing near the bonfire, arms folded, listening closely to Finn. Finn's jeans are dirty, his sleeves are rolled up, and his blond hair is even wilder than usual. He's gesturing at the hedge, the tree stumps and the ransacked borders, as if he's a director of a play.

'She's taken leave of her senses,' Paul says, who has always admired Aunt Edith's garden. He turns to Sarah, expecting answers, but she's as confused as he is.

'I know as little as you do,' she says. Aunt Edith and Finn are walking slowly towards them, deep in conversation. She feels a sudden twinge of envy. 'I hope he still has time for our garden,' she says, the words tumbling out before she can stop them.

'Yes,' Paul says. He is quiet for a moment. 'Should we be jealous?' She wonders if he's teasing her, the way he sometimes does about Finn, but there isn't a trace of amusement in his voice. They still haven't talked about the argument they had when her mother was here. The anger between them is like a dying fire, smouldering, ready to ignite.

Aunt Edith joins them, breaking away from Finn for the briefest of moments to kiss them. 'Isn't this exciting?' she says, her eyes sparkling. She is wearing a twinset, tweed skirt, white tights and wellington boots; her cheeks are dusted with rouge and she's wearing pearls.

A drop of sweat slides down Finn's neck. He draws his arm along his forehead, and the hairs on his arm glisten.

Aunt Edith looks every bit the royal on tour, and Finn could be one of her subjects from the shires.

'Well,' Paul says. 'It's a project.'

'It certainly is,' Aunt Edith says brightly. If she's detected the scepticism in Paul's voice, she shows no sign of it. 'Tell them, dear,' she says to Finn, giving him an encouraging smile.

Finn licks his lips. Sarah feels her stomach lurch, the way it does when Jack appears on stage for the nativity at Christmas.

'I know it looks a mess now, but those conifers were

242

blocking the light and the hedge was dead,' he begins, a little hesitant at first, but growing in confidence. 'Once this is cleared, we can sow grass and start planting. The end of the garden will be an orchard of cherry trees and pear trees, with wild flowers in the summer, and daffodils and tulips in the spring. The rest of the garden will be more formal, with a water feature and borders, and a privet hedge.'

It's the most words that Sarah has ever heard Finn say all at once. She doesn't know enough about garden design to judge his ideas, but he seems enthusiastic about his scheme. Aunt Edith seems to be quite taken with Finn, and Sarah knows only too well how magnetic he is.

'It's going to look lovely,' Aunt Edith says. She looks at Sarah expectantly.

'Yes,' Sarah says. 'It will be a different garden.' She doesn't point out that the garden has lost its seclusion and shelter, or that Charlie and Jack will miss the dark, wild part, where they hunted for caterpillars and beetles.

Aunt Edith seems satisfied with her response. 'Good. Let's have a cup of tea and a biscuit,' she says. Somehow, despite the noise of the chainsaw, Jack hears about the biscuit and comes running. Charlie jumps down from a tree stump and jogs after Jack, dragging a stick behind him.

'It's going to cost a bomb,' Paul says to Sarah in a low voice, as they go inside.

In the kitchen, Aunt Edith puts the kettle on. Sarah takes four mugs from a cupboard and puts tea bags into the blue-and-white Royal Doulton china teapot. Aunt Edith opens the fridge and takes out a carton of long-life milk. She looks in the larder, searching behind packets and jars, and eventually produces a festive-looking tin of cranberry biscuits; no doubt a Christmas present, and not a recent one. Aunt Edith arranges the biscuits on a plate and Sarah opens the carton of milk. She pours milk into two plastic cups for Jack and Charlie, and into each mug for the tea.

There is laughter from the boys, who are sitting on Finn's feet and clinging to his legs. Finn could be Gulliver, pinned down by the Lilliputians, but he doesn't seem to mind. Paul is speaking to Finn, but his words drown in the clamour of the children. In the company of the two men, Jack and Charlie seem to be even more unruly than usual.

'Biscuits,' she calls. As if she's incanted a spell, the boys immediately release Finn. She'd usually make the boys wait until everyone was sitting at the table, but they need to calm down and she's knows this will do the trick. She hopes her aunt, who is now wiping a silver tray, won't mind. She carries the plate of biscuits and the two cups of milk to the round wooden table, the boys leaping around her like pups. Charlie crams a biscuit into his mouth, makes a face, and spits it into his hands. 'Horrible,' he says, spraying crumbs. Jack erupts into laughter, knocking over his cup. Milk pours over the edge of the table and pools on the floor.

'Jack,' Sarah snaps. 'Look what you've done.'

Jack goes crimson. He doesn't speak.

The kettle is boiling. Sarah doesn't want her aunt to have to make the tea. She glances at Paul, hoping to catch his eye, but instead, Finn sees.

'Yes, it will take a few weeks,' Finn says to Paul. He walks over to the kettle, picks it up and fills the teapot.

Paul follows, frowning. He doesn't seem to notice that Finn is making the tea, or that their children are misbehaving. At times like these, her husband is as blinkered as a carthorse.

'Jack, get the kitchen roll,' she says, holding Charlie's sticky hand to stop him wiping it on his clothes or the fabric seats of the chairs. Jack does as she asks, and they both wipe up the milk, with Sarah still holding on to Charlie.

'Your manners are dreadful,' she says to them. 'What will Aunt Edith think?'

'Sorry, Mummy,' Jack says, solemnly. 'We'll be good now.'

Charlie nods, looking contrite. 'Sorry,' he says.

From sinners to saints. She never stays cross with them for long.

Aunt Edith is still preoccupied with the tray, arranging a bowl of sugar and teaspoons on a doily. She doesn't seem to have noticed the commotion about the biscuits or the spilt milk.

'Aunt Edith, why don't you sit down and relax? I must take Charlie to wash his hands, but I'm sure Paul can help,' Sarah says, emphasising her husband's name.

At last, Paul is propelled into action. He puts the teapot and the mugs on the tray, and carries it to the table. Aunt Edith follows, and Finn joins them.

In the cloakroom, Sarah washes Charlie's face and hands, and the cold water makes them both shiver. 'You're a monkey,' she says, scolding his reflection in the mirror. His blond hair is sticking up and his pink cheeks look almost edible. He gives one of his huge smiles. 'I love you,' he declares. He turns around and hugs her tightly, and her heart melts.

She takes Charlie back to the kitchen. She sits down beside Jack and puts Charlie on her other side. It's better if she is between them; the boys are more likely to act up if they sit together.

'You must know all the gardens in Littlefold,' Aunt Edith is saying to Finn. 'I expect you have your favourites.'

'Your garden is one of them,' Finn says, not missing a beat.

'Of course it is,' Paul says, under his breath, but loud enough for Sarah to hear.

Aunt Edith laughs, almost girlishly. If she's heard Paul, she doesn't show it. 'You're sweet,' she says to Finn.

'I'm serious. There aren't many gardens like yours left,' Finn replies. 'The new builds are huge, but their gardens are postage stamps.'

'True,' Aunt Edith says, leaning forward. 'I can't understand it.'

'No,' Finn says. 'I prefer the original gardens.' He glances sideways at Sarah. She knows that he's talking about her garden now, not Aunt Edith's.

Paul sips his tea. He doesn't speak.

'I must come and see your new home,' Aunt Edith says to Sarah. 'You've been here for . . . it must be a year.'

'Time has flown,' Sarah says. She doesn't say that it's nearly two years since they moved to Littlefold. She knows it's easier for Aunt Edith if they come to her at the Laurels. 'You're always welcome, of course.'

'It's a lovely spot,' Finn says. 'Good walks.'

'Yes. Sarah's quite the rambler these days,' Paul says, an edge to his voice. 'She's always off in the woods.'

Aunt Edith turns to her, looking concerned. 'I hope you don't go alone,' she says. 'You never know who you might meet. Surrey isn't the safe place it once was.'

'There's no need to worry,' Sarah says, trying to sound reassuring, bristling with annoyance at Paul. 'It's always the same people. Neighbours with dogs or housewives out for a jog.'

'What about the scary man?' Jack says, looking from Sarah to Finn, and then back again. 'The one who frightened you all in the woods?' He seems to be addressing both of them.

Sarah doesn't know what to say. She hadn't realised that Charlie had told Jack about the stranger in the woods – his speech wasn't as fluent then – but somehow Jack's pieced it together. Charlie must have also mentioned Finn.

There is a silence. Her heart begins to pound. She doesn't

dare look at Paul, for fear of what she might see. 'Oh, that gypsy. He was harmless,' she says, hearing the breathlessness in her voice.

Jack begins to say something, but Sarah catches sight of the kitchen clock and cuts him off. 'Goodness, it's eleven o'clock.' She stands up. 'I'm so sorry, Aunt Edith, but we must go. Jack has a birthday party.'

'Yes, of course,' Aunt Edith says. 'You don't want to miss the fun and games.'

In the car, Paul is silent, looking straight ahead, and the short drive to the village hall seems to take much longer than usual. Sarah isn't sure if Paul's realised that she knows Finn better than he thought, or if he's worrying about her aunt's garden; perhaps she's got it completely wrong, and he's fretting about the office. It's hard to tell with Paul. Her husband gives so little away.

At last, they arrive at the village hall. Paul stays in the car with Charlie while Sarah ushers Jack inside. The party has begun and the animal man is arranging a snake around a boy's shoulders as if it's a scarf. The boy looks hypnotised, his face is pale, and he doesn't blink. Two girls in flouncy party dresses nudge each other and giggle. The animal man unwinds the snake, there is scattered applause, and the boy joins the other children sitting on the floor, the colour flooding back into his face.

'You don't have to do that,' Sarah says to Jack, who is standing quietly beside her. She's wondering how to settle Jack in, when a girl turns around and beckons to him. It's Emma, looking very grown-up in a midnight-blue velvet dress and a faux-fur stole, her fair hair pulled back in a bun. Jack lets go of Sarah's hand and sits down beside Emma. Emma cups her hand to his ear, whispering, and Jack smiles.

Sarah knows it's time for her to leave, but she feels as paralysed as the boy in the serpent's embrace, somehow unable to move or look away. There have been times when she's wanted to fast forward through these early years that demand so much of her, more than she could ever have imagined, but now she suddenly wishes time would stop, that she and her children could stay just as they are; happy, close, forever young.

A woman touches her arm and her thoughts evaporate. It's Claire, the birthday boy's mother. She smiles, revealing perfect, white teeth. 'Max is over the moon,' she says, and Sarah isn't sure if she is referring to the party or the presents or something else. 'He loves Jack,' Claire continues, her voice as smooth as silk. 'I do hope they're in the same class next year.'

Jack doesn't talk about Max and they don't play together, but Sarah says, politely, 'Yes. That would be nice.'

Claire folds her arms, and the diamond rock on her finger glitters. 'I'm so pleased you agree. I will request them to be together, and you must do the same. Max will be super-excited.'

It is telling that excitement alone isn't enough these days; super-excitement sounds unnatural and ill-advised, like a child who has been given too many sweets. Sarah remembers a conversation at pick-up last week. 'The classes will be mixed up next year. Parents can request one friend to be in their child's new class,' Jessica had explained. They'd agreed that Sarah would request Emma and Jessica would request Jack. Jack would never forgive her if she asked for Max.

Before she can reply, Claire carries on, 'I'm so sorry, darling, but I must dash. Crisis with the party bags.' She gestures at two toddlers chasing each other around an enormous bunch of balloons. She lowers her voice. 'Siblings. Not invited.' She sighs, as if her own manners are beyond reproach. 'Enjoy your two hours, sweetie,' she says pointedly, as if Sarah is now indebted to her for this small freedom, and disappears into the village-hall kitchen, no doubt to fill two gift bags with stickers, sweets and bouncy balls.

Sarah walks back to the car, mulling over her new dilemma. Managing the other mothers at Jack's school is exhausting. She wonders if she's wearing a sign. *New and disoriented; caves in a conflict.* She imagines the signs that some of the other mothers might wear.

*High-flyer in the city; talk to the nanny.*

*My shoes are more expensive than your car; don't waste my time.*

*Bubbles and Botox. I'm plastic fantastic and high as a kite.*

*Social climber with a chip on my shoulder. Watch your back.*

She could explain, hoping that Claire will understand, or she could do nothing and feign surprise if the boys aren't in the same class. Perhaps there's no point worrying. She has a feeling that Claire will take offence, no matter what she says or does.

In the car, Paul is reading emails on his BlackBerry and Charlie is in the passenger seat. The windscreen wipers are on, the hazard lights are flashing, and Charlie is pushing a button to make his window go up and down. He looks as serious as an engineer carrying out final checks before a rocket launch.

She speaks to him through the closing window. 'Hello poppet. Are you having fun with the car?'

'It's not a car,' he says patiently, as if she's the child. 'It's my ellaplane.'

'I see. Shall we fly home?' And then, because it's the easiest way to get him back into his seat, 'You can watch TV while I make lunch.'

She's said the magic words: Charlie obediently climbs back into his seat and Sarah straps him in. Paul slips his BlackBerry into his pocket and starts the car.

She's thinking about Claire again, wondering if she ought to have a word when she collects Jack, when Paul says, in a bullish voice, 'I can't believe what your aunt's done to her garden. It was perfectly nice as it was.'

She doesn't understand the rationale for the works either; the garden was lovely, if a little overgrown before. Still, it is Aunt Edith's garden, to do with as she likes. 'She seems very keen on the project. Perhaps she wanted a change.'

'A change?' Paul laughs, as if she's a fool who knows nothing. 'That boy's ruined it.'

She feels herself bristle at the accusation, but she says, as evenly as she can, 'It's a work in progress. I'm sure it will be fine.' She doesn't understand why Paul is upset. It isn't their garden.

'Can't you see? Are you so blind?' Paul looks at her, his eyes darkening to black, but she still doesn't know what he means. 'This boy wants to launch his garden-design career and he's somehow persuaded your aunt to fund it. Your aunt is elderly and vulnerable, and he's taking advantage.'

For a moment, Sarah is too shocked to speak. Paul is right: this would never have occurred to her. Finn has his demons, but he's not evil. 'No,' she says. 'Finn isn't like that. And no one could make Aunt Edith do anything.'

Paul takes the bend too quickly, the car swerves, and she grips her seat.

Charlie laughs, delighted. 'Faster, Daddy,' he says.

If Paul has heard Charlie, he doesn't show it. 'You seem to know Finn very well, perhaps more than I realised,' he says, quietly. 'He's in and out of our home. Our children treat him like family . . .' His voice trails away.

Silence fills the car, like water. She imagines herself sinking, her lungs emptying, her hair floating like weed.

'You're right, something has changed,' Paul says. 'It's this boy.' He pulls the car into the driveway and switches off the engine. He looks at her as if he doesn't recognise her, as if she disgusts him. 'For God's sake, Sarah. What a fucking cliché.' He gets out. He slams the car door. He walks away.

She looks down at her hands, still gripping the leather seat. Her hands look like they belong to someone else. She hears the muted beeping of the house alarm and then it's quiet again.

'Mummy?' It's Charlie, in the back seat. His innocent voice stabs her.

She gets out, fumbles with his straps and lifts him to her, burying her face in his hair. He clings to her, and she feels their hearts beating. She wants to stay like this always, close to her little boy. After a moment, he gently pulls away. He strokes her wet cheek. She puts him down, he slips his hand into hers, and they walk together into the house.

It is dark inside. Paul hasn't turned on the lights. She takes off her shoes and Charlie's, Charlie climbs onto the sofa in the playroom, and she switches on the TV. In the kitchen, she pours herself a glass of water and drinks it down in gulps. Then she sees Paul, appearing like a spectre in the glass panes of the conservatory. He's standing outside, legs planted, arms folded. A lord surveying his land. The lawn glistens, the willow tree sways and the field is rippling in the breeze.

She goes out and stands beside him. He doesn't look at her or speak.

'Paul,' she says. 'This isn't fair.'

He stays silent and she tries again. 'We've gone for a walk once or twice, that's all. He's just a boy. It's nothing.' She knows this isn't completely true. Still, she doesn't deserve Paul's condemnation. She isn't having an affair. 'Please trust me. This isn't about Finn.'

'I don't trust him,' Paul says, avoiding her implied question.

'I don't want him near my children. I don't want him in my garden. I don't want him in my house.' He doesn't need to say it, but she hears it all the same: I don't want him near my wife. He looks at her. It's that same look that he gave her in the car. It makes her feel unclean.

'Fine,' she hears herself say, sounding more indignant than she feels, feeling more frightened than she sounds. 'But you're overreacting. When you see that, you'll owe me an apology.' She feels a cramping pain inside; she's not completely blameless, but no one should be punished for something they haven't done.

She'd have liked to storm off, take the car, drink the afternoon away in a bar, but there are Marmite sandwiches to make and sticky fingers to wipe. A child to collect from a party. Homework to supervise.

She's lying in bed, alone, in the dark. It is late and the children have been asleep for hours. Paul is in the spare room. He'd said something about an early start and not wanting to disturb her, but they both know the truth. They fear the words that might be said. Neither of them want to touch.

It is a warm, humid night and she's thrown off the covers. She is wearing a nightdress, and her arms and legs are bare. It is quiet and still, the kind of heavy silence that compresses the air.

Something has changed. It's this boy. How convenient to blame someone else, and in doing so, make her culpable. It isn't fair. Paul's absence from family life, leaving her to raise the children alone, their dislocated lives; this is the cause of the discord between them.

She sees the boy, his blond hair falling into his eyes. Finn. He has a hold on her that is so taut, it's almost painful.

Light flashes through the curtains, fracturing the sky, and

there is a loud bang, like an explosion. Rain is falling, gentle at first, then hard and insistent, hammering on the roof and the windows. If the boys have woken, too frightened to leave their rooms, she might not hear their cries. She gets up and hurries down the dark corridor. Jack is curled up on his side, the sheet twisted around his legs. Charlie is on his back, his arms flung above his head. The thunder booms, the rain pounds, but her children are deep in dreams. She needn't worry. The spare-room door is shut and the light beneath it has disappeared. She goes back to bed.

After a while, the rain eases, the thunder softens, and the storm moves away. The trees are whispering in the woods. An owl cries, and its lament seems to be meant for her. She drifts, rising and falling, carried by the currents and tides of sleep. A boy is sending stones skipping across the lake. The water sparkles, the stones dance, and his arms are strong and brown. The surface of the lake sets, turning to glass. The stones bounce, ricochet, spin . . .

She sits up, suddenly, completely awake. There it is again: the sound of stone hitting glass. Someone is throwing pebbles at her window. She sees the stranger again, his dark eyes flicking over her. He has come out of the woods, crossed the field and climbed over their gate. The vagrant is here to claim her and her children. He will drag them into the woods, bind their hands, press his blade to her throat. The Medusa will watch her undoing. She creeps over to the window and looks out, hiding behind the curtains. There is a full moon and the black sky is scattered with stars. The garden is washed in pale light and the field is silvery; beyond, the wall of dark, towering trees.

A shadowy figure is standing beneath her. She recoils, her heart knocking in her chest, but before the scream breaks from her, the man looks up. It's not the vagrant. It's a boy.

Finn's face is white and drawn. His lips are moving, but she can't hear the words. He is gesturing, urgently.

She runs downstairs, her hand skimming over the bannister, her nightdress swishing against her legs. Something has happened. Someone is hurt. She finds the front-door key and puts it in the lock. Her hands are trembling. The key won't move, it's stuck, she must have the wrong one, but at last it turns.

Finn steps out of the shadows. The porch lantern flickers on, bathing him in amber light. His skin glistens and his hair is wet. His shirt clings to his chest. He stares at her for a long moment. She's aware of her silk nightdress, fitted close at her waist; her bare arms and legs. Her hair is long and loose around her shoulders.

He takes her hand. 'Come,' he says.

She follows him through the moonlit field and into the woods. The trees almost seem to be alive, watching them, moving their branches. There is silence under the mantle of darkness, but also the sounds of invisible creatures rustling in the undergrowth and flying above. The long wet grass clings to her legs and arms, and stones cut her bare feet. Nettles sting her ankles. She trips over a tangle of roots and nearly falls.

'Wait,' she says, but Finn doesn't seem to hear. He is taking long, purposeful strides, almost dragging her behind him. He doesn't speak. She wonders again if something has happened, but somehow, she can't ask; fear of what may lie ahead stops the words.

There is the scent of wild things, of dank soil and musky fox. Rainwater drips from the canopy of trees. They cross the wooden bridge; the planks creak and the sharp fragrance of the marsh lilies catches in her throat.

They stand together beside the lake. The moon shines a path along the still water. The bench for Samuel Thomas is brushed with silver; not for the first time, she longs to touch it.

The neighbouring houses are dark and shuttered. It is quiet. No one is hurt, no one else is even here, and the anxiety she'd felt in the woods disappears.

The wind sifts through the trees. She closes her eyes for a moment, feeling the caress of the cool air on her face, her neck, her shoulders. Her skin tingles. She could step out of her nightdress and slip into the lake. The water would be silky. She could be a mermaid.

'Why have we come here?' she says softly, but even as the words leave her lips, she knows. He turns to her. His damp hair is tousled and his eyes glitter like the water. He pulls her to him, folding her into him, and she feels his heart beating, loud and fast. He presses his mouth to hers and she tastes him. Vodka, cigarettes, vanilla. He gives her his breath and she burns. His hands sweep up her nightdress, brushing over her thighs, her stomach, her breasts. Blood thuds in her head.

She slips her hands beneath his t-shirt. His skin is warm and smooth, and his body is strong and firm. They are pressed against each other, but it isn't enough. He unfastens his belt and then she's undoing his jeans, her hands trembling over the buttons. This is wrong, the words whisper in her head. Her body throbs and she pushes the thought away.

He draws her down to the forest floor that is still wet from the storm. They lie together in the shadows, beneath the trees. Her nightdress is rucked up around her hips; twigs and stones press into her shoulders and the small of her back. The air is scented with washed grass, soil, and the green scent that is him. Her heart is rocking against her ribs. He is moving over her, covering her. In a moment, everything will change. She will be changed, for ever.

The clouds shift and starlight falls across his face. Flawless, glowing skin. He is so young. Innocent, even as he readies himself to take her.

'No,' she says. Her voice sounds far away, as if it belongs to someone else.

He slips a finger inside her. The shock, the wetness, makes her gasp.

'Yes,' he whispers.

A moan breaks from her. She tries to twist away, but he pins her down.

'You want this,' he says.

Her chest tightens, squeezing her lungs. 'Wait. Stop,' she says.

Slowly, reluctantly, he lifts himself, allowing her to move away. She gets up, smoothing down her nightdress. Her legs feel shaky. She must get away. She must leave this place before it's too late.

'You're a tease,' he says. He gives her one of his knowing smiles. 'All right. I'll play.'

Anger flares inside her. 'This isn't a game,' she says.

He is quiet for a moment. 'No, it's not.'

She feels the tension between them and is suddenly afraid. If he puts his arms around her again, she won't be strong enough to resist. And once that line is crossed, there will be no way back. Paul will find out somehow; he already suspects. He might forgive her, but his resentment, her guilt, would ruin them. Her children would suffer. She could lose everything.

Finn is coming towards her, reaching out his hand. Time slows and she seems to float away from herself, hovering above her body, as if she's her own tortured, tethered ghost. He strokes her arm. He is saying something, but she can't make out the words. His voice sounds muffled, as if they are underwater. All she can hear is the keening of her heart.

A cry breaks from deep inside her. She pushes him away, as hard as she can. She doesn't care if she bruises him, or if her nails scratch his skin.

He staggers backwards, his mouth slack, his eyes widening. He is close to the rim of the lake, too close, and the dark rippling water seems to rise up behind him. He stumbles, the ground slides beneath his feet, and he is falling. The lake will claim him, just like it did with Samuel Thomas. She feels herself brace, preparing to run, she will dive in after him, but the crash of his body hitting the water doesn't come.

He lies on his side, silent and still. She wants to go to him, but she folds her arms tightly, as if to bind herself. Moonlight touches the curve of his cheek, his lips, and shimmers in his hair. The lake breathes behind him.

After a moment, he pushes himself up. His shirt is dirty and torn, and his arm is grazed and bleeding. His eyes are full of shadows. 'You're like me,' he says, but she doesn't understand what he means.

'No. I'm not,' she says.

She turns and runs into the woods. She hears him calling her name, but she doesn't stop. Her breath is ragged, her chest aches, but she flies through the trees, hardly feeling the claw of brambles, the whip of low-hanging branches.

In the morning, she finds leaves in her matted hair and there are insect bites on her arms and legs. Her nightdress is stained with grass and mud, and carries the briny-earthy scent of the lake, the woods, and the boy. She wraps it in newspaper and hides it away, burying it in the depths of her wardrobe.

The presence of the nightdress troubles her. It's unlikely that anyone will discover it, but it's a testament to her guilt. At night, surfacing from disturbing dreams that she struggles to remember, the dark, looming wardrobe seems to pulse, as if the dress concealed inside has malignant powers.

She could throw it away, put it in the bin that is emptied by the council, but it would still exist. She imagines a man in overalls at the refuse centre, unfolding the newspaper, fingering the sullied silk. The thought of it is repugnant and fills her with shame.

She sits on the patio step, the newspaper parcel beside her. She flicks the lighter, once, twice, watching the flame dance. The sun is high in the sky; in the field, the long grass glimmers. Her children are at school. Paul is at the office and won't be home for hours. Mrs Jones might see, if she happened to look out of her bedroom window. She'd wonder why Sarah was burning a dress, but she'd never mention it. Mr and Mrs Jones keep to themselves, just as Sarah and Paul do.

Perhaps the parcel will be empty and she will wonder if that night in the woods was a reverie. She feels inside the folds of paper. Silk slips beneath her fingertips.

She lifts the nightdress to her face. There is a faint trace of his musky-green scent. She closes her eyes, remembering. His hands sweeping over her. The urgency of his kiss. The dark sky, pierced with thousands of stars, as they lay together in the shadows of the trees. It took all her strength to leave.

She flicks the lighter again, touching the flame to the silk. The fabric shrinks and writhes, the edges glowing amber. White smoke, as delicate as mist, curls away. There is an acrid aroma that conjures singed feathers and scorched wings. The nightdress doesn't burn as quickly as she'd expected it to. The flames keep going out and she has to keep lighting it again. The silk burns slowly, almost reluctantly, leaving cinders that crumble to dust between her fingers. When it is done, she wraps the ashes in newspaper again and puts it in her jacket pocket.

The lake is achingly beautiful. A swan glides on the water, sunlight dapples the full-leafed trees, and birds are soaring above. The night that she was here with Finn feels far away, as if she read about it in a book or watched it in a film. She takes the parcel from her pocket and unfolds the newspaper.

She scatters the ashes into the lake. The dust settles on the water, drifts, dissolves and disappears.

# Finn

## *Autumn 2011*

Mist lies along the water. The trails are carpeted with the curls of russet and brown leaves. A squirrel is foraging for acorns among the oak trees.

Finn kneels beside the lake, digging with his trowel in the damp clay soil. Four holes, with plenty of space between them, for the seedlings that he has been nurturing indoors in pots. Tender green shoots that look like the cress he used to grow from cotton wool in eggshells when he was a child. One seedling for every year that has passed. If he plants them now, before the first frost, there will be flowers next spring.

He puts his trowel to one side and sits back on his heels. *Are you here, brother? And if not, where have you gone?* The soul must go somewhere, but the Bible stories of Heaven and Hell seem far-fetched. He often finds himself talking to Sam here. It isn't because of the accident. The lake was their place. *I can't come as often as I used to. Got to get my head down. Make something of myself.* He draws his sleeve across his wet face.

He's forgotten his gloves. No matter. He takes the first

pot, turns it upside down, gives it a tap, and the seedling drops into his palm. He carefully settles it into the ground, raking the soil over with his hands, gently pressing down. It is a shady spot, here on the lake shore, perfect for forget-me-nots. Tiny blue flowers with slender stems. *They're delicate, but tough, like you.* In a few seasons, there will be a blanket of powder blue in front of the memorial bench. The scientific name, *Myosotis*, means 'mouse ear'. *That should make you smile. You used to call me Mouse, remember? Because of Nonna's name for me. Topolino.* Three seedlings are planted. He taps the last one from its pot.

He submerges his watering can in the lake and the soil is washed from his hands. He waters the seedlings, anointing them, binding the roots to this place.

He sits on the bench, pushing his hands into his pockets. There is a break in the cloud and the sun comes out, slanting through the trees. The lake dazzles. The woods glow crimson and gold.

The last time he came here was with Sarah, that night after the storm. She was bewitching in that silk dress. Her bare shoulders. Her long, loose hair. He'd ached for her, desired her so intensely, it seemed unstoppable. He wonders if this was how Sam felt. In the end, there was too much at stake.

He hasn't seen her since then, but he often hears her children when he's helping his father with the Joneses' garden. There is laughter from the trampoline or the thump of a ball kicked against the fence. Sometimes, he hears her calling them in for tea, or if one of the boys has fallen and hurt himself, she runs into the garden and comforts him. Her voice still feels so familiar, as if, somehow, they have always known each other.

He stands, brushing the dirt from his jeans. He should be getting on. It's nearly time to meet Mia. 'So I'm guessing you like espresso,' she'd said yesterday after class, as if they were in the middle of a conversation and not speaking for the first time. She tucked a strand of hair behind her ear and he glimpsed an intricate tattoo on the inside of her wrist that looked like Sanskrit. Her eyes were green; her hair the colour of red wine. Something fizzed inside him. 'Good guess,' he said. The door swung open and students began to file in for the next class. The lecturer was loading his PowerPoint slides. 'I'll be at the Java Club tomorrow, at around ten. Maybe I'll see you there,' she said. 'Maybe you will,' he answered, and she'd returned his smile.

He stacks the empty pots. He picks up the trowel and the watering can. The wind moves through the trees. The sun has burned away the mist, the lake is smooth and calm, and the sky is lightening. He walks away, along the path through the woods.

*Forgive me Sam, but let me go.*

# Sarah

*Midsummer 2012*

Greenish sunlight filters through the veined leaves. The woods are scented with white wisteria and flecked with the deep purple of rhododendrons. Apples hide in the boughs of the old tree that stands like a guard beside the wooden-fenced fields. Beyond, the long, feathery grass is scattered with buttercups and blood-red poppies.

In the distance, a train sounds its horn, and Sarah imagines families with children in pushchairs, ladies in shift dresses and men wearing blazers, gathering on the platforms at Littlefold and Wickford, glancing at the clock counting down.

The sun pulses, bleaching the hair on her arms. The heat hangs in the air, shimmering. Clouds of midges part.

The two mares are grazing in the next field. They lift their heads, regarding her with their liquid brown eyes. She picks a dandelion and blows the seeds away.

The woods are shady, coloured lights dance while her vision adjusts, but her feet know where the gnarled roots are, each rise and dip of the path. She slips beneath the overhanging branches, skirts the brambles, lifts her arms above the stinging nettles.

The wooden plank bridge is dusty and the stream beneath it has disappeared. Skunk cabbages have sprung up again in the dank, black soil, lacing the air with their sharp scent. Marsh marigolds shine like yellow stars.

The lake is as smooth as glass. A swan glides past, trailing her cygnets, and mallards are paddling in the dappled shade of the willow tree. A moorhen bobs up and down. The red-brick houses, the striped gardens, the swept jetties; it is as peaceful as it was the first time.

She slips off her shoes and sits beside the lake, dangling her legs into the cool water. Butterflies flit and emerald dragonflies are hovering. The ivy-wrapped oak and chestnut trees teem with invisible insects and bees. Gulls circle above, calling. The clouds, the trees, the houses, the birds, are all captured inside the lake like an upside-down painting. A woman with hair floating like weed looks up at her. Her face shifts, fragments, and is whole again.

She sits on Sam's bench, running her fingers over the dark wood, feeling the knots and the grain. Finn isn't here. She didn't expect him to be, although there have been signs of his visits. She guesses that he planted the forget-me-nots. Sometimes, she finds little offerings on the bench that he's left for Jack and Charlie: a collection of gleaming conkers, black-berries, and once, sticks fashioned into a rudimentary bow and arrow. In return, she takes posies of roses or camellias, flowers cut from their garden, and places them on the bench. The flowers are for the drowned boy, but also for Finn. She imagines meeting him again, by chance, in the village. He will give one of his sudden, warm smiles. The night they were here together, that moment of madness, needn't haunt them; they can be friends.

Aunt Edith says that Finn calls in on her, from time to time, on his way back from college, although his work at the Laurels has finished. Her aunt's garden has become a light-filled oasis. A lush, velvet lawn. An orchard of fruit trees. A pond with tadpoles and darting fish, and a statue of a boy gazing into the water for eternity. Sarah still misses the way the garden used to be – the seclusion, the hidden nooks, the wild woodland, but the change has been good for her aunt. Aunt Edith's face is softer, her eyes are bright, and although her hand trembles, it doesn't seem to trouble her the way it once did.

Sarah won't be able to come here for a while. Tomorrow, the builders arrive with their ladders, saws and drills. The house will be purged, stripped of stained carpets, peeling window frames, the fractured fireplace. Bathrooms will be ripped out; walls will come down. The bones of the house will be excavated, the dust falling like rain. And then, when it is a shell, emptied of everything that is broken, they can begin again.

When she told Paul her decision, that she would renovate the house, she felt something soften in him. He is spending more time at home. He travels less. On the weekends, she notices that he switches his BlackBerry onto silent. Occasionally, he leaves the office early to collect Jack from school. He's even talking about joining the local golf club. Small changes carry weight.

New memories are made. Paul on his hands and knees in the garden, helping Charlie to plant the sunflower that he'd brought home from nursery. Jack hovering with a watering can that Charlie grabs in his enthusiasm and inadvertently tips all over Paul. A moment of stunned silence, and then peals of laughter. Paul and the boys setting off for the garden centre and returning jubilant, with slug pellets to protect the sunflower, a rounders set, croquet and a giant Connect 4. They'd spent all afternoon outdoors. Tea was a picnic on the lawn: scones, finger sandwiches, a jam roll. It reminded Sarah of when she was a child, staying with her grandparents in Littlefold. They'd smile, she thought, if they could see her here now, with her own family.

The sun dries her feet and polishes the bench until it shines like walnut. She traces the blackened inscription with her fingers, etching the words into her heart. *A flower in His garden*. It is time to go. Paul is waiting for her, and so are Jack and Charlie.

# Acknowledgements

Thank you to those who read early drafts of the manuscript, shared their wisdom and encouraged me to keep writing: Tricia Wastvedt, Fay Weldon, Ella Berthoud. Thank you to Sarah Beal and Kate Beal for championing this novel and being such a delight to work with – I couldn't ask for more supportive publishers. Thank you to my wonderful agent, Megan Carroll, for taking me under her wing, and to everyone at Watson, Little. Thank you to Kate Quarry and Laura Macfarlane, for their meticulous attention to the text. Thank you to Jaimie Keenan for the beautiful cover art. Thank you to Fiona Brownlee for guiding this novel into the world. Thank you to Jane and Stanny, for giving me the time to write. Thank you to Paul Ellis, for talking to me about quarries. Thank you to Gus, Alex and Beau who encouraged me to write this story, but are not in it. Thank you to my parents, Pauline and Bijan, for everything. To my grandparents, Dick and Phyl, whose wartime romance in Italy inspired the beginning of this novel, thank you for sharing your memories. I think – hope – you would have enjoyed reading this. To my paternal grandparents Mansureh and Esmaeil, and surrogate grandparents Zari and Marashi: never forgotten. All my love and gratitude to my family and friends who have accompanied me on this rollercoaster ride of a writer's journey.